MOTHER TONGUE

Mother Tongue

a novel by

Vassilis Alexakis

translated from the French by

Harlan R. Patton

with an afterword by

Marianne Bessy

AB

This is an Autumn Hill Books book
Published by Autumn Hill Books, Inc.

1138 E. Benson Court
Bloomington, Indiana 40401
USA

First Published as La langue maternelle

Cet ouvrage, publié dans le cadre d'un programme d'aide à la publication, beneficie du soutien du Ministère des Affaires Étrangères et du Service Culturel de l'Ambassade de France aux États-Unis.

This work, published as part of a program of aid for publication, received support from the French Ministry of Foreign Affairs and the Cultural Services of the French Embassy in the United States.

Cover design and layout by Justin Angeles

Autumn Hill Books ISBN: 978-0-982746691
Library of Congress Control Number: 2017931903

www.autumnhillbooks.org

AHB

For Marie-Claire

1.

I'm in a classroom. The students are all older and poorly dressed. They're immigrants. The place is squalid and dim. I got here late. A woman I find very unpleasant, a Frenchwoman, arrived at the same time and sat behind me. "I'm going to have to have it out with her," I thought. I'm hardly paying attention to what the teacher is saying, a vague silhouette in the distance. I'm not even sure he's speaking. I suddenly turn toward her: "I know all about what you said, everything you've done against me," I tell her. She has tiny eyes and I can't tell whether she's looking at me or at the teacher. I notice five words she's written in her notebook: when did she write them, when did the teacher dictate them? They're written in the singular and in the plural. The first, *rizi* (it has nothing to do with rice), takes an n in the plural, *rizin*. I'm learning a foreign language in the company of a dreadful woman.

I took the metro to Omonia. The smell from the tunnel hasn't changed since my childhood. The stations in Paris don't have the same scent, the darkness smells different there. At the far end of the platform there's a two-meter electronic sphinx that reads the lines in the palm of your hand. A screen built into its chest displays messages in several languages encouraging people to discover their fate. The French text has spelling errors in it. A man slipped his hand into the slot without putting in any money: a whistle went off and made him pull his hand back quickly. There were quite a few people around the sphinx examining it, but by the time the train came no one had wanted to learn his fate.

The landscape has changed around Athens. It's been built up. They're building the same style of unsightly apartment building with narrow balconies everywhere. Leaving the city by metro takes longer than it did before. The first trees I saw were the ones in the new cemetery. Theodoris and Marilena came with their car to get me in Kifissia. We went to Stamata.

"A strange name," I said.

Stamata means "Stop."

"Indeed," said Theodoris.

Marilena turned out the collar of my shirt to see the tag.

"How much did it cost you?" she asked.

"Twelve hundred francs."

"I'm surprised you'd spend that much on a shirt! Why is it so expensive? It's not a major label."

"Maybe you just don't know the label," said Theodoris.

I don't dress very well as a rule. My friend Vaguelio had to insist before I updated my wardrobe. We were together when I bought the shirt. She had come to Paris for a few days. I also bought an Irish sweater with a number of pockets and a raincoat. We crossed Drossia, or the Cool.

"It really is cooler here in the summer than in the surrounding villages," Theodoris remarked.

I asked him if there was an etymological dictionary of place names. Apparently there isn't. Costas, my brother, couldn't tell me why the mountain that overlooks Ioannina is called Mitsikeli. He told me that we systematically Hellenize all Albanian, Vlach, and Slavic place names in northern Greece to prevent any challenge to our control in the region.

"Marilena is really good to me, she really loves me," Theodoris confided a bit later while we were walking in the country. "You remember what Niki was like, don't you? With Marilena I get bored. She always agrees. No matter what I say, she agrees."

Niki never did, not her. She didn't have any children with him. Before they were married, they had agreed that they would have six. He was afraid of her. He hesitated to make a comment about a movie for fear that she would contradict him.

"You can't imagine how relieved I was when she agreed with me."

"You're not going out," she used to tell him. "You're not going anywhere!" She fought him, screaming, and Theodoris ended up giving in.

"One time she made me think she was having a heart attack. She was lying half-conscious on the floor. I called an ambulance, but as soon as she heard me calling the emergency number, she recovered. She got up and even criticized me for my initiative."

I hadn't known what the emergency number was at the time. I decided to keep it handy, I might need it someday. We took a diagonal path across several open fields grown over with weeds and the occasional tree. We skirted chicken coops. I don't remember hearing any dogs barking. We went to the village oven to ask what time we should bring the lamb tomorrow. How was he able to put up with Niki for twenty-five years? And why, after so many years, did he stop putting up with her? He couldn't give me a satisfactory explanation. He said that they'd been at school together, that he felt sorry for her, that she was completely dependent on him.

"I was positive she'd never leave, and you know how hard it is for me to live alone. She didn't have any friends and wouldn't allow me to have any. She was convinced we would grow old together. When we bought the apartment, she had another door to the bathroom put in so that the cleaning woman could get there without passing through our room: she was already thinking about a time when one of us would no longer be able to get out of bed."

Theodoris' mother is convinced that Niki had him bewitched. I had lunch with her one day — she was one of my mother's closest friends. She told me that her husband, who passed away several years ago, had such an aversion to his daughter-in-law that he made a habit of turning her photograph to the wall. I wondered if Theodoris knew that.

"I have a hard time understanding you," I admitted.

There were ten or so people at the house. Others arrived the next day, Easter Sunday. Most of them were students, Theodoris' pupils. He likes to get them together, eat with them, chat with them. They listen respectfully, even when he starts in on a subject that has nothing to do with the art history he teaches. They show affection for him, boys and girls both, captivated by his strangeness. Several girls are probably in love with him, but they avoid showing it. They love him discretely, without asking for anything, probably guessing that they're only entitled to a small measure of his affection. He gives the impression of being interested in each of them, of having no favorites.

The women worked all afternoon to prepare the meal. They squeezed lemons, washed lettuce and placed it into earthenware salad bowls. I watched television. In the library I found a book by Condylakis and read one of his chronicles devoted to those unfortunates who lose their money playing cards on New Year's Eve and return home disillusioned at dawn. I used to read that author with a certain pleasure when I was a teenager.

"There's a hole in your sock," Marilena told me, laughing.

She has a cheerful, pleasing voice, but what she has to say is almost always unpleasant. She notices only what's defective, inadequate, bad. She predicts catastrophes and always expects the worst. Her expression is bitter, her face a bit dull. Her presence darkens the place where she finds herself. "Maybe she's jealous of Theodoris' students," I thought. She became his mistress well before he and Niki separated. "Maybe she cried a lot before."

Toward eleven in the evening, before we left for church, I called my father. I was hoping he would pick up the phone, the night before Easter, but he didn't. Maybe he wasn't home. My father rarely answers the phone — the ringing paralyzes him, terrifies him. He doesn't dare approach the phone when it's ringing. I once saw him tense up in his armchair, squeezing the wooden arms as hard as he could. He was staring at the phone as if it could attack him.

"Want me to answer it?" I asked.

"No," he said softly, "I forbid it."

"What are you afraid of exactly?"

He looked at me, no longer afraid. The phone had gone silent. He seemed somehow sorry. "There are fears which can't be explained."

Even when he knows it's me calling — I call him every day at one o'clock — he takes his time picking up. He lets the phone ring twenty times before answering. I imagine him inching toward it, reaching out with a hesitant hand. He claims that he sometimes answers immediately.

"Sometimes the ringing is so unbearable that I prefer to stop it right away. I answer before I have time to be afraid."

On the other hand, he has no trouble making a call. He calls me quite often, most of the time for no real reason, to chat or to tell me about a dream he's had. I'm rather surprised my father still dreams. I thought people stopped dreaming after a certain age, just as they stop making plans. I thought old people's nights were mute. My father is eighty-three.

We stayed out on the square in front of the little Stamata church, which filled with people. Theodoris drew my attention to the legs of a blonde woman in a very short red dress. She was wearing high-heeled shoes, also red. The mass was being relayed on loudspeakers. I only went into the church for a moment to get candles. There were mostly old people inside. Light from the candles gave their faces a soft, almost youthful color. I hadn't been inside a church in years, at least for as long as I've lived in France. I didn't go often as a child either. I don't ever remember our parents forcing my brother and me to attend mass. I was astonished to see women make the sign of the cross when they walked past churches. I noticed they made the gesture quickly when the building was small and ostentatiously when it was more imposing. I've opened the Bible now and then — I even stole one from a hotel — but have never got beyond the middle of the second page. I haven't read the Gospels. My knowledge of religion is limited to a few scenes — the first that comes to mind is the sacrifice of Abraham — to the first verse of two or three psalms, and to some scattered phrases: "Forgive them for they know not what they do," "Let he who is without sin cast the first stone." No ceremony ever thrilled me, not even the Good Friday procession. I didn't find religion attractive. It inspired feelings that were rather morose.

The announcement of the Resurrection was met with firecrackers, smoke bombs, and fireworks. Firecrackers were going off like machine gun fire. I wondered how my father would have reacted if he'd heard this racket. He might have found it funny. A big white cloud filled the air, making the church and the people around it seem as if they were high up in the sky. The lit candles, growing more numerous, were like the stars.

We tried to keep our candles lit all the way home, to keep the flame from the church alive. If one stayed lit, that was enough, since we could light the others from its flame. Mine went out only once. When we got home, we traced a black cross with the smoke from the candles on the lintel of the front door. I'd forgotten that custom. "I don't have any history," I thought. There are still traces of dripped wax on the cuff of my trousers from that night.

"You'll burn the sofa if you keep smoking so much," Marilena told me.

I slept on the sofa. A woman peeling potatoes in a corner of the living room and tossing them into a bowl of water woke me at dawn. She had long gray hair and muscled legs, her skirt pulled up to her knees. I met her friend, a pale, thin man of about thirty-five who kept to himself and spoke little. He barely moved and gave the impression that he was conserving energy, as if he could feel himself growing old too soon, as if he were as old as she. She was about sixty and was nearly a head taller than him. They were no doubt aware of how different they were, since they stayed some distance away from one another. He smiled at her from afar. Even his smile looked a bit forced, a tired, joyless smile. She, on the other hand, was terribly busy, coming and going, taking care of everything. She even danced after the meal, though not gracefully. The effort they were both making to lessen the peculiarity of their relationship finally wearied me, like a play that goes on too long.

"Some night," I said to Theodoris, "he'll get up quietly, put on his shoes, and kick her in the face."

"He really likes her, I swear. The two of them get along very well together."

I was in a good mood until dinnertime and for a bit after. We had finally decided to have two lambs cooked at the village oven, and we bought grilled liver and tripe kebabs. We had trouble getting the spit into the car and finally put it diagonally over the back seat after wrapping the meat in newspaper.

"Who's going to eat all that?" said Marilena. "We won't be able to even eat half of that!"

She was right. One of the lambs was barely touched. The table was covered with food at the end of the meal and there was more in the kitchen. When we were children, my mother used to make bread slices with margarine for us. She put little bits of olive on the margarine. The slices looked like playing cards. Later on, the olives were replaced with cheese, hard-boiled eggs, even meatballs sliced in half. I saw the progress of the Greek economy in my bread and margarine.

We ate in the garden. Big clouds sailed through the sky, their shadows sweeping across the table. Someone tried to fly a little white kite, but it got caught in the power lines as they always do. I spoke with two students. Theodoris had told them that I was a cartoonist living in Paris. They used the familiar "you" form with me. That made me happy. I thought about certain French people whom I've known for a long time and with whom I still use the formal "you." Even with Véronique Carrier, the editor in chief of the *Miroir de l'Europe*, I still say *vous*. She invites me to dinner at her apartment once a year, in June. She's married to an ethnologist who has spent much of his life in the Amazon. He's brought back a number of objects made by the Indians, but nothing in his behavior would suggest he had lived among them. I have a lot of trouble imagining this elegant and aging man on a raft with a revolver in his hand. I leave their home at a quarter to eleven: I get the impression that they would consider my visit too short if I left at ten thirty, and too long if I stayed until eleven. They say goodbye without ever crossing the threshold of their apartment. I have to turn my back on them to push the elevator button. They don't wait for the elevator to arrive. The door closes behind me the moment I press the button. I hear their door closing long before I go for my visit, from the moment Véronique gives me her annual invitation. This happens toward the end of May. It wouldn't be an overstatement to say that from the beginning of spring I hear the Carriers' door closing behind me. I'd like to explain to them how much their haste upsets me, but I've never found the right moment or the right words. Friendly as they are, the impending click of the door does not allow me to feel really at ease in their home. Charles Carrier always recounts some episode of his life with the Indians. He talks about the Kaxinawá, his friends the "bat-men." They live along the banks of the Purus River in Peru. I listen with interest and with some vague sense of regret. It occurs to me that I'll never know the bat-men. There are other trips I'd like to take, but I probably never will, for lack of time. I'm starting to say goodbye to countries that I haven't visited, people I haven't met. My experiences will remain just as limited as they are today. I don't know whether I like the Carriers or even whether I think they're nice. Perhaps they inspire no feeling in me at all.

A girl brushed against my arm. She was constantly looking elsewhere, she didn't want to miss anything that was happening around her.

"What are you drinking?" she asked me.

I was drinking raki. My glass was half empty. I thought she was going to get the raki bottle, but I was wrong. I saw her start a conversation with someone else.

I also spoke to a blue-eyed poet. His hair was carefully pulled back and ended in a tiny ponytail held by a green rubber band. His suit was green too. He was wearing a loud tie with geometric patterns. Theodoris introduced us just before lunch.

"There's an interview with him in *To Vima*."

He lowered his eyes modestly. He asked me if the French read poetry. I told him they preferred novels.

"Here too," he said. "The public is turning more and more toward the novel, but poetry is still popular."

"We have a great poetic tradition," Theodoris reminded us. "The young need references for writing. The novel doesn't give them any. It doesn't have any real roots here. Poetry, however, has roots and theater does too. Theater certainly expresses Greek reality today better than the novel does."

The poet was talking about a conversation he had once had with the novelist Costas Taktsis. "He considered the novel to be the mirror of industrial society. That's how he explained its success in developed countries."

A small woman with a sweet face, dressed in black, came up behind him and put her arms around his neck. He showed no surprise — he didn't even turn around.

"Don't you want to put your hat on?" she asked him. "The sun might be bad for you."

"He has a hat," I thought. He didn't answer her. He wanted to know if I spent time with the circle of Greek artists in Paris. He used the formal "you."

"No. Manthoulis is the only one I see. We get together for bean soup from time to time."

He seemed disappointed.

"All you do is cartooning?"

"Yes."

"He draws remarkably well," said Theodoris.

I don't draw remarkably well. My drawings are about the same as all the rest of the press cartoonists. I look at the same topics as they do. We hijack the same symbols, the American flag, the Star of David. What would I think of my cartoons if they were done by someone else? I probably wouldn't notice them. The poet had a notepad in the outside pocket of his jacket. He went off alone to write.

"You aren't going to start in on an epic, I hope," said his girlfriend. "Write something short, something pithy! Dinner is almost ready!"

I went into the house too. The living room was empty. I picked up the Condylakis book on the floor beside the sofa and put it away in the library. In the old days there weren't any fireplaces in houses. Recently I've even seen them in apartments. "My compatriots discovered the fireplace while I was gone," I thought. I could see the guests through the bay window, but I couldn't hear them. Theodoris was busy telling a story. I saw him make a series of short hops. It must have been a funny story since everyone laughed. Marilena walked through the living room.

"You've had enough of us?" she asked.

I turned on the television. Kilaïdonis was singing an old song that sounded like the music of the islands:

Keep smiling, captain
This storm too shall pass.

Vaguelio loved that song, she sang it in the car. We got to the port late. We had just enough time to board the boat. It was still night. The streetlights along the quay were lit. A team of young people were filming an advertisement on the empty bridge. I'm not so much nostalgic for Vaguelio as for the time when I got along well with her. Things were simpler. I figured she must be with her parents in Vrilissia and that she was perhaps watching the same program on television. "I absolutely have to find the origins of those names: Vrilissia, Mitsikeli, Stamata." Marilena came through the living room again, carrying a white chaise longue. She showed it to me.

"Do you think it's mildew?" she asked.

There were indeed countless little dots of greenish mold, concentrated in the middle of the cloth. I suddenly noticed they formed a human silhouette — I could make out the head, the shoulders, the hips.

"I know what must have happened," Marilena said. "The mildew grew on the sweat that soaked into the fabric. They must use this chaise longue for sunbathing in the summer."

I helped her carry it outside. We cracked red eggs together as Easter tradition requires. I don't know why we make them that color or why we play the game that ends when all the shells are cracked except the most solid one. I listened very carefully to the noise the eggs made when they were cracked together, as if I expected that one note to remind me of some forgotten music. Just for a moment, I saw my mother's hands with the pot she used to boil the eggs. I think she used to put coloring into the water. She was holding a wooden spoon. The egg I selected proved to be quite solid, but a woman finally broke it by striking the pointed end of hers against the rounded side of mine, which just isn't done.

"I'm sorry," she told me. "I hadn't noticed that I was holding it backwards."

"It doesn't matter," I said.

"In countries where they don't play this game, they probably don't know that the small end of the egg is always harder than the big end." I imagined my father at home, all alone and cracking two eggs together, playing a game with himself that always ended in a tie.

The music was playing very loudly. The older woman's friend turned down the volume of the stereo several times until she finally told him, "But young people like it loud."

He smiled at her and didn't move. The girl beside me was eating quietly. The movements she made when she served herself made her hair shift slightly. Her hair was very thick, but I could see each strand as if it were drawn with India ink. Each hair had its own luster. Her shoulders were bare. Her dress was held up by very thin straps. She glanced quickly at my plate and continued eating. Her shoulder split her hair in two, left a tiny dark gap like a delta. From time to time I crossed through that opening as if I were seeking shelter from the light. I thought that the skin near her neck must be very soft. I couldn't see whether she was wearing earrings. But I decided that an earring was visible from inside the hiding place formed by her hair. I imagined it set with blue stones. I was disconcerted when she spoke to me, as if I'd forgotten she was there.

"Theodoris told me that you're very well known in Paris. Is that true?"

"The newspaper I work for isn't a really big one, but I've been working there for a long time. I'm known mostly by people in the profession."

She didn't have what you'd call a beautiful face, but nonetheless she was very attractive. Her chin stuck out slightly and her nose was round like a child's. I imagined the sketch I could make. It wouldn't take me more than thirty seconds.

"What sort of sketches do you do?"

"Political cartoons. … I did funny cartoons when I was starting out, but the newspapers don't want them. It's a genre that's been abandoned, like the short article, and I don't know why."

She looked at me curiously. She threw back her hair. She wasn't wearing earrings.

"Nowadays the newspapers only publish caricatures and comic strips. I've never liked comic strips. Inventing a story and creating characters tires me out."

"So you don't really like what you do then?"

"I have a huge number of research materials at home, thousands of photographs of politicians and celebrities. Other photos, too, since I have to know how to dress a cardinal, an Indian, an American soldier. I have to be able to draw an Exocet, a Middle Eastern landscape, an operating room. The photos are all filed in green boxes that take up the biggest wall of my apartment."

"I can't even talk clearly about my work," I thought.

"I dream of one day being able to throw away all those pictures, the boxes, the shelves, of freeing up the wall."

"Do you have an address in Athens?"

Theodoris came over to us and sat beside her on the arm of the armchair. He tilted his head back. His eyes were red.

"You aren't feeling well?" she asked him.

"I don't know whether it's the sun or the wine that's making me dopey."

He turned to me: "I'm thinking about calling Niki. What do you think?"

"I wouldn't do it if I were you."

"She may be alone … . She has a boyfriend, of course, but he's from Sparta. He probably went to Sparta to celebrate Easter."

"Then Niki must be in Sparta."

I started to laugh. He laughed too.

"He didn't offer to show you his drawings?"

"No," the dark-haired girl answered, "but I'd like to see them."

"I live on Thebes street," I told her.

"Really? I have a friend who lives there, number 42."

Someday I'll meet her friend. We'll drink a glass of ouzo in the neighborhood, then we'll take her motorbike and go to the seaside. She'll lose a clog along the way.

"I've lost a clog," she'll tell me, showing me her bare foot.

I'll get off the motorbike and look for her clog on the street, paying no attention at all to the cars flying headlong down Syngrou Avenue. I'll find it and put it back on her foot. We'll go to a nightclub called the Amazon across from the airport.

"You haven't seen my wife by chance?" Charles Carrier will ask me.

He'll shake my hand and move on quickly. We'll drink gin. We'll sit on the floor, in a row of artificial plants. She'll put her head on my shoulder. I'll stroke her chest. I'll suggest that we go have coffee at the airport.

"Do you think it's open at this hour?"

She'll have trouble getting up. She'll get tired out while we're crossing the parking lot. I'll put her beside a scrawny bush. The airport will indeed be open, and the bar too, but there won't be anyone in the immense waiting rooms, which are usually packed. Only one flight will be listed on the arrivals board, expected at four ten in the morning and coming from New Delhi. I'll go back with the two plastic coffee cups. The girl will have disappeared. I'll walk around the tree.

A voice will say, "Are you looking for the girl?"

It will be a soldier carrying a machine gun pointed toward the ground.

I'll empty one of the coffees at the foot of the tree and drink the other as I walk away. I won't find the motorbike where we left it. A taxi will speed by in front of me. In the back seat, I'll see Véronique Carrier.

Theodoris didn't have the energy to take care of his guests. I took the jug and served wine to everyone. They wanted to know how I sign my cartoons.

"Pol," I said.

"*Pavlos* is *Paul*, in French," Marilena added.

"I think I've seen some of your cartoons," said the woman who had broken my egg. "My sister lives in Montpellier. She's a psychiatrist."

The students were dancing to popular music at the far end of the terrace. They were jumping up and down without moving their feet, so their shadows did not move, as if they were dancing on little gray mats. Some of them were doing a very slow dance from Epirus. The music was as monotonous as the wind. "It could be that this dance is older than the music that goes with it, that it was first danced to the sound of the wind." My brother lives in Ioannina, the capital of Epirus. He's a pharmacist, but he's mostly interested in studying the local folklore. He publishes the journal *Epirotika*. I'm planning to go see him. He has a big house outside the city between the lake and the mountains. "Maybe he can explain why we crack Easter eggs together?"

"Have you seen the time?" someone said.

It was five o'clock.

"Good heavens," said someone else.

They began leaving the table, scattering around the house. They lay down in the grass. "Everything eventually tires us out, the meal, conversation, music." I sat down in a corner of the garden where there was a faucet connected to a green plastic hose with a little yellow lattice pattern. Right beside it was a big flat rock with a deep groove in the middle that looked like a capital "I." That made me think about the epsilon of Delphi. I learned by accident, thumbing through a guidebook at Vaguelio's, that the letter conceals a mystery. I'd opened the book mostly out of boredom. I was at her place to stay with a plumber who was trying to fix the dishwasher. I don't remember why Vaguelio wasn't there. If the plumber had been competent, I would not have read that book. He had taken the appliance completely apart and was examining the parts one by one, taking them over to the light. He blew on them, cleaned them, but wasn't able to figure out what was wrong.

"Strange," he said from time to time.

He sat down on the floor without the slightest hesitation, despite the water that had flooded the kitchen, to inspect the bottom of the dishwasher. At regular intervals he thought he had found the solution: he would put it all back together, plug it in, but water still ran out onto the floor.

"That must not be it," he'd say and then take it apart again.

It was already dark.

"Leave it, we'll take it to the dealer. I'll pay you for your time, of course."

He gave me a dark look.

"I'll manage," he said. "And I certainly won't accept any money if I don't fix it."

Then he lay down on the tile to find a spring that had slipped under the electric stove. "Let's hope he doesn't break the stove." That's when I went into the living room and started the book. I learned that at the entrance to the Temple of Apollo, where the Pythia officiated, certain maxims of the Seven Sages were engraved: "Know thyself," "Nothing in excess." Among them was one isolated letter, a capital epsilon, whose meaning is still unknown. The E has given rise to a number of hypotheses, the text's author continued, but none of them has proven satisfactory. This discovery delighted me, and since I felt that it was due to the plumber, I stopped persecuting him. I didn't even complain when he broke the two glasses that were drying on the sink. The enigma of the E reminded me of problems in crossword puzzles. "It has to be a very difficult word to find since we don't know the definition or the number of letters."

"Give me a word that starts with epsilon," I asked Vaguelio when she came home about one in the morning.

"*Éndélos*, completely," she said.

The plumber convinced us to let him have one more try. "He'll never leave," I thought. "He'll spend his whole life trying to fix the dishwasher. We'll all stay awake together." At two in the morning, he finally agreed to leave. He did indeed refuse the money I offered him. I can still see him on the landing, loaded down with his toolbox and a bag of spare parts, waiting for the elevator with his head down.

"Don't worry about it," I told him.

He didn't look at me, just moved his head slightly. He must have felt defeated.

A little green lizard was sitting about ten centimeters away from the stone, examining it. He turned around and stopped. I suppose he sensed that he wasn't in any danger because he turned toward the stone again and held up his head as if he wanted to see the top of it. There was nothing there but dried pine needles. He started to go around it. His hind legs, the ones he used to move forward, were much more powerful than the front ones. They were only used to change direction. He stopped in front of the hose, which was about the same color as his skin. He climbed halfway up, then back down. He did not think it worth the effort to cross the hose just to get to a place that wasn't really different from where he was. While I watched him move, I thought about the only ancient inscription I had ever felt the need to copy. I saw it at a museum in Berlin. I think it wouldn't have drawn my attention if my mother's health had not already begun to decline. I know it by heart because I recopy it every year into my new calendar: "Attalus to queen Apollonis, his mother, for the affection that she showed him." I saw in the encyclopedia that Apollonis, queen of Pergamon, wife of Attalus I, was known for her kindness. The inscription is from Attalus II. I imagine that it's from after his mother's death.

I don't know exactly when I started feeling gloomy. I emptied my pipe by knocking it lightly against the ground. I didn't want to worry the lizard. Before I could crush out the ashes, which were smoldering a bit, I heard someone cry, "That's how forest fires start!"

It was the girl with the long dark hair. Her irritation completely dismayed me.

"Couldn't you empty your pipe somewhere else?"

I crushed out the ashes. Pictures of forest fires on television last summer went through my mind. She turned away from me and walked away quickly. "I'll never meet her friend who lives at 42 Thebes Street. We won't take her motorbike to the seaside. She won't lose a clog on Syngrou Boulevard." I got up. The lizard had gone away.

"I'm leaving," I said to Theodoris.

He was at the edge of the terrace looking down. When I stood next to him, I realized that he was staring at the chaise longue.

"Come look at this," he said.

"I know," I said. "The mildew forms a silhouette on the fabric."

"It's Niki's ghost. She was the only one who used that chaise longue."

He didn't have the energy to go with me, he had a headache and his back hurt. So it was Marilena who drove me to the Kifissia metro station.

"When are you going back to Paris?"

"I don't know."

I didn't feel like answering any more questions. I regretted having confided in the dark-haired girl during the meal. We crossed a street of low concrete houses, beautiful in the late afternoon sun.

"I'm happy that you're with Theodoris," I said. "I didn't much like Niki."

It's probably because of her that Theodoris and I stopped seeing one another over the past few years. Long ago, I used to bring Niki miniature things, chairs, plates, to decorate the dollhouse she had made. She played with the house while I talked with Theodoris. She didn't participate in the conversation, although she followed it carefully. I noticed that Marilena, too, sometimes acted like a little girl: she asked naïve questions, asked Theodoris to help her carry something not especially heavy. I wondered if she didn't collect dolls: besides the miniatures, I had brought Niki a few dolls.

"He goes out with his students three evenings a week. Doesn't that seem a lot?"

"What do you do when he's out?"

"I watch television, I draw. But my teacher tells me that electric light changes the colors. And on television, there isn't much to watch."

I imagined they both must check their watches often during those three evenings and that time certainly passed much more quickly for Theodoris. She got out of the car when I did at Kifissia, she had some errands to run. She took her backpack from the trunk. It was shaped like a panda with a big black and white head. When she put it on her back, the animal's muzzle nestled in her hair. I thought that Theodoris would have a hard time leaving Marilena, if he decided to do so someday.

I saw the cemetery from the metro window again. A bit farther on there's a football stadium where I went occasionally as a child. At the time I didn't even suspect that our wild applause might bother visitors to the cemetery. I went there for the first time fifteen months ago. I glimpsed the gray mass of the stadium through the cypress trees, but I didn't pay it any more attention than I had paid the cemetery years ago. I went back again a week later. I thought it would be easy to find the grave. I took the first path to the left and started to read the names on the stones — dozens, hundreds of unfamiliar names. I finally found the place, three paths farther down. "What are you doing here, among all of these strangers?" I thought. I sat down on the ground and I looked at the gravel between my shoes. That was when a huge roar went up from the neighboring stadium, which had been quiet up until then. It was so loud I thought I was back in the bleachers, thirty years ago.

Night had begun to fall when I got out at Omonia. I don't know what they talk about, all the people who meet on the square every night. I never went near enough to listen. "I've seen enough people today." I stopped for a moment at the intersection of Patission and Chalcocondyli. I decided that I liked the orange of the trolleys and the yellow of the taxis. I crossed Patission Street and started climbing up toward the Lycabette, avoiding Exarchia Square. There are two very lively neighborhoods between Exarchia and Kolonaki, but my own is completely deserted and dark at night. I'd even say it's dark during the day: all it has is shabby stores selling outdated women's underwear, electrical materials, and plastic toys. Their display windows look dusty. There are also some book binderies and a few print shops that seem gray and sad, as if they had never had the chance to print anything but death announcements. The neighborhood's lone restaurant is in a basement. The streets bear the names of obscure figures or small provincial towns. It's a quiet and fairly dirty neighborhood that survives outside the world of fashion and excitement. I bought a ground floor apartment here cheaply. I prefer to live here rather than in Ano Patissia, where I grew up and where my father still lives. Ano Patissia makes me sad. The apartment buildings that have replaced the old houses depress me, and the houses that are still intact depress me too.

I walked past a café where a few old men were playing cards. A little farther along on the same sidewalk I saw a funeral home that was open. Inside, a man was watching television. "He's waiting for the old men playing cards. He's waiting for them to finish their game."

I put the pullover I was carrying away in the bed's storage drawer, emptied my pockets onto the marble table attached to the wall, and lit the water heater. My apartment looks big since I had the walls taken down. I have very little furniture. Just the corners are filled, by the desk, the bed, a bookshelf, the refrigerator and sink. I'm thinking of putting a Ping-Pong table or French billiard table in the middle. I really like both games, though I have no talent for either. The Ping-Pong table's advantage is that it can be moved, folded up in a corner. Maybe I'll invite some people. It's difficult for me to accept the idea that it won't happen, that there will never be a party here. The billiard table would certainly give the apartment a stern look. It doesn't like music, I think, except maybe opera. But opera, too, gets in the way once the game starts. All you should hear then is the music of the game itself, the soft movement of the balls, their imperceptible bounce off the rails, the perfect muted note they make when they come together. It's as if they're apologizing to one another. Ping-Pong is much more cheerful: it sounds like a woman in spike heels coming down a marble staircase. The ball is barely heavier than air. It is made to fly away. It makes sense to wedge it under a paddle when the game stops. It's very fragile but that doesn't weaken its joie de vivre. I suppose that if it met a billiard ball, especially the red one, it would view it with respect, maybe with fear. The problem with Ping-Pong is that you can't play alone. I probably would have opted for it if Vaguelio were still with me. When I'm in a good enough mood to wish there were a woman here, I lean toward Ping-Pong.

Coming back from Stamata, I was happy to be in this empty apartment. "Maybe I won't buy a billiard table or a Ping-Pong table." I called my father. He answered relatively fast. He'd gone to church the night before with the neighbor ladies.

"Then we ate at Fanny's," he told me. "We stayed up until two in the morning!"

My father lives among a group of ladies, widows and spinsters, who help him with his housework, run his errands for him, iron his shirts. Fanny is the youngest. She was in school with my brother. She was popular at the time, but unapproachable. She was waiting to get married, to be freed from the burden of taking care of her father. But her father, who was disabled, took his time freeing her: he died a year ago. She's been dressing in black ever since.

"She went to the cemetery yesterday," he told me. "She watered our mimosa and the geraniums."

I concentrated on the mimosa for a moment. I tried to see it in the dark. A light wind bent it over from time to time. My father told me he was going to get his teeth taken care of.

"I don't like to hide behind my hand when I talk."

To thank the neighbor ladies for all the help they give him, he tells them imaginary stories. I think he passes them off as true.

"Your father has really led a surprising life," one neighbor told me.

He worked as a cashier at the main office of Emboriki Bank: I don't think he ever did anything wrong, but he liked to joke with the customers. My mother confided in me one day that he had nearly been fired because of that. A few years before he retired, he got a promotion that was really just a way of pushing him aside. They gave him a tiny office upstairs where he never saw anyone. Since he didn't have much to do either, he read books about Africa.

"Africa interests me," he used to say.

On his office walls he had hung pictures of African warriors with big bellies and skeletal legs. Some of them had bones in their noses, like in the picture books. They reprimanded him about those photographs, too. He left the bank as soon as could, before the age of sixty. He had started working very young. He didn't tell us stories when we were children. He left that to my mother.

I remembered the face of the dark-haired girl as I could have drawn it. I saw that nonexistent drawing clearly, though I could not see what it was drawn on. I saw a lot of little black lines in empty space. I sat down at my desk and looked at my colored pencils for a moment — they make a pretty bouquet in a heavy pewter jug — and the little bottles of acrylic paint. Most of them are dried up. In Athens I've rarely had the chance and the time to draw. I remember the sketches I've done here very well, for the cover of a book, a newspaper, a friend's wedding, my brother, and five or six for Vaguelio. I did her portrait on typing paper. She was sitting on the bed with her head tilted. She was smoking. Sometimes she held the cigarette in her right hand, sometimes in her left: as I was finishing I noticed that in the drawing she had a cigarette in each hand. I entitled it *Vaguelio with two cigarettes* and gave it to her. I'd like to see it again. I used the entire range of reds, no other color. I also drew my mother in her hospital bed, with a black felt-tip pen. Her hair is not combed, it sticks out in all directions, as if it were panicking. Her eyes are closed. Her mouth is quite good. I kept that sketch, of course. I put it in a brown paper envelope. I can see it from here. It's on the bookshelf, between two black volumes of the encyclopedia. *Éleuthéroudakis*. I haven't looked at that drawing in months. I want to see it, but I don't want to see it.

It seemed to me that I wanted to write. I took the typewriter out of its case, an old typewriter given to me by one of my mother's cousins. I've never used it. The ribbon looks brand new. I put a sheet into the roller. The desire to write was strong, but lacking substance. "Maybe I took out the typewriter just to see the letters of the alphabet." My eye paused on the accents and breathing marks, recently done away with. I wondered if it would be easy for me to break the habit of using them. The keys were slightly hollowed out. They looked like theater seats. "The letters are watching me," I thought. I had lit a pipe. I was wearing a white shirt whose pocket was full of bank notes.

My apartment is situated at the back of the apartment building, and looks out on a garden where there's only one tree, a laurel. "The Ping-Pong ball will end up in the garden all the time. I'll have to climb over the railing to go get it. I might have to get rid of the railing." I ended up accepting that I wouldn't do anything that evening. I would not draw, or write, or eat, or take a bath, or watch television. I'd smoke another pipe or two then go to bed. But I didn't want to get up from the desk without trying the typewriter. I pushed on the key that raises the roller and in the middle of the page typed a capital epsilon.

2.

I don't have much to tell. I go out with friends from time to time. I go to one café in Kolonaki fairly often. I went for a walk near the central market. I wanted to buy a saw and a bronze coat rack, but I couldn't find a coat rack that I liked. I bought a pound of sheep's milk cheese. The refrigerator purrs softly: if I can't get used to the noise, I'll find a way to make it stop. I pinned the sheet of typing paper with the capital epsilon to the wall beside the desk. The summer after I moved to Paris I brought my mother a map of the city.

"Here's where I live," I told her.

She marked the spot with an "x," and she put the map up in the bedroom. Each arrondissement was a different color. Mine was pink. Then I moved to the thirteenth, which was green, then to the sixteenth, which was dark red. With every move, my mother added an "x" to the map. She had also marked the addresses of the newspapers I worked for. She was really upset when I moved to the suburbs, as if I had deprived her of the chance to follow me around.

"Where are you now?" she said.

I made a dot on the wall with my pen, about ten centimeters south of the map. The ink soaked in, and made the dot visible even from a distance. The map is still in the same place. On the wall facing it, my father hung a map of the world.

"What do you use that map for?" I asked him.

"I study it," he answered.

The bed has stayed in the same place, too, but no one uses it anymore. My father has made a habit of sleeping next door, in our old children's room.

"I'm really comfortable in my apartment," I thought, but without real conviction. My thoughts don't concern me. I use them to keep busy and amuse myself. I open the door hesitantly, as if I weren't really at home. My steps have a hollow ring to them. The walls and the objects view me with mistrust. They haven't learned to know me yet. It's only natural that they should have some questions about me: "Who's that? What's he doing here?"

I feel like I have to justify my presence. I sweep, I wash out the bathtub, I do what I can. I try to make my apartment feel friendly toward me. It has to understand that it can trust me. I'm sorry there aren't any roaches, because if I exterminated them I could move up in my apartment's esteem. I suppose that our relationship will improve once I decide to repaint it. Traces of cement and plaster mark the places where the walls stood before they were removed. Which means that the memory of those walls is still intact. Pacing in my apartment, I have a pleasant illusion of passing through those walls.

I'm frightened when a glass slips out of my hand, as if I were going to be scolded. Costas was telling me that the custom of breaking plates during celebration dinners is based on the belief that noise drives away evil spirits. I think that the noises I make attract them, that the spirits are only a few steps away from me while I'm picking up the pieces of glass.

About ten years ago I stuck a black and white photograph of Rita Hayworth to my refrigerator door in Paris. I thought I'd get tired of looking at it after a while. That hasn't been the case: I got used to it, time has legitimized its presence. I have no desire to get rid of the picture. I even told Martha, the cleaning woman, to be careful not to get it wet when she cleans the fridge. She must not be paying much attention to my recommendations, since the paper has taken on a few ripples. Over the past ten years Rita Hayworth has aged.

The total absence of any professional obligations has added to my perplexity. I've always had lots of work in Paris, far too much even, and now suddenly I'm not doing anything. I don't feel like drawing. What would I even draw? The green sweater Vaguelio gave me, lying on the black toilet cover, that I glimpsed through the half-open bathroom door? I read in the encyclopedia that the adjective "green," *prassino*, comes from *to prasso*, "leek." It seems to me that the French think more of a grass green when they use the word, that they tend to grant it a brighter shade. "Only black is the same everywhere." I don't feel like uncapping the India ink bottle. Its odor will remind me of my office at the newspaper, the waiting rooms of several other daily papers, my debut in the profession. I spent twenty-four years in Paris. I take no joy in looking at the inkbottle, as if that black ink were the quintessence of my life in Paris. I didn't find Mitsikeli, or Stamata, or Vrilissia in the encyclopedia. I did discover that Mount Penteliko, which rises above Vrilissia, was once called Vrilissos. "I could start writing an etymological dictionary of place names." Apparently I'm in need of a drastic change.

It's getting light outside. I see the silhouette of the laurel tree through the French doors, but the leaves aren't clearly distinguishable until seven. I get up very early, as if I had urgent work to do. I've already drunk one cup of coffee. I'm going to fix a second one. My text is moving along slowly. I'm happy every time I find the right word. "I'm building sentences … . I'm looking at myself in a new mirror." A well-known Steinberg cartoon shows a man rubbing himself out with an eraser. I don't have the intensity that funny cartoons require. My thoughts are vague, they bloom only in half light. When the sun rises, I stop writing. In the journal I kept in my teens, I was already complaining that nothing was happening, that I had nothing to write. I had just discovered the ability of words to dress the emptiness. They make me think about clothes hung on hangers. All I'm doing is continuing to write that same journal after an interruption of more than thirty years.

I used to draw mostly on Sunday mornings. I'd take my sketchpad, a pencil, and leave the house. I'd cross vacant lots and get to a stream where reeds and trees grew, then draw the houses that were there, a dog, a mulberry bush. I often sat at the foot of a tree. I remember the shadow of its leaves on the white page. I'd go home around noon, happy and famished. My mother would have liked for one of her sons to be a writer. She read a great deal, she admired writers. She may have thought that I would fulfill her dreams, since my compositions had a certain originality to them, but it wasn't enough. She was a bit disappointed when I told her that I planned to attend the Beaux-Arts School, and even more when I announced my decision to dedicate myself to drawing. She considered drawing to be the poor relation of an art that didn't really interest her to begin with. Costas' compositions were no better than mine, for the very good reason that I was the one who wrote them, usually, though my mother didn't know. He helped me in math, physics, and ancient Greek. Without ever reading them I was convinced that the classics were boring. Spending time with my ancestors depressed me. They had the same austere look as the saints on Byzantine icons. My eyes move to the paper pinned to the wall. Why did I start being interested in the epsilon when I never seriously studied the ancient language? For me, it's enough just to look at it. My mind stops at the threshold of its mystery. The E keeps me company.

My mother finished secondary school in Amphissa. She was proud of her school. It was a public school, which, nonetheless, had at its disposal the substantial fortune bequeathed to it by a businessman by the name of Yagdzis. That money allowed them to pay their teachers generously and, of course, to hire the best. In my mother's view, it was the quality of local teaching that explained the city's intense cultural activity. My mother claimed that Amphissa published more journals than Patras, in the Peloponnese.

"The Peloponnese isn't making progress," she said, "because they don't read."

She lived in Amphissa until she finished school. Then she came to Athens with her father and mother. Her father, who had been in construction in Amphissa, invested his entire savings in a passementerie shop he opened on Lekka Street. At the beginning of the 1930's, unfortunately, people didn't need braids and ribbons. My grandfather was ruined and sank into a lengthy depression. His mood didn't improve until the day war was declared. It seems he left for the front with a feeling of relief. Perhaps he thought the war would put an end to his troubles. He was among the first killed, in the mountains of Epirus, not far from the place where he had been born. My grandmother died a few years later. I knew her but don't remember her at all.

As a child, I imagined that Amphissa was like the kingdoms in stories, with houses made of chocolate and fat shopkeepers wearing red vests. Over the years, my mother's stories became fewer and fewer, as if she were beginning to forget, or as if she hadn't enough energy to travel that far in time in order to remember. Her desire to see Amphissa again faded too. She was afraid she wouldn't recognize it anymore. She had no relatives at all left in the region. Toward the end of her life, I'm sure she only thought of it when she was buying olives. She was angry when she couldn't find the famous Amphissa olives at the grocer's.

"I don't want any of your savory olives," she would say to the grocer, with a bitterness that wasn't like her at all.

She talked to us about the bell makers of Amphissa, who were "known to all Greeks," just like its tanners. She told us how the shepherds would try out bells for hours, sitting cross-legged on the floor.

"They would hold them about fifty centimeters off the floor, about the height of a goat's neck. The sound of each bell had to be unique, so that the shepherd could follow the animal's movements by ear. The bells were a kind of identity card for the animals."

They also had to harmonize together so that the movements of the flock would produce a pleasant music.

"The shepherds chose them as carefully as musical instruments, and the bell makers made them just as carefully. One of the best-known stores in town used the name Liszt after the musician, it was called Chez Liszt!"

Her memories of Amphissa weren't all good ones. Her mother worked in a tannery, washing hides. They were soaked, apparently, in a mixture made from dog excrement, which opened the pores and made cleaning the hides easier.

"The foul smell from the tannery followed my mother home," she told us.

"When I came home from school, I could tell at the front door whether she was there. People called tanners 'turders.'"

She sometimes smiled when she said that word, but she usually didn't. Scatological terms displeased her deeply. She didn't even approve of the words "pipi" and "caca." She just simply replaced them: she said "one-two" for pipi and "two-three" for caca.

"Do you want to go two-three?" she would ask me.

It was at school that I learned, to my great surprise, that this terminology was not widespread.

I think Costas' interest in folklore was first awakened by our mother's stories. He reminds me of her when he explains some popular tradition: he speaks slowly, with circumspection, and weighs his words carefully. It's only when he's less interested in questions and doesn't know much about them that he becomes verbose.

"Be precise," my mother used to say.

I try to be precise. I often use the dictionary, especially Vostandzoglou's *Antilexico.* That gentleman had the excellent idea of classifying words by themes, grouping them around some fifteen hundred basic terms. The verb *awaken* that I used above is under the rubric *encouragement.* The beard entry informs us that a little beard growing just below the lip bears the pretty name of *bamterlélé.* My *beard* covers a good part of my face. It has turned nearly white. During my first year in Paris, I let it grow out. I was a student at the Beaux-Arts then. I've since forgotten the shape of my face.

I had the chance to meet Vostandzoglou a long time ago in a magazine office. He was born in Asia Minor. I remember his kindly smile. He wanted to become a novelist, but since he wanted a better dictionary, he decided to write one himself. It proved to be more work than expected: he classified about twenty thousand words and wasn't able to do anything else before his death. His Antilexico reminds me of forgotten words that move me. It amuses me by reminding me that the condom is also called a "cock-cover" (*périkavlis*). It invites me to stroll through the language. Sometimes when I'm glancing through it, I have the feeling that I'm reading the novel that the author didn't have time to write.

I think the Greeks of the diaspora have contributed a great deal to enriching the language — I'm thinking especially of Coraïs and of Psicharis, who both lived in Paris. I myself largely forgot it over the years I was gone. Surely I would have a harder time writing down the insignificant things I'm talking about (I wonder from time to time why I keep writing) if my liaison with Vaguelio, which lasted two years, hadn't allowed me to get back in contact with Greek. We called one another every day when I was in Paris and saw one another every day in Athens. Her presence sweetened the atmosphere in my apartment, and the expectation of her arrival did too.

Love that's just beginning needs new words. Vaguelio and I invented several. I gave her another name, and she changed mine as well. Then we discovered that those nicknames had a host of diminutive forms. We gave completely new names to the games we played. She would hide in the armoire and call out, "Where am I?"

I'd pretend not to know: "Where are you?"

She would suddenly leap from the armoire and throw me to the floor. We tried to smother each other under the covers. She'd keep me from getting to my pipe or a newspaper. We'd wrestle.

"Bring me something red," I'd say to her.

"And you bring me something black!"

We'd both start searching, she for a red object and I for a black one. We'd race on hands and knees. We'd go from the door of her apartment to the bedroom. The one who got to the bed first was the winner. We'd bump each other, push each other against the wall, grab each other by the feet. Vaguelio's dog would stand off to one side, unmoving and almost pensive, and observe the game's progress. It was a white dog with floppy ears. She'd found it in the street and called it Gaour after the hero of a popular novel set in the jungle.

We changed the meaning of certain common words. We made up words that had no meaning at all so we could talk without saying anything.

I would say to her, for example, "Where did you put the *varsoumas*, sweetie?"

"The *varsoumas*?" she would say, stalling for time. "It's in the *yenditsa*!"

"Oh is it?" I'd say, disapprovingly.

"Absolutely! In my family, we always put the varsoumas in the yenditsa," she would add and burst out laughing.

She laughed easily and often got angry. She was convinced that I was seeing other women. She didn't listen to what I said, but she tried to guess what my words were hiding. When that happened, space got dangerously tight. I once asked her to leave.

"Do you really want me to leave?"

She was standing at the door, with her hand on the knob.

"Wait a second."

I took a felt pen and traced the outline of her shadow on the floor.

"No," I said when I finished.

"Erase that, please," she asked me a bit later.

I was never able to erase that drawing completely. You can still see the outline on the floor. We once had an argument about Macedonia. She was planning to attend a government-sponsored demonstration against the Macedonian Slavs, "people of Skopje" as they called them. Athens planned to block recognition of their state under the name of Macedonia. Vaguelio claimed that only Greeks had the right to use the term, since the main northern region is already called that. "Macedonia is Greek, and only Greek," was the government slogan that had been relentlessly repeated by the media for several days before the demonstration.

"You can't really understand because you don't live here," she said. "It doesn't matter to you if a war breaks out, does it? You have French nationality, don't you?"

She had already asked me that question twice, but apparently my answer hadn't convinced her. I maintained that we should recognize Skopje as North Macedonia or New Macedonia.

"We can't let them take over our history. They only got there a few weeks ago! They're tourists! What do they have to do with Alexander the Great? If we recognize them as Macedonians, we're opening up the door of Greek Macedonia to them!"

"We're the ones who claim that there's only one Macedonia, not them."

That discussion caused a long-term resentment between us. Afterwards, we always avoided broaching the subject. She ended up not going to the demonstration, which took place in Athens, on the Field of Mars — perhaps the government chose that spot to show that it was ready for anything. There was a huge crowd. Loud protests from the demonstrators shook the windows in my apartment.

We met at The Greek Film Festival in Thessaloniki, where she'd gone with an actress friend. I'd been named a member of the short film jury. We drank ouzo at noon in a back street. There were other people with us. I didn't see her over the next few days and thought that she had left. On the closing evening, she was waiting for me at the door of the Movie Palace.

"Shall we?" she said.

The room had a high ceiling. A transom over the door let in the blue light from the hallway. It lit the lower part of the bed. Our legs were blue. We went out late at night and sat down on a grassy median. Workers on ladders were taking down the letters of the "31st Film Festival" sign. They were huge letters in bright colors. The workers were barely visible in the pale glow of streetlights, but the letters were perfectly clear as they descended to the sidewalk one by one.

We stayed one more day in Thessaloniki. We walked on the quays. The sea was calm and about the same color as the sky. From time to time bells would ring. It was a Sunday. The endless curve formed by the quays seemed ideal to me. We walked across Aristotle Square, which seemed festive, and another square where there were hundreds of Russian immigrants, disillusioned and badly dressed. Vaguelio tried to take pictures of them, but they stopped her. On Egnatia Avenue she took a picture of a funeral home. It had the same gray furnishings and the same beige walls as most of those businesses. They're gloomy, as befits a place where no one ever hears anything but bad news.

"Why are you photographing that, my lovely?" asked a giant of a man in a white apron standing in the door of a neighboring pastry shop. "You should be taking pictures of me!"

That's how we met Mr. Aphthonides — his name means "abundance." He must have weighed about one hundred and twenty kilos. We went into the shop and ordered two stuffed galettes. He sat down at our table. He told us that he was originally from Constantinople and he named several cakes with Turkish names that aren't made anymore because no one appreciates them. He informed us that yogurt must be made from buffalo milk, which has become nearly impossible to find. I supposed that his last name was originally a first name, but I didn't ask him about it. He was angry with women, found they were all hypocrites.

"And when I say all of them, I'm including my mother," he insisted.

He had us taste several pastries. In the end, he wouldn't even let us pay for anything, not even the galettes. At noon we returned to the little street where we'd drunk ouzo a few days before, as if we were in a hurry to form habits the two of us shared.

I remembered Mr. Aphthonides' judgment of women during one of my last arguments with Vaguelio. She admitted that she was still seeing one of her old lovers, something she'd categorically denied up to then. I was beside myself.

"So Aphthonides is right!" I spat.

She was perpetually angry at someone. She got mad at her sisters and sometimes she wouldn't speak to her mother. She lived feverishly, worked a great deal — she's a photographer — went to bed at dawn and drank tremendously. I think she was afraid of being bored. I was less accustomed to domestic scenes than she was. I haven't had any stormy relationships in Paris. My love stories ended peacefully. Greek television series invariably describe a conflict, between the father and the mother, the son and the daughter, the father and the son, the daughter and her fiancé, the mother and a neighbor, the employee and his boss, the boss and his secretary. "You can't talk to me like that!" is the key phrase in Greek television series. The short films I saw at Thessaloniki, all by young directors, often had family discord as their subject, but they were more dramatic in tone. They expressed the sufferings of children confronting authoritarian parents.

Through the bathroom window, which opens out onto the apartment building's air duct, I can hear a young couple or the security guard and his daughter arguing. Now and again an old man lets out a lengthy growl, as if he were trying to spit. In summer, when all the windows are open, shouts can be heard from the other side of the apartment building. In Paris, my neighbors are more discreet. I barely know them, really. I've never seen the man who moved in on my floor several months ago. But one night when I was looking out the window I saw his shadow beside mine on the white wall of the apartment building across the way. I almost gave him a friendly wave by way of my shadow, but I didn't especially feel like getting into a conversation, even indirectly. So we've never met, but at least I can say that our shadows are acquainted.

She was surprised when I told her that I planned to leave her. She was convinced that I needed her more than ever. I really was very distressed. Apparently there are misfortunes that cannot be shared, or that one doesn't feel like sharing.

"I need to be alone," I told her.

We were in the living room of her apartment, each of us sitting on opposite ends of the corner sofa. On the coffee table there was a sky-blue fruit basket full of coins. She didn't say anything. She got up and put on a record of Nino Rota. She turned the sound way up, as if music we had often listened to together could reduce the distance already stretched out between us. She lit a cigarette, then went into the kitchen, which opens directly into the living room. She was bent over the sink doing something. I'm not sure if she noticed when I left. Walking away down the street, I could still hear the music. It was *Nights of Cabiria*.

When I stop writing and am drinking my third cup of coffee, about nine in the morning, the apartment's tranquility makes me happy. I don't hear any voices at that hour. People have gone to work or to run errands. I don't even hear the old man. I imagine he's sleeping. I stare at the laurel tree in the garden or the steam rising from my coffee. Writing tires me out, torments me, but nonetheless gives me a certain pleasure. I think it's because of the contact with words. I'm breathing right next to the language, that's what I'm doing. As for the content of my text, I've already said that it doesn't seem important to me. I have the feeling that there are silences between the words, long silences, as if I were writing in order not to say anything, rather than to express myself.

The ease with which I got rid of the habit of using the *périspoméni*, the circumflex accent, convinced me that it was superfluous. I write with a Staedtler pencil. Now and then I draw a head or a running man in the margin. I also drew a cube framed by a woman's hair — a cube wearing a wig. I'm not using the typewriter. I put it back in its case. Its noise disturbed me and so did the stilted look of its letters. They made my text unusually solemn. I've invented a game that keeps me busy when I'm short on inspiration: I compose sentences using only words that start with the letter E. So far I've produced three.

Erpéton échon énochlissin ex éntonou ellipséos édesmaton éphagen éteron erpéton: Reptile suffering a severe lack of nourishment devoured another reptile.

Ekchristianisménos eidololatris éviassen épamphotérizonta épiscopon eis ecclissaki érimikon: Idolater converted to Christianity raped an ambiguous bishop in an isolated chapel.

Écho épiskephthi eidon-eidon épaguelmatiès, emvrithis éntomologous, eccentrikous ephoplistès, émbirous ergatès, euprossigorès étairès, émpathis eirénodikès, ékolaptoménous éthnosotérès, eukolossymvivastous éphoriakous, exantliménous épétès: I visited all sorts of professionals, erudite entomologists, eccentric shipbuilders, experienced workmen, hospitable courtesans, hateful magistrates, providential men in gestation, obliging Treasury agents, worn-out beggars.

I almost went to Delphi one summer, a long time ago.

"How can it be that you haven't been there yet?" my mother asked me.

She looked at me with the same deep surprise that my spelling errors had inspired in her years ago.

"What a strange idea, to write it that way!" she would say.

She advised me to look very carefully at the statue of a smiling young girl, but I've never managed to make the trip. When did she visit Delphi? When she was in secondary school probably. The shrine is quite near Amphissa. I could go there now. "Maybe the time has come," I thought. I'm still looking at the laurel tree in the garden. "Maybe."

I don't know how long I'll stay here. I've been back for two weeks and have only called France twice. I called Martha and a colleague at the paper, Marie-Christine. I asked her to send me twenty packets of tobacco.

"That many?" she said.

"I may ask you for more."

I smoke three or four packets a week. This is the first time I've been here without a return ticket. "If I knew why I came, I could plan my return." I study the burned bits of tobacco in the bowl of my pipe: some are sticking straight up, others form parentheses, question marks, or even little waves. They remind me of Arabic calligraphy. Martha takes care of my apartment and pays my bills. I asked her to open the mail. There were mostly invitations to exhibits, wine-bar openings, some flyers.

"The Two Cubs are selling their leather goods at prices…."

"Throw it away," I had to keep telling her, because she was quite prepared to even read the flyers to me.

A letter arrived from Greece. Was it from Vaguelio? She doesn't know I'm in Athens. Unfortunately, Martha couldn't decipher the signature.

"Is the writing slanted?" I asked her.

"Fairly slanted, but there are straight letters too."

I realized that I didn't remember Vaguelio's writing very well. Was it really slanted? She rarely wrote to me.

I listen attentively to everything around me. I'm examining Athens as if I've come to study it. My previous trips didn't allow me enough time to really look at it. I was constantly thinking about Paris. Athens fascinated me less. I can't say that I don't know the city, nor can I say I know it well. I was convinced that Callidromiou Street ran parallel to Alexandras Avenue, and I was stupefied when I was going up the former and chanced across the latter. One day I found myself on Strefi Hill, thinking I was on Lycabettus. Reality often forces me to revise the city map that I keep in my head. I move streets, hills, even entire neighborhoods, and replace them with others. My map is like those ancient charts where nothing is in the right place.

I do, however, know the pitiful look of Athens' trees. They're bitter oranges, for the most part. They never grow over two meters high. The stake that's meant to support them is usually pulled out of the ground — someone probably gave it a kick — and leaning against the tree. They carry their stake like a cross. They suffer from the city's polluted atmosphere as well. At night they're even worse off because neighborhood residents pile their garbage around them in plastic bags. Late in the night garbage men deliver them from that disagreeable company, but never completely. Either because the bags weren't closed properly, or because they were torn open by cats, parts of the contents stay on the sidewalk.

I walk with my head down most of the time, so I know the sidewalks better than the buildings. All I'm really familiar with is their basements. The tops of their windows just barely protrude over the level of the sidewalk. There's a little well between those windows and the sidewalk that pedestrians use as a trash bin. They're occupied by elderly people who look out rather hopefully toward the sidewalk. They wear faded pajamas. It's surprising that the authorities allow people to rent basements that flood regularly from the rain. One gets the clear impression that the state is on the side of the owners and builders whose abuses have been growing for decades, encroaching on streets, devouring public spaces — Mount Lycabettus is built up practically to the summit — and building apartment houses that are far too high. Walking in the streets of Athens, I can almost hear a constant whispered conversation between a builder and a ministry official. Every building, in its own way, is a testament to an official finally giving in.

Sidewalks, mostly very narrow, are invaded by mountains of bricks, sand, or marble dust. In this outrageously overbuilt city, construction work never stops. Sometimes the sidewalks simply aren't there at all: they're regularly demolished to repair a pipe, to install new phone lines. The materials used to repair them, once the work is done, are extraordinarily varied. Sometimes smooth slabs, sometimes cement stepping-stones mixed with gravel, sometimes beige or orange tiles with an oblique wavy striated pattern. Such cacophony displeases the elegant shops, which hide their own bit of sidewalk beneath a green carpet or black linoleum. I've grown so used to Athens as it is now that I've forgotten its face from another time. I just remember that there were very few cars and that you could see carts passing in the streets. They were pulled by stocky horses with long manes. I've been told that they were Hungarian. I don't have the heart to remember anymore. Perhaps I've reached the age of my mother when she stopped talking to us about Amphissa.

My interest in the city and its inhabitants isn't constant. It can end abruptly. My eye wanders over the round café table, takes its time going from my thumb resting on the edge of the table to the ashtray. I slide my thumb. My hand falls into my lap. The uneasiness I feel is satisfying. "I don't want to feel good." A moment ago, I was curious to hear how the woman sitting a few tables away would answer her companion. She was obviously about to say something to him, but she didn't say anything and she even squeezed her lips tightly shut. I have trouble gauging the sincerity of my interest in people and things. I don't know what sets it off or what reins it in. I was moved by a taxi driver's story about the death of his twelve-year-old son. The boy suffered from a bone marrow disease.

"I had to sell everything so that we could have him cared for in France," he confided. "This taxi isn't mine anymore. Now I work for a boss. I went around to all the ship owners, and they all gave me some money, two hundred, two hundred and fifty thousand drachmas. All told, it cost me fifty million. Social Security only reimbursed half. The doctors took the marrow for the graft from my daughter, who's fifteen. The boy spent eight months in the hospital. The operation was a success, but his liver just couldn't take the shock, and we had barely enough time to bring him home. They fixed up a little hospital room in the plane for him. He died just as we arrived. God did not take pity on him."

"I came here to listen to this story," I thought.

"I still owe eight million."

"You'll pay it back," I told him.

"I just don't have the energy. I'll pay it back, of course. No one is rushing me. Someone will marry my daughter with no dowry. But I have no energy anymore."

As I was getting out of the taxi, I asked him his daughter's name.

"Callirhoé," he said.

I'm more easily touched than I used to be, my equilibrium at the mercy of the tiniest event. Even the pathetic soap operas on television can move me. Tears come to my eyes when Alexandrakis is finally accepted by his wife's family and when his decrepit old middle-class mother-in-law tells him, "Come, my son, give me a hug!"

That scene gets to me, my chest tightens, and I can't control myself anymore. Maybe I just didn't cry enough in my own life, or I didn't cry when I should have, and now I'm externalizing forgotten emotions. The tears falling now are old ones.

I managed to control myself fairly well that day. I only went out of the house two or three times so that my father wouldn't see me. I went to the far end of the garden. I'm the one who called my family to let them know. I showed a certain composure, despite the pain I felt when I had to say that sentence. I repeated it thirty, maybe forty times. With every call, I had the feeling that I myself had just found out the news I was breaking to them.

"You know . . . ," I began.

They didn't know, of course. It had just happened.

I can't claim that I came to take care of my father because I don't take care of him much. I've only gone to Ano Patissia twice. He came to visit me, too. He's reassured by the fact that I'm in Athens, I think. He's happy when I call him. But he doesn't want me to do anything more for him. He can't stand it when I take his arm in the street. His walk has become halting. He moves lightly, like a dancer. My father will not admit that he's aging. It's true that he has no serious illnesses, though he sometimes complains about his liver or his kidneys. I, too, have trouble admitting that he is getting old. I'm outraged when the neighbor ladies call him "grandfather." He's happy for any help he gets from them and sees it as an expression of tenderness rather than an act of pity.

Every time I've gone to see him, I've found Fanny at his place, cleaning up the kitchen. I hadn't seen her in over a year. I was in Paris when her father died. Her skin looked extremely pale to me, perhaps because she was dressed in black and wasn't wearing makeup. She'd lost weight. Her forehead reminded me of her father's. We talked very little the first time. She avoided looking at me, stared at the door, the refrigerator, as if she were embarrassed by her appearance and wanted me to look elsewhere.

"I've aged," she said.

She's forty-nine, like my brother, but she looks younger. I found her depressed, rather than older. She still reminds me of the girl she was. She has very nice legs.

"What story is my father telling you?" I asked her when we were alone for a moment.

"The adventures of Pim, a boy who ran away from home and who's crossing the United States, trying to earn a living. We meet every Wednesday, we make tea, and he tells us the next installment."

We talked a bit more the second time while my father was upstairs working on something. I learned that Pim's parents, Italian carnival people living in New York, aren't his real parents. They kidnapped him while on tour in Europe.

"He promised us that Pim would travel around the world!"

I told her Costas' news. She talked to me about a friend of hers who had a good job, three charming children, an understanding husband, and who jumped from her apartment balcony one day. She assured me that I knew her, we'd been in English class together. I couldn't remember.

"She died the same week that . . . ."

She began to cry. I put a hand on her back.

"You have to try to forget him."

She turned and looked at me.

"I don't want to forget him," she said coldly.

She wouldn't stay to have lunch with us. She left after she finished her work. I asked my father if he paid her.

"She got angry when I talked to her about it . . . . She has her father's retirement, and it's fairly generous. She spends almost nothing, doesn't buy clothes, doesn't go out. She goes to the cemetery every morning, then she comes to see me."

My father has an impressive appetite. He likes to have several dishes around him, and he always does. Some he prepares himself, the rest are gifts from the neighbor ladies. He didn't cook before and didn't use to be nearly so fond of food. Before he's even swallowed the zucchini and the tomato he's just speared, he's already casting a hungry look at the rice with spinach and the pasta au gratin. I used to be embarrassed by the noise he made slurping his soup, probably because I knew it annoyed my mother. Now it bothers me less. I think he eats too much, of course. I try to get him to understand that by barely touching the dishes myself when we're together. The sacrifice I make by way of example means that I am always hungry when we leave the table. But he scarcely notices what I eat. We have coffee in the living room. He swore to me that he didn't need any money to pay the dentist, that the entire cost would be picked up by the bank's employee health insurance. He's missing two or three upper incisors.

"You're right," I told him. "You should get it taken care of."

"Of course I'm right!"

Her picture is on the buffet. It's a color photograph taken in the country, the trees visible behind her. You can see her shoulders, her arms. When we divided up her things, I took the woolen jacket that she's wearing. You can't see the cigarette she's holding in her hand, but you can see the smoke rising along her left arm and dissipating at her shoulder. My father doesn't smoke.

"Women clearly have more money than men," he once declared unexpectedly. "The richest are about forty years old, they have brown hair, wear glasses, and are rather thin. They don't look rich, but they have huge wallets in their purses. Young women don't have a cent, they spend everything, they're superficial. They even owe money to the grocer! I know what I'm talking about. I was a cashier for thirty-three years!"

He repeated "thirty-three years," then said nothing more. Memories of the life he led bother him. That troubles me. He doesn't see any of his former colleagues. He has no friends at the bank. He made friends with only one customer, Stelios, a photographer. He's the one who took the photograph of my mother on the buffet. Their friendship does not upset me. Stelios isn't an ordinary man either. The walls of his studio are covered from top to bottom with hundreds of photographs where he's standing beside De Gaulle, Kennedy, Brigitte Bardot, Gagarin. Every time he went to the airport to report on famous visitors, he managed to have himself photographed beside them. He'd hand his camera to a colleague and pose alongside the important person. What was he hoping for? To steal a bit of their glory? He's a collector of celebrities. All the Greek politicians know him. He claims that Caramanlis, when he was hosting Giscard d'Estaing in Athens, spontaneously invited him to shake the French president's hand. I think I've seen a photograph where Stelios is between the two men, and it seems to me he has taken them both by the arm. I've had the chance to visit his studio. The celebrities usually have a rather sullen look, while Stelios wears a triumphant smile in all the snapshots. The fame of some of those important people did not last long — former champions whose records were soon broken, former husbands of actresses, forgotten after the divorce — so I sometimes wonder who in the world the person beside Stelios might be. My ignorance both surprises and upsets him: "That's Manfred Germar! How can you not recognize Manfred Germar if you're so interested in track and field?"

He's probably afraid that all these people will fall into obscurity and that his collection will, consequently, lose its value. Fortunately, he himself managed to become rather famous: a few years ago, the weekly *Tachydromos* had a long illustrated article about him, entitled "The Don Quixote of Photography." Other papers have also talked about him. During the military junta, he stopped going to the airport — he had no desire to be photographed with people invited by the colonels. For that period, he had to earn his living photographing baptisms and weddings that took place in his neighborhood.

I went upstairs to the bathroom. The door to the bedroom was partially open. I looked at the brown bedspread with big orange flowers, the only thing covering the mattress. On the wall, I saw the world map that my father studies. I was going to go into the room, but the door creaked slightly just as I pushed it. I think it was the noise that kept me from going in.

I don't like to stay alone in the living room — my father came upstairs too. I couldn't avoid thinking about that afternoon when we had to move all the furniture. We took out the chairs and the coffee table, folded up the big table, and pushed the buffet into a corner. We made a big empty space. I remember the glasses clinking in the buffet while we were moving it. All the furniture was put back the very next day.

The telephone did not ring. Costas calls him every evening at eight o'clock. I asked him if the ring had bothered him for a long time.

"It always has," he said, "but I didn't pay any attention to it before. Now I do pay attention, and that's the difference. Sometimes the phone stays quiet for hours and then I get two or three calls one after the other. Once it rings, it's a sure thing that someone will call again in the next few minutes."

I offered to buy him a phone with a softer ring. He has an old black telephone.

"That won't change anything."

He glanced at the phone sitting near the front door on a little chest. There is a big mirror just above it that reflects part of the stairs up to the second floor.

"So what are you doing?" he asked. "How are you keeping busy?"

He didn't use to ask me questions. I spoke mostly with my mother. The man who chatted so much at the bank didn't say a word at home. He got our news from my mother. I would never have heard anything of his troubles at the bank if my mother had not talked about them. There's no doubt that she played the leading role. Both Costas and I confided much more easily in our mother than in each other. She intimidated us less. We spoke to her for hours. She didn't say much. She listened mostly.

"I don't do anything."

"That's not possible . . . ."

He said it in a small, hesitant voice, as if he were afraid of seeming indiscreet. I was touched by his interest. I realized that he was sitting in the armchair where our mother sat. Since I had nothing else to tell him, I talked about the mysterious E of Delphi. He clearly found it interesting:

"That's astonishing," he repeated two or three times.

When I had finished, he added, "You know what that letter makes me think of? Messages in bottles thrown into the sea by shipwrecked sailors that finally arrive years later, when they've become nearly illegible. There's a half-erased message like that in *Captain Grant's Children*. There are just a few letters and a number left, and no one knows if they mean longitude or latitude."

I admitted that Fanny had told me about Pim. He didn't seem either pleased or displeased. He seemed to be waiting for me to say more. I remembered that my mother made fun of his taste for tall tales.

"Is it true that you're going to have him go around the world?"

"Maybe," he said, maintaining confidentiality.

"Have you chosen an itinerary?"

He grasped that I wasn't planning to make fun of him.

"I think he's going to cross the Americas, all the way to Tierra del Fuego, and then go to Africa. I don't invent everything, you know: I borrow things from novels and films. I'm reading a book on Mexico City right now. I have to stay informed, I don't want to be talking nonsense."

He asked me for two Jules Verne books, *Captain Grant's Children* and *The Lighthouse at the End of the World*.

"I'm certain that the lighthouse at the end of the world is on Tierra del Fuego," he said.

I thought about the next part of Pim's travels and offered to bring him the adventures of *Tarzan*, too.

"But I have Tarzan!" he exclaimed, as if it were unthinkable that he might not have it.

At the end of both visits, he went with me as far as the garden gate. He stayed there, like my mother used to do, waiting until I turned the corner.

I was walking fast, as if I wanted to escape the memories I still have of this neighborhood. They aren't bad memories, but they're so distant that they naturally make me a bit sad. "This neighborhood isn't a place, it's an era. I'm walking through an era." I felt an inexplicable pain when I saw a schoolgirl about twelve years old with a stack of books under her arm, opening the door to her house. I walked along the edge of my old elementary school. The wall around the schoolyard has been raised. It's four meters high. I heard children shouting. Suddenly, a basketball came over the wall and landed almost right in front of me. It bounced on the hood of a car, then into the middle of the street, and ended up in front of an apartment building. There was no one on the street. I picked up the ball and with a kick sent it back into the schoolyard. From the children's shouts, I could tell that the game had started up again. "I came here," I thought, "to give you back the ball."

3.

I saw the poet I met in Stamata and I waved at him, but he didn't wave back. He was wearing the same green suit. The bookstore was packed. It wasn't easy to get to the buffet and pour myself a plastic glass of retsina. I noticed a middle-aged man with a white beard wearing a wide-brimmed black hat and a black cape with a red scarf around his neck. He reminded me of the Toulouse-Lautrec drawing by Aristide Bruant. I recognized several writers in attendance and a young blonde woman with a crew cut who hosts the *Portraits* program on television. The event was organized by Manos Acridakis, the editor, to present a new volume devoted to *The Eternal Greek Woman*, with a preface by Amalia Stathopoulou, the current minister of culture.

Amalia is an old friend of Manos. We were waiting for her to start the press conference. People were looking out the front window of the bookstore, watching for the arrival of the official car.

"A reporter mentioned you a few minutes ago." Manos told me, "She wants to meet you. I'll tell her you're here."

He looked around, but he didn't see her.

"How long are we going to wait?" asked the blonde television host.

"We can spare another ten minutes or so, Ionna."

I remembered her name, Ionna Calogridou.

"No more than ten minutes, okay?" she said, eating a little triangular sandwich.

I noticed that she was the center of attention. She was wearing heavy makeup. As soon as she'd finished the sandwich, she took a little round mirror out of her purse and checked her mouth. She made faces, as if no one could see her. People were watching the man in the black hat too. He was talking to two writers slightly younger than him, both of them pensive and a bit sad. He, on the other hand, looked delighted. He seemed to take pleasure in talking. One of the writers lifted his glasses and wiped his eyes with a big white handkerchief. I thought he was crying. The few writers I knew in Paris were equally morose, as if they never thought about anything but stories that take place in rainy little towns. The poet from Stamata — I call him that because I don't remember his name — started trying to get through the crowd. We looked at one another again, and he avoided greeting me.

There was a copy of *The Eternal Greek Woman* open on a glass table. I paged through it: it was a series of portraits of famous women — Sappho, Anna Comnena, Bouboulina, Penelope Delta, and others. It was a luxury edition, copiously illustrated. The preface stressed the contributions of women to Greek culture, social struggles, and the fight for freedom. The Minister declared that the Greece of today is worthy of its distant ancestors and that its achievements will grow ever better thanks to laws guaranteeing equality of the sexes. The text was about twenty lines long. Stathopoulou's signature took up the rest of the page.

Back during the dictatorship, I once drew a fat woman holding up one leg, threatening to crush a tiny little boy under her heel.

"Do you love me?" she was asking him.

I was feeling a distinct hostility toward the Greeks. Not knowing how to explain the timorous attitude of most of my countrymen toward the junta, I had decided that it was their mothers' fault. I wasn't upset with fathers: in my eyes, women alone were responsible. I flew into a rage every time I saw a mother slap her child. After the student uprising at Athens Polytechnic, I had to revise my judgment a bit, but I didn't change my opinion. It's very easy to form an opinion, and it's just as difficult to get rid of one. I don't know the reasons for my animosity toward women. My mother was rather gentle. I was far from feeling as oppressed by family as the Thessalonica short film directors seemed to be. And I have to admit that I wasn't very daring under the dictatorship. Two years after the coup d'état, I left for Paris. I participated in the demonstrations there against the colonels, of course, but stayed in the back of the room to avoid being photographed. I knew that several photographers were collaborating with the embassy to draw up lists of the opposition. A few of the cartoons I published back then could have irritated the Greek authorities. That wasn't the case, apparently. Maybe the embassy didn't know who Pol was. I doubt they ever tried to find out.

The cover of the book shows Bouboulina standing at the bow of her ship and directing operations against the Turkish fleet. The scene takes place during the 1821 War of Independence. The men of her crew look frightened. The ship — a very large barque — is named *Agamemnon*.

I looked at the crowd again. Some were impatient with the Minister's late arrival, but the ambiance was still friendly. It was obvious that they all knew one another well and all I could hear around me were first names: Yorgos, Nicos, Socrate, Eleonora, Dimitra, Caterina. In Paris, under the same circumstances, it seems to me that I would have heard mostly family names — Delbourg, Grandmont, Carrier, Caumont, Nicolaïdès — since that's the way my name is pronounced in French. In Greek they say Nicolaïdis, with an accent on the next-to-last syllable. I was jealous of those demonstrations of friendship. It was as if I weren't part of the same society, as if I were an intruder. I got some more wine. I had to protect my glass constantly from the guests' sudden movements. The poet handed Calogridou a book, probably a collection of poetry since it was in large format with few pages.

"She's here!" someone said.

A black Mercedes with tinted windows had just appeared. There was a general movement toward the door. The poet and Calogridou were the first to set foot on the sidewalk.

"Get ready, Thanassis!" cried Calogridou to a young guy carrying a video camera on his shoulder while busily eating ice cream by a newspaper kiosk across the way.

I remembered kiosks selling ice cream when I was a child. They were equipped with a cooler. Thanassis wasn't overly concerned. He just bent down to look inside the vehicle, which was moving at the pace of a hearse.

"Throw that ice cream away!" Calogridou shouted again.

Someone pointed out that the car was from the diplomatic corps.

"It might be for the Nigerian ambassador," said Manos. "He lives near here."

The car turned at the corner. They all went back inside the bookstore, slightly annoyed. Calogridou alone stayed outside and kept shouting. She had taken the cameraman's lack of alacrity as a personal affront.

"When I tell you to do something, I mean right now. Understood?"

Thanassis thought it best to make at least a slight effort: he crossed the street and stood in front of the bookstore, still eating ice cream.

"You can't count on anyone in this country!" said an exasperated Calogridou, going back into the bookstore.

She turned toward Manos: "Call Amalia. We really need to know if she's coming or not!"

I could feel that the mood in the room was taking a turn for the worse. Manos no doubt felt the same, because he went straight to the phone. I hadn't known that television, which was almost nonexistent when I left Greece, had become so influential. It was clear that Calogridou's broadcast would guarantee the book's success.

"It's busy," said Manos.

The press conference started without the Minister. The three men who were the work's authors were the first to speak. They assured us that their texts, based on serious historical sources, dispelled the myths surrounding some of the book's heroines, like Sappho. I learned that Anna Conmena and her brother waged a ferocious war on one another to win the throne of Byzantium. I'd like to know more about that. Anna lost, finally, and dedicated the last years of her life to writing the *Alexiad*, a very long biography of her father, Alexis I. She was in love with the Greek language.

"She claimed that she loved the language even more than the air she breathed," said one of the authors.

The man in the black hat had slipped away. The poet was now standing between the two writers, whispering something to them. The cameraman, flanked by his two assistants holding a spotlight and a microphone, was alternately filming the speakers and the audience. Manos was the last to speak. It was his opinion that Turkish expansionism and the awakening of Balkan nationalisms represented a threat to Greece and that all Greeks must rally. At first I thought he was attempting to mock speeches made by politicians but realized quickly that wasn't the case.

"Not long ago, our borders were the line between the West and the Communist Bloc. A chasm separated us from our neighbors. Our security was guaranteed. The fall of the communist regimes has completely changed the rules of the game. New alliances are being formed. We can't count anymore on our strength alone. The West, which discovered we were Orthodox like the Russians and the Serbs, looks upon us with suspicion."

I wondered whether we should really be afraid of our neighbors. Neither Albania nor the new Macedonian state seemed capable of attacking us. Were we supposed to fear Bulgaria? Just before leaving Paris, I saw a Balkan map in the *Miroir de l'Europe* with hand-drawn revisions by the Russian Jirinowski and on it Bulgaria went all the way to the Aegean Sea. This is, I suspect, the way great powers control the destinies of smaller peoples, by taking a marker and drawing a few lines on a map. Turkey, of course, is our eternal enemy. I think it would be impossible for us to view them objectively. A fear of Turkey is part of our national identity.

People didn't seem very interested in Manos' speech. He finally got around to the book. He spoke lyrically of the eternal Greek woman, as if she were a single person traveling through the centuries. We heard a toilet flush and then saw the man with the black hat come through a door at the back of the bookstore. The spotlight turned to him, and stayed on him as he came toward me. Manos looked up, as if he was having trouble making out his text once deprived of the light.

"Unassuming and kind, understanding and generous, the Greek woman is transformed into an enraged tiger when our nation, our civilization, and our religion are in danger."

The man in the black hat stopped beside me. He whispered in my ear: "I must — alas — go to the bathroom very often."

He stepped away from me and squinted while staring at me, the way one studies a painting. My astonishment seemed to satisfy him.

"Shhh! Let's let our friend talk!" he added, nodding toward Manos.

I met Acridakis Manos in the late 1960s. He was part of a clandestine organization and was considered one of the most gifted activists on the extreme left. He was arrested during the uprising at Athens Polytechnic and spent the last months of the dictatorship in a prison camp on an island. He went into publishing after the junta fell. Several publishing houses were created then, but very few have survived. Manos understood earlier and more clearly than his colleagues that the revolutionary texts he was publishing would quickly lose favor with the public. Perhaps he simply stopped believing in the revolution, but the fact is that he adapted perfectly to the laws of the marketplace. The works of Gramsci, Rosa Luxemburg, Althusser, and Lucás, are only a minute part of his catalogue, which is dominated by novels, psychoanalysis books, and contemporary politics. He has avoided getting mixed up in politics, which has allowed him to maintain good relations with all the political parties. He has also published tourist guides, books about astronomy and about medicinal plants, and a cookbook entitled *Greeks at the Table*, with one of my drawings on its cover. I imagine Rosa Luxemburg, Gramsci, and the others looking down with disappointment, from the high shelf where they're kept nowadays, on the books displayed in the window.

I only see Manos when he comes to Paris for the Paris Book Fair. He stayed with me once, and he desperately wanted to make love with Martha. I warned him that he ran the risk of getting beaten up by her husband and he settled down.

The man in the black hat leaned toward me again: "I've enjoyed your cartoons in the *Miroir de l'Europe* for years," he said.

He offered me a cigarette. Other people were chatting here and there. The cameraman wasn't filming anymore and the spotlight had been shut off. Manos' speech was getting tiresome. I thought about what he would have said twenty-five years ago. In no uncertain terms, he would have accused the two major parties and the Church of exacerbating popular nationalism. He would have stated that these dangers weighing upon Greece are nothing more than a myth designed to turn people's attention away from the real problems. When I first met him, he could never find words strong enough to denounce the Holy Synod's support for the junta. He wouldn't have neglected to remind us that extreme right-wing sympathizers always control the Church. I seemed to be hearing two speeches at the same time, both delivered by the same voice, and each contradicting the other.

"I decided to publish *The Eternal Greek Woman* now because it seemed essential to me that we recall the sacrifices that have been made in this country to protect certain values. Malevolent shadows fall upon our borders. I would like to stress both the book's historical interest and its currency."

The applause was rather lukewarm, but Manos looked very pleased, as if through his speech he had been able to push back the malevolent shadows.

"What are you working on at the moment?" I asked the man in the black hat.

I asked the question in hopes that his answer would help me figure out whom I was dealing with.

"I'm writing an essay on the Homeric poems. My thesis is that the books of the *Iliad* and the *Odyssey* are an homage to the letters of the alphabet, book I to alpha, book II to beta, and so on. Book I of the *Iliad* sets forth a number of characters whose names begin with A: Athena and Apollo intervene in a conflict between Achilles and Agamemnon."

Several people had approached and were listening to him. He noticed and wasn't speaking just to me anymore.

"Homer is inaugurating the alphabet, celebrating its birth. Song XVI of the *Odyssey*, which corresponds to the letter *p*, is built around the word *pater*: Ulysses meets up with his son Telemachus. In the *Iliad*, the poet tells of the exploits and the death of Patroclus. The two poems are composed according to the same rules, which proves they're from the same author."

I thought I should ask him about the epsilon at Delphi. A woman asked if he was planning to publish his articles. It was then that I realized it was Professor Caradzoglou, who teaches literature at the University of Athens. He's best known for the ill-tempered columns he publishes in *Embros Sunday*. In the photo that appears alongside his article, he's not wearing a hat. He told the woman "yes," and then turned his back to the small group listening to him.

"What do they say about Greece in Europe? They laugh at us, don't they?"

We were suddenly surrounded by the television people and the spotlight was trained on Caradzoglou. Calogridou, holding the microphone, asked him, "Professor, what do you think of the Greek woman?"

"I think very highly of her," he said. "Very highly.... The only thing that bothers me about her is that she washes ashtrays that are only slightly dirty and then puts them by the sink. She doesn't dry them, but waits for them to dry themselves, which explains why ashtrays are always by the sink. I think that the Greek woman looks upon them as plates in which certain people have the bad habit of crushing out their cigarettes."

Calogridou gave him a dull look. "She doesn't understand what he's saying," I thought. She thanked him. I asked if I could continue the discussion with him after the event. He was supposed to meet his wife at two o'clock in a café in Kolonaki.

"Come along, if you like," he offered. "I warn you that she's crazy, but she won't bother us. She's not as talkative as I am."

"Quiet, my friends!" said Manos. "The Minister's on the line."

Everyone stopped talking instantly and turned toward the phone.

"We waited for you until ten after one .... Yes, I understand. I'll have someone bring you a copy .... You haven't forgotten what you promised me, have you? Okay, I'll arrange it with her. Would you like to talk to them? I'll plug in the speaker. Kisses, see you soon."

He pushed a button. There was a sort of echo, then a whistle followed by complete silence. We heard a small cough.

"Can you hear me? I hope you can hear me."

It was Stathopoulou. Her astonishingly young voice, nearly childlike, is well known to all Greeks, as my mother would say.

"I'm very sorry for canceling on you. I would sincerely love to celebrate this exceptional publication with you, dedicated to women who have honored Greece with their talents and their struggles. I'll even let you in on a secret: when I think of Penelope Delta's suicide the day the Germans entered Athens, it brings tears to my eyes."

Her voice became famous when she was on stage. Newspapers still talk of her interpretation of Electra at the Epidaurus Theater in the late 1950's. Apparently she was so touching in the scene where Electra recognizes her brother Orestes and speaks the famous line "Long-awaited voice, are you really here?" that everyone was deeply moved, even Orestes, who forgot his lines. Despite claims from the envious that she's at least sixty-five, Amalia has managed to keep not just her voice, but also her looks. Those very same envious people allege that she's had quite a number of plastic surgeries done. Her picture appears in the paper very often. I don't think that her popularity is due to her acting abilities—it's been over thirty years since she last acted — or her cultural policies, since her ministry's budget is tiny, but rather to her astonishing youth. She gives the impression that she has overcome time, that she has won a rare victory. When she goes to the provinces, people crowd around her, want to touch her. She's a true star, the heroine of a fairy tale. She goes through life the way the eternal Greek woman moves through the centuries.

"I can guarantee," she continued, "that the government has decided to extend women's rights and recognize their role in society. As you all know, we've already adopted certain measures toward that end. We'll adopt others too."

Several people were looking up toward the ceiling as if they expected to glimpse the Minister through the long cloud of cigarette smoke. A phone rang in Stathopoulou's office.

"In a very few words, that's what I wanted to say to you. Along with you, I drink to the Greek woman ... To our country!"

The applause was very enthusiastic this time and covered up the dial tone after she hung up.

"Why didn't you film any of it?" Calogridou asked the cameraman, rather calmly.

"Film what, Ionna?"

"Those people listening, for heaven's sakes. It was a special moment!"

People were indeed under a spell. They took their time continuing their conversations. Caradzoglou had left. I went over to Manos to say hello. He was chatting with the two writers. "Those two will surely have lunch together," I thought.

"She may not be very intelligent," Manos was saying, "but she knows instinctively what she needs to say or do."

"She's an actress," one of the writers observed scornfully.

"She doesn't read," added the one wearing glasses.

Manos' shirt with its blue and white stripes looked like the Greek flag.

"But she looks great on television," he said, "and that's what counts nowadays. I know for a fact that she doesn't read: she told me that she hasn't opened a book since she left the Dramatic Arts Conservatory."

"I'm leaving," Calogridou announced.

"You'll lead off the broadcast talking about my book, right?"

"We'll see about that," she said jokingly.

"She'll have to start with it," Manos confided, as she walked away. "The channel where she works is run by Stathopoulou's youngest brother, Pandelis."

"He really does know everyone," I thought. I suddenly felt that I couldn't stand being with him or with his guests. I left quickly, like I did at Stamata. The poet was waiting for me on the sidewalk.

"How are you doing?"

"Okay."

I tried to continue on my way, but he stopped me again.

"May I go with you? I know you're meeting Mr. Caradzoglou. I'd like to speak to him. He really doesn't like us poets and I think he may even despise poetry. Unless you have personal things to discuss, of course."

I didn't ask him how he knew about my plans. I simply assured him that the conversation would be of a strictly confidential nature.

"He's in love with my sister," I explained.

I felt better and better as I got farther away from the bookstore and the poet. "He's worming his way in," I thought. "He's one of those people who worms his way in. Manos worms his way in too. Maybe they all worm their way in?" Repeating the verb *élissomai*, to worm one's way in, seemed so funny to me that I started laughing as I waited for the light to turn green. I decided to buy a little notebook and to write down all the words starting with epsilon that attract my attention, one to a page. "I'll write the verb *élissomai*. What word did Vaguelio say? *Ektaktos*, exceptionally? *Éndos*, inside?" I remembered that she'd said *endélos*, completely. The name Vaguelio starts with epsilon in its outmoded form too, but I never called her Evanguelia. Just as I was crossing the street, I realized that I was still holding the plastic cup in my hand. I placed it atop a mountain of garbage bags after drinking the little wine that was left. I considered my description of sidewalks satisfactory. "I'm done with sidewalks. I won't talk about them anymore, I don't need to look at them anymore."

It was a superb springtime day. A soft wind was blowing, purifying the atmosphere and lightening the walk. I saw a lemon tree blooming on a square. A white dog was in front of me. It looked like Gaour, Vaguelio's dog. At the far end of the square, the dog turned right. I went straight.

It occurred to me that I could spend an entire day following a wandering dog. "I'll note where he goes and how much time he spends in each place." Sunlight was flooding over the two rows of tables, which took up nearly the whole sidewalk. Caradzoglou was sitting inside. I saw him through the window. He hadn't removed either his hat or his scarf. His wife looked seventy. She had big eyes and waxy skin. She didn't react when I approached them. It was only when I sat down and began to chat with her husband that she shifted her position slightly, but without looking at me. Her hands were folded in her lap, resting on her black woolen skirt. Caradzouglou was drinking hot milk. She was drinking tea. Her cup was full.

"Have you seen the UN soldiers on television? Don't you think some of their faces are disturbing?"

Two drops of milk clung to his white beard. On the terrace there were mostly young people and forty-five year old men in black leather jackets reading the newspaper. He told me that he appreciated *Le Miroir de l'Europe*, that he thought it was a fairly objective newspaper despite its constant defense of the French government's foreign policy.

"Did you know that Véronique Carrier was once an interpreter in the Foreign Affairs ministry? That was back when I first met her. She'd just finished her studies in Switzerland."

I know that she has a lot of friends at the Foreign Affairs ministry, but I didn't know that she had worked there. I was surprised and disappointed to learn it from Caradzoglou. I remembered the click of the Carriers' door as it closed behind me. "In a month, if I'm in Paris, I'll go dine with them." The thought seemed unbearable to me. I called the waiter and ordered an ouzo. I tried to explain to Caradzoglou how French journalists see Greece: "Quite a number of them want Turkey to take our place in the European Union. They think they'll get along better with Turkey. They don't approve of our friendship for the Serbs and they don't understand our opposition to recognizing the Macedonian state., There's a very wide consensus on questions of foreign policy in France. It's rare that you'll hear any differing points of view. Discussions of Bosnia, like the Gulf War a few years ago, get everyone's hackles up. The print media are the only ones reminding us from time to time that these problems aren't so simple."

"But television's role is just that," he said, "to simplify things and make examples of the guilty parties! Here too, it's gotten difficult to express a different opinion. People who want to open a dialogue with the government in Skopje are seen as traitors. We should give in on the name and in exchange ask them to teach Greek as a foreign language in their schools. If they're going to claim our national heritage, the least they could do would be to learn our language. I wrote all that in one of my columns. They let me write anything I want, probably because no one reads me."

"Do you remember Paris, Marika?"

The name touched me deeply. I had to bend down and pretend to tie my shoes.

"I'm talking to you, Marika!" said Caradzoglou harshly.

Marika said nothing. I think she tried to smile. Her lips moved hesitantly, then she stared at a spot under the table. "That's the third spot she's stared at since I got here." She was looking at the bottom of her skirt, or the foot of the table, or the floor, or maybe her husband's shoes, or something beyond all that, which was perhaps nothing at all. Caradzoglou shrugged his shoulders.

"We lived on the Rue des Feuillantines. I have very fond memories of those years."

It was undoubtedly the Toulouse-Lautrec poster that had inspired his choice of outfit. People always steal something from the places they've lived. Greek artists who have spent some time in Paris usually buy a beret. I don't have a beret and I don't really think that my clothes would let anyone guess where I live. My beard doesn't give anything away either: it's not in fashion in France or in Greece. But the tobacco I smoke is French. It's one of the very few sold only in France. A truly French cloud rises from my pipe.

Aristide Bruant's clothes were in perfect harmony with the theatrical poses that Caradzoglou assumed. He gestured like a silent film actor. Every time he delivered an important sentence, he said nothing for a few seconds and held the same pose, as if he were expecting the audience to applaud. He leaned back when he spoke, which made me think he lectured in an amphitheater. But his voice wasn't that theatrical. It was high-pitched, though he spoke clearly. Like all good actors, he was acting even when he wasn't speaking: he stroked his beard, took the bottom of his cape that was touching the ground and placed it on his lap. I wondered if he was bald. I couldn't remember clearly his picture in *Embros Sunday.*

We talked about the political situation in France. He knew about the rise of the extreme right and the impact of its message within the government. I told him that poverty is visible everywhere in the streets now, that the homeless have become an army. He didn't know that they were called SDF ("*sans domicile fixe*," "no permanent address"), or that there were publications dedicated to their problems, which they distribute themselves.

"Unemployment has wounded the French, humiliated them," I told him. "Not all of them, of course: apparently capital revenues are huge, and the stock market is in fine shape. But multitudes of people have lost their jobs or run the risk of it. They're an eclectic group, including Atlantic fishermen, Air France employees, many of the young. Nowadays, creating a business that employs even five people is considered a feat, and the television news talks about it at length."

On the way from my place to the metro station, I told him, I see seven panhandlers sitting on the sidewalk, each with an empty can next to him for change from passersby.

"Did you notice what sort of cans they are?" he asked quickly, as if he thought the detail was very important.

"I believe they're tuna cans."

"I think people are getting along better here. They don't declare their income. They have money abroad. They often work for several employers at once. A female colleague at *Embros* has four salaries: from the newspaper, radio, television, and a public relations firm. She may also be getting money from a political party. I'll introduce you, if you come by the office. She's very beautiful and, of course, very rich."

It was already three o'clock. I was afraid he'd leave before I could ask him about the epsilon at Delphi. His wife didn't seem to be following the conversation. "She only hears some of the words we're saying and makes up her own sentences."

"She bought an enormous rosewood bookcase," Caradzoglou continued, "It must have cost five million! She showed me a picture of her bookcase, and it's empty. She doesn't have a dozen books!"

The waiter brought the ouzo with a few pistachios in a saucer. I remembered the ouzo café in Piraeus we used to go to when we were in high school. It was known for its varied hors-d'oeuvres. Every new glass of ouzo was accompanied by a more substantial plateful. By the time we finished, they were bringing us hors-d'oeuvres on a platter.

I saw a big cockroach — black and immobile — on the ground. Caradzoglou saw it too. He gave me a panicked look and glanced toward his wife. I understood that she mustn't see the cockroach. Fortunately, she was sitting on the other side and was looking outside now, rather than under the table. The cockroach took two or three steps and stopped. He looked lost or exhausted. "Maybe it's his first time out in the light of day, his first walk." His wings glistened like metal. He didn't look at all like he'd come through filthy underground passages. He came a little closer. The quick movements of the lizard in Stamata came back to me. I pushed the cockroach away with my foot. Caradzoglou looked at me with wide eyes and gestured for me not to crush it. "It would make a sound like a twig snapping," I thought. Marika hadn't noticed anything. "She thinks she's afraid of cockroaches the way my father thinks he's afraid of the telephone. They're actually afraid of something else." I asked him what word starting with E is central to song V of the *Iliad*.

"*Éris*, the dispute. Disputes among warriors, which explains the frequent use of the word *énchos*, the lance."

The word *éris* reminded me of Vaguelio. I looked outside as if I expected to see her. The two writers were walking along the edge of the sidewalk, one behind the other. Both of them were looking down. "They walk like I do." I decided to call Vaguelio. "I'll ask her if she wrote to me in Paris." I finally asked Caradzoglou about the epsilon at Delphi.

"We'll never know its meaning," he said. "Ancient texts scarcely touch on it. Plutarch alone mentions it, much later, at the beginning of the second century

A.D. He was a priest at the shrine in Delphi and would've been in a position to know its meaning. Well, he doesn't. He makes assertions that aren't really convincing or are ridiculous, just pointless.

"How should we interpret the silence of the ancient Greeks? Did they know its meaning or not?"

Marika turned toward me for the first time.

"Why aren't you drinking your tea?" her husband asked her.

"I forgot about it," she said in a weak, scratchy voice.

She touched the cup of tea with her index finger, as if she wanted to make sure it was really there. Then she placed her hand in her lap and looked outside again.

"Maybe they knew it and maybe they didn't. I prefer to think that they knew nothing about its meaning and thought it superfluous to worry about a problem that couldn't be resolved. Was the E a mystery or not? Yet another enigma!"

"So no one knows anything." The thought gave me a certain satisfaction. I realized I was in no hurry to be done with this problem. To me, the ancient epsilon looked like a good-as-new toy.

"Why are you interested in that letter?"

"I don't know .... I hope I can at least clarify the mystery."

"As far as the epsilon is concerned, don't fool yourself, you won't find anything. You'd be wasting your time."

At the end of our conversation, he concluded the portrait of Greek society he'd started to sketch out.

"You have to understand that Greek society is a jungle. We, too, have changed. We've become wild beasts. The crisis we're going through is basically a moral one, like in Italy. Do you remember the greed of gold prospectors in the old western films? We have the same feverish look they had. The disclosure of certain scandals, which gives the impression that we're living in a transparent society, has really pushed us farther into the shadows."

The scene outside wasn't nearly as ominous as his description. People would walk by, recognize a friend among the customers, and stop to chat. The friendly ambiance I'd noticed at the press conference also held sway on the sidewalk. I had the feeling that I was in a village rather than in a city as huge as Athens. There was always someone smiling, sometimes at one table and sometimes at another. It looked as if the same smile was making the rounds of the café.

"Don't let the sun fool you," he said. "You're doing the right thing, living abroad."

I wasn't convinced. The torpor I was beginning to feel was vaguely amusing. I chalked it up to the ouzo. There wasn't a drop left in my glass. There was nothing but an ice cube. Caradzoglou paid, and we exchanged phone numbers. A girl walked by us, lightly perfumed. She was searching for someone. She looked around the room and then left.

"The ancient Greeks believed the gods smelled good," said Caradzoglou.

All three of us were standing. I said goodbye to them. I didn't think that Marika would say anything, but she let her husband get a few meters away.

"You'll find it!" she said in an urgent tone, as if she really wanted to convince me.

She walked away hastily. I gathered in those words like an unexpected gift. "I'll find it, since Marika said so." The idea that the word "to find," *eurisko*, begins with epsilon — I naturally thought of Archimedes' famous *euréka* — made me even happier. My good mood wasn't altered by the noise I heard beneath my feet as I was moving toward the door a few moments later. It was like the sound of a twig snapping.

I walked around Kolonaki for a long time. The aristocracy of Athens, once centered in this neighborhood, gave the streets distinguished names. Solon Street crosses first Homer, then Democritus, Pindar, and Heraclitus. Side by side, just beyond the square, are Herodotus, Lucian, and Plutarch. Another neighborhood, Pangrati, is also fond of ancient Greeks, but since it was built after Kolonaki it had to make do with the less famous among them: Hellanikos, Pyrrho, Chremonides, Astydamas. Vaguelio lives in Pangrati, on Vryaxidos Street: I imagined that it was the name of a hetaira, but it's not — it's the name of a sculptor. It really bothered me, back when I often went to see her, that at every intersection I came across were two ancient Greeks whose names didn't mean anything to me. But I thought that their limited fame partly excused my ignorance. I was not, alas, much better informed about the celebrities gathered around Kolonaki. I didn't know when Plutarch lived or that he'd been a priest in the service of Apollo. I only remember two or three sentences from Heraclitus. I only know the very little that it's impossible not to know. Kolonaki reminds me of the extent of my ignorance, shows me its true dimensions, pulls my ears like my strictest teachers used to do.

"The gods smelled good." It was pleasant to recall Caradzoglou's words, they appealed to my ear. "There is a music I know nothing about." I wondered why ancient Greek courses at school were so boring, so dreary. We followed along, as unhappy as children being led on a walk through a cemetery. Sometimes we were paralyzed by the marble faces of our ancestors. Sometimes we wanted to make fun of them — to dress them up with fake noses or smear lipstick on them. We made fun of Homer, especially. I remember a pornographic verse version of the *Iliad* written in a notebook that we passed around. It was more or less universally known in schools and was most likely the work of generations of pupils who had suffered at the same desks, trying to understand Homeric dialect. We commented on where the poet came from: "Nine cities claim to be his birthplace, but in fact he was born in only three of them."

The *Iliad* and the *Odyssey* interested us only when in the form of comic books or films. I clearly remember Kirk Douglas playing Ulysses. I didn't read the *Odyssey* until many years after I'd left school, when my memories of that era were already fading, and I read it in a French paperback edition. I was at the newspaper when I got to the part where Ulysses reaches the land of the Lotus Eaters. It was noon. My colleagues had left for lunch. The big newsroom was empty. Maybe the episode left a huge impression on me because I could see that my memory would abandon me little by little. That was when I first wondered how teachers responsible for teaching us such a text could manage to put us to sleep. Ulysses should have been at least as appealing to us as Robin Hood. We were all familiar with the sea that handled his boat so roughly. We lived on its shores. It was the theater of our own fears and dreams. It was also in Paris that I read Plato and certain Pre-Socratic philosophers. Now and again, I would page through a voluminous introduction to Greek mythology. My perplexity was revived with each reading: why had we been so disgusted with Greek courses? My teachers' religious convictions kept them from viewing classical antiquity impartially. Only those myths with a moral lesson interested them. When I arrived in France, I was very surprised to see that there were many fans of Greek mythology in that country. I myself didn't really like it because I didn't know it very well.

I went into a big bookstore on Solon Street and asked for Plutarch's text on Delphi, but they didn't have it. I bought the Iliad in ancient Greek with a translation in Modern Greek. I still haven't read all of it. I know only parts of it, like most things where I'm not totally ignorant. I also bought *Captain Grant's Children* and the *Lighthouse at the End of the World* for my father. Did he invent Pim's name, or did he find it in a novel? Among the stacks of notebooks in the office supply section, I found exactly the same ones I used in school. On their cover, in a yellow frame, is a full-color illustration from the 1821 War of Independence. On the third or fourth in the pile was the same picture as on Acridakis' book, but not nearly as well printed. So I came upon Bouboulina again, standing in the bow of the *Agamemnon*. I selected that notebook to write down words starting with epsilon. It has forty pages. Was it the dislike I felt for the commander of the Greek army that kept me from reading the *Iliad*? I was aware that Agamemnon had sacrificed his daughter to get the favorable winds the boats needed before leaving for Troy. I reflected that Iphigenia must have been about my age. It seems to me that as a child I confused Agamemnon with Abraham.

I turned right on Pindar Street and started walking uphill toward Mount Lycabettus. It was twenty minutes to four. The streets were deserted. I wasn't hungry in the least. The first streets parallel to Solon Street are among the very few which don't bear names from classical antiquity: they honor the memory of three instigators of the Uprising of 1821 — Scouphas, Tsacalof, and Anagnostopoulos. They reminded me of those poems where Victor Hugo compares the rebels of 1821 to the heroes of the Trojan Wars. The name of Bouboulina's boat leads me to suppose that the rebels themselves were thinking about the ancient heroes. I stopped at the corner of Anagnostopoulos and Pindar to catch my breath. I sat at the edge of the sidewalk, looking down Pindar Street, which goes straight into the heart of Athens. The rock of the Acropolis rises much farther away, well beyond the city center. In engravings from the last century, Athens in 1821 is only a village built at the foot of the Acropolis. Around it there was a yellowish plain, a little desert, where sometimes a woman passed carrying a pitcher or a shepherd passed with his small flock. The Acropolis today is hidden by buildings and by the smoke rising from the city. You can make it out through a thick fog, but only from the tops of surrounding hills. I think the decision to transform the nineteenth-century village into a capital was made for purely sentimental reasons, since the name allowed them to associate modern Greece with ancient Greece. The Greek state declared that it was resuming a very old story.

I opened the *Iliad*. I hadn't seen the original text since school. I read two lines and went straight to the translation on the left-hand page. I read another line and its translation. I went on like that for a while: my eyes moved from one page to the other as if I were watching a tennis match. I had to admit that the original was just as hermetic to me as it had been in high school. I recalled that we didn't have translations of classical texts in school. We had to learn Ancient Greek flawlessly if we were to appreciate Homer or Plato. The *Iliad* was a series of rebus puzzles, as were the *Banquet* or *Antigone*. The intention was not to school us in poetry or philosophy, but to teach us a language, which, though it was not completely foreign to ours, was nonetheless very difficult. We might have been captivated by the classics if we'd been able to study them in translation, like French and German students do, and then we would have studied the language willingly. But rather than starting with the works to get to the language, we started with the language and never got to the works. We weren't concerned with the spirit of the texts, but rather with the letter of the texts. I lit my pipe and stood up. I didn't have the energy to continue climbing up toward Mount Lycabettus. I took Anagnostopoulos Street toward my neighborhood. Kolonaki had begun to bore me.

My thoughts slowed my walking, I moved carefully, as if my path were strewn with little invisible obstacles. I constantly felt like stopping. The real obstacles in my way — bricks and garbage bags — bothered me less. I knew how to get around them. My teachers were inspired by the same romantic ideology that had made Athens into a capital. They dreamed of reducing the distance between Ancient Greek and Modern Greek. Language was the umbilical cord that connected us to our ancestors, the major proof that we were indeed their descendants. It was important that it be reinforced, that it be obvious. Not only were we to learn Ancient Greek, we were also supposed to give up Modern Greek. The language we spoke was considered vulgar. We were obliged to write in a curious artificial idiom, halfway between Modern Greek and Ancient Greek, which was called "pure," *catharévoussa*. In any case, we had no grammar book apart from the Classical Greek one. My teachers were trying to forget the time that had passed between Homer and the 1950s.

We did the same sort of acrobatic leaps over centuries in our history courses, so the most ancient events seemed relatively recent to us. We went from Alexander the Great straight to the year 1000, to witness the resurgence of Hellenism within the Byzantine Empire. Roman domination was almost completely ignored. After mourning the fall of Constantinople and of Constantine Palaiologos, we crossed all the centuries of Ottoman occupation with amazing speed and came to a stop in 1821. It isn't as surprising as foreigners think that the Macedonia of Alexander the Great is so strong in our memory: that is the Macedonia whose map we study in school.

I think Kolonaki ends at the stone stairway connecting Anagnostopoulos Street to Didotus Street. There are about fifty steps. I went down them very slowly. Some days we were proud to be Greek, especially during national holidays, or when we dealt with foreigners. But the rest of the time we felt no pride at all. Constant references to classical antiquity made us doubt ourselves. We had been brought up with the certainty that no text of any quality could be written in the language we spoke, that we'd never have anything better to show than the works of the past. We spent thousands of hours studying classical antiquity without ever really seeing it. All we'd really learned was how to draw our genealogical tree. "Too bad," I thought as I went down the stairs. I repeated it with every step. I regretted not knowing sooner that the gods smelled good.

I thought that Didotos was an ancient Greek, too. He wasn't. He was Firmin Didot, a French editor and Hellenist of the nineteenth century. The French archeology school, which was responsible for the dig at Delphi, is on that street. Around it there's a garden with big trees. Plutarch's book would surely be in their library. The numbers on houses reminded me that the number 5 was once written as the letter E. But why would the Temple of Apollo, considered the center of the world, bear the number 5? "The center of the world doesn't need a number." I had a hard time accepting the indifference of the Ancient Greeks to the epsilon. "If it had been elsewhere, they might have ignored it, but at the entrance to the temple at Delphi it must have intrigued them ... Why did they think that a simple letter of the alphabet was an impenetrable mystery? Even if they were convinced they'd never find the answer, they probably would have discussed it in a dialogue about exactly that: the attitude one should assume when faced with problems reputed to be unsolvable." I leaned more toward thinking that they don't mention it anywhere because they all knew what it meant.

On the sidewalk, at the corner of Didotos and Zôodochos-Pègè, a taxi was parked. Through the open door, I could see the bare feet of the driver. He was lying on the front seat, his face covered by a newspaper probably revealing some new scandal, since the headline in gigantic letters was "ΑΙΣΧΟΣ!" *eschos*, which means shameful or awful. I thought of the epsilon again, since the *ai* diphthong is read as "è" in Modern Greek. I have no idea if it was pronounced the same way in classical antiquity. But that didn't keep me from imagining that the E of Delphi was a colossal spelling error, like those I used to make in school, and that it stood for some word starting with ai. I thought of the word *ainigma*, enigma.

Acridakis' bookstore was on my way. It was closed. Several copies of *The Eternal Greek Woman* were displayed in the window. "We're constantly travelling backwards," I thought. The Greece of my teachers lived in the past. It was trying to hang on to its youth. It defied time, just like Stathopoulou. "We're an old country speaking with the voice of a child." I could see the outline of my silhouette on the window and behind it books on shelves. The shelves made stripes on my body, divided me into floors. I could make out my face and beard a little better.

I didn't call Vaguelio. "We'll have a pleasant evening, but just at the moment when we leave one another we'll think about that other separation in her apartment. We'll hear the Nights of Cabiria music again." She'd no doubt be surprised if I called her. Maybe she wouldn't recognize my voice. I called Theodoris. He told me that Niki calls him at home every day.

"I think she calls me just to make Marilena jealous. She asked me if she could use our washing machine until she gets hers repaired."

"Did you say yes?"

"I couldn't really say no."

I could see Marilena's hurt look. So why does Theodoris have so much trouble breaking away from Niki? He still hasn't divorced her. He told me that the girl with the dark hair who was sitting beside me at Stamata — her name is Penelope — had asked about me.

"Don't you want her phone number? I'm sure she'd be happy if you called her."

I wrote it down. I was inclined to forgive her the reprimand about my pipe ashes. The parody of the *Iliad* I mentioned had circulated in Theodoris' school too. He couldn't remember any lines, but he promised to find at least part of it for me.

I opened my collection of ouzo labels. They're filed in a green folder, pasted to sheets of typing paper. I started the collection in Paris, I don't remember when: maybe after I'd read the *Odyssey* and learned what happens to visitors to the country of the Lotus Eaters. The first one I kept bears the brand name "*Léthé,*" forgetfulness. I unstick the labels by putting the bottles in water. Doing that reminds me of Greece, of the stamps I once collected. My mother made the books where I kept my stamps. We didn't have money for superfluous expenses. She would attach three or four strips of glassine paper to sheets of orange-tinted light cardboard with her sewing machine. Then she would punch holes in the sheets and tie them together with a ribbon that she tied into a rosette.

The names of most of the ouzos sound like the titles of poems or songs: "the Surroundings," "the Labyrinth," "Renown," "the Breeze." Stelios Kazandzidis, the singer who went into producing ouzo, used the title of one of his hits, "I exist" as a brand name. The illustration on the label is most often inspired by classical antiquity (there's the Acropolis, Athens, a trireme, the Venus de Milo, Sappho, Achilles, Pyrrhus, Apollo on a dolphin), much less frequently by the Greece of today (represented by an evzone, a flag, the Arta bridge, a windmill, a *komboloï* — the beads older Greeks keep in their hands at the café). They are sometimes erotic. The most unusual label I've found has a hole through which you can see a girl in a bathing suit on another label pasted on the other side of the bottle. The contents of the bottle magnify the picture of the girl. It's like seeing her through a keyhole. My collection contains over one hundred fifty labels. While I was putting the folder away in my bookshelf, I glanced at the brown paper envelope between two volumes of the encyclopedia, but I didn't touch it.

In the notebook, I recorded the words starting with epsilon that I'd found: *éndélos*, completely (in parentheses, I added Vaguelio's name), *élissomai*, to worm one's way in, *éris*, the quarrel, and *eurisko*, to find. I hesitated, but finally wrote down the word *ainigma*.

I heard Marika's words again: "You'll find it."

I remembered the voice of another Marika saying: "Be precise."

And: "What a strange idea, to write it that way!"

I suddenly took the brown paper envelope and looked at the portrait of her I'd drawn in the hospital. You can just see her hand, her fingers pulling up the covers. I felt no emotion at all, which seemed strange to me. But walking through the apartment I remembered the empty space we'd made in Ano Patissia by moving the furniture that afternoon. Fifteen months have gone by since then. It was winter. They put the coffin on the arms of two chairs placed side by side. Costas arrived at dawn, he'd driven from Ioannina, he'd travelled all night. He absolutely wanted to get to the house before they took her away. He arrived in time. They didn't take her away until around eight thirty in the morning. We went with her as far as the street. Then we went back into the house and closed the door. We found ourselves facing the two armchairs placed side by side in the middle of the room.

4.

Why is Neoptolemus at Delphi and why do the priests of the temple want to kill him? I really don't know. But he climbs on the Altar of Chios, which stands before the door to the temple, and there he's attacked by his pursuers. I imagine they're armed with swords and sticks. What else might they use? Snakes, perhaps. The place is full of them. When he first arrived in Delphi, Apollo had to do away with the serpent Python. Our hero has to keep jumping to stay away from the swords and the sticks and maybe the snakes they throw at him. They say that his gyrations inspired a new "pyrrhic" dance (Neoptolemus is also called Pyrrhus). I'm learning the existence of a dance whose steps are inspired by fear of having one's legs broken. I imagine the scene taking place at night, the flames of a nearby fire casting Neoptolemus' giant shadow on the temple's façade. The flames climb high, die down, then flare up again quickly. "The best way to learn the pyrrhic dance, if you're not being pursued by furious priests, is to watch how flames move."

A small fire burns perpetually inside the temple on the Altar of Hestia, fueled with pinewood and laurel branches. A parabolic mirror and the sun, the symbol of Apollo, are used to relight it when it goes out by accident. I remember how carefully we tried to keep the flames of our candles alive, coming back to Theodoris' house Easter night. The inside of the temple is rather dark. It's lighted mostly by the door opening. The Pythia officiates from the far end of the room, the darkest part. She sits in a small square space, about one meter deep and inaccessible to the public, called an adytum. We don't know if she could be seen performing her duties. The adytum may have been protected by a partition like the one used to screen off the sanctuary in Eastern churches. I suppose that people move quietly inside the temple, that the dim light imposes a certain silence. I don't know if their clothes have pockets, or what sorts of small objects they might have with them. The walls are decorated with weapons sacred to Apollo. Herodotus tells us that they came down off the walls and took up combat positions to defend the temple against Persian soldiers.

The epsilon was made of wood, most likely suspended above the main door. It too was an offering. Small square pillars, shaped like the mile markers along roads, carried the maxims of the Seven Sages. Atop each was a head of Hermes, and each was adorned with a phallus, placed in the right spot. Hermes, protector of travelers, greeted pilgrims at the door of the temple. It's possible that the E was dedicated to him: his name does indeed start with that letter in Greek (ʽΕρμῆς), the "h" in other languages being nothing more than a reminder of a rough breathing mark. It's also possible that it was dedicated to Hestia (ʽΕστία), goddess of the home, vigilant guardian of the sanctuary. Perhaps it was meant to protect the place, like the cross above the door in Stamata. "It was the temple's good luck charm," I thought. In my notebook, I wrote the name of *Hermes*, on page six, and that of *Hestia* on page seven. None of the pillars placed on either side of the door has been found. We don't know which maxims were there, apart from the two I've mentioned — "Nothing too much," and "Know thyself." The archaic wooden epsilon has not survived, nor have the bronze and gold ones, gifts of the Athenians and the Romans. I get the feeling that I'm looking into a bottomless well. Neoptolemus' dance ends with a leap: he flies over the heads of his attackers and lands in front of the temple. It's a remarkable jump of over thirteen meters. His father, Achilles, had also made an impressive bound, from his boat onto Trojan shores. In the end, Neoptolemus won't get away from the priests. They show no mercy to their enemies. Aesop called them social parasites and they hid a sacred vase in his luggage, accused him of theft, and threw him into an abyss. The shrine is on a slope of Mount Parnassus. It receives a good deal of snow in winter. The Pythia does not prophesy during that season. Apollo abandons it and goes much farther north. They both resume their activities in the springtime. In summer, the heat is often unbearable. The sea is distant from Delphi and considerably lower. Fortunately, the area doesn't lack for water. The Castalia Fountain, which slaked the thirst of the Pythia and inspired poets, still flows. It forms a little stream that nowadays runs under the paved road.

I finally found a way to spend my time: I read. I read from eight thirty in the morning until one in the afternoon in the library of the French Archeology School. I bought a second notebook with a different illustration on the cover: this one shows an orthodox priest hanged by bloodthirsty Ottomans. I come here with my two notebooks and two well-sharpened pencils. At eight thirty, no one is in the library yet. It's below ground level, but through the bank of windows at the top of the wall you can see the trees in the garden and the feet of passersby. I saw a blind man walking fast, barely touching the graveled path with his cane. He probably works here. He didn't look all that young to me, despite his energetic gait.

I sit at one end of the long table under the bank of windows. I'm not alone for long. The other readers are mostly students, Greek and French. We exchange a quiet "bonjour" in a low voice, as if we were afraid to awaken the spirit that lives here. Their notebooks are much larger and thicker than mine and don't have pictures on the covers. I am undoubtedly the oldest and the least serious student in this silent class. Now and then I cast a glance at my neighbor's bust. I can see a bit better when she bends down to read the notes at the bottom of the page.

Every half hour, three quarters of an hour at most, I go out to smoke in the courtyard. I can barely hear the noises of the city. The School's garden is an oasis in the center of Athens. Its trees are high enough to mask the buildings all around it. I smoke on the marble steps leading down to the garden. Then I go back in by way of the spiral stairway. I feel more and more comfortable every day. I discreetly remove my shoes under the table and put them back on just as discreetly before going out.

I have a goodly stack of books in front of me. The School's publications are bound in burgundy leather. The pages are yellowed and very smooth. I placed the palm of my hand on one page and it was rather cold. Sometimes they're lightly stuck together. When I turn the page, I hear exactly the same sound as when you rip off a Band-Aid. I haven't read Plutarch's treatise *On the E at Delphi*. I don't think I could appreciate it just yet. I did open it, however, and on the first page I saw two black and white photos of Delphic coins from the Roman era in which the epsilon appearing between the columns of the temple. On one of the coins, there are two columns. On the other, there are three. It's a plain epsilon, with no decoration at all.

I read two pages of one book, three pages of another. I can't manage to concentrate my attention. I'm wandering aimlessly on the surface of things. My neighbors have a dissertation to write, I imagine. I don't know what I'm working on. "I'm learning," I think. But here I am, writing too, and on a subject I don't know about. I'm astonished by my daring. I've probably been influenced by Athenian taxi drivers, who can talk comfortably about anything. They start with the weather and traffic problems, but move along quickly — before the meter gets to 300 drachmas — to politics and economic problems. The poor quality of our country's leaders sometimes saddens them, sometimes makes them angry.

Changes in social attitudes evoke ambivalent comments from them:

"I remember ... " they say.

With the meter at 500 drachmas, they pose the question: "I ask you, sir, where will it all lead?"

When the trip is longer, the debate broadens. It isn't just the Greek situation that worries them, but those of other countries too, the entire planet.

"Because, after all is said and done, what are we, really? We're nothing but a pile of manure!"

At times they start feeling friendly toward the customer and at a red light or on a curve, quite unexpectedly, they ask: "So where are you from?"

Scientific questions don't intimidate them at all. After looking at a mole on my left arm, one rather fatherly driver told me:

"You've got to have that removed! It might turn ugly!"

He even told me about a clinic where they do that sort of thing. I was relieved that he didn't propose operating on me himself. Most taxi drivers tackle a wide variety of subjects, but some are specialists who delve deeply into one single question. One of them lectured me about octopus fishing. It was his favorite pastime. He spent his days off fishing for octopus. We arrived at my place before the end of the lecture. He parked, turned off the meter, and kept on talking. I've been told that one of his colleagues is wild about literature. His taxi is filled with books that he praises highly and that he might perhaps agree to sell. I'd like to meet him. The Athens taxi is a little university that also allows you to get around town.

Did I come to Athens to read these books? They're written by specialists for specialists. Their intended audience is fewer than five hundred people. I could probably have found them in Paris. It's true that I would have read them differently there. Places transform texts, paintings, and music. I feel like I'm in the right place to study this literature. The lighting in the library seems perfect to me.

I learn from the librarian that Delphi is often bombarded by rocks falling from the surrounding cliffs.

"But there was never any question of moving the oracle elsewhere," he says. "Various forms of worship were well established at Delphi beginning in the Mycenaean era, before Apollo and the Pythia got there."

He lent me a magnifying glass so that I could look more closely at a photograph of the statue of Antinous shortly after it was discovered. It was unearthed in 1894, two years after the dig began. It's standing in front of a pile of earth and stones. It doesn't have any arms and the legs are probably broken. In any case, you can't see them in the snapshot. Antinous is about as tall as a little boy. The body is softly curved. He has a child's cheeks. Here and there, you can see the stains from his long stay under the earth, which sheltered him for I don't know how many centuries. It makes you think of a newborn baby before it's been washed.

I don't know why this black-and-white photo fascinated me. "I'm looking at it to try and understand why I'm looking at it." The young man's male member is either missing or really small. On the other hand, you can easily make out his balls. The pressure of his thighs pushes them slightly forward. He's looking down and to the right, away from the sun, but he doesn't look like he wants to shield himself from the sun. It's as if he's avoiding the eyes of the workers surrounding him, as if his nudity made him uneasy. But the workers aren't looking at him. They're all turned towards the lens. Their expressions are serious. One adolescent, about the same age as Antinous, looks particularly worried. They're all standing, almost at attention, a few meters away from the statue. They probably didn't expect to make such a find. It's the snapshot of a meeting between a celebrity from the second century A.D. and a group of workers from the nineteenth century. I thought about Macriyannis, a nearly illiterate general from the War of Independence, and the admiration he expressed for ancient statues: "Don't sell them to foreigners," he told his comrades. "They're what we fought for."

I owe that information to my mother, who was a regular reader of the general's *Memoirs*, a clumsy but remarkably vivid text, apparently. She liked Macriyannis all the more because he came from the same region as she did. I met a taxi driver who was also an admirer of ancient art. Like Macriyannis, he was especially impressed by the veins that can be seen on the statues.

The workers are split into two groups, one on either side of Antinous, who occupies the center of the picture. The way they're arranged makes you think of a military unit welcoming a head of state. One soldier or gendarme stands among them, you can make out a sort of kepi. Several are wearing straw hats. Some of the faces reminded me of one of Buñuel's Mexican films, but I don't remember the title. They're warmly dressed and wearing canvas shirts, vests and jackets. The statue's nudity is nearly provocative. "They don't look at one another because they can't look at one another. They belong to two different worlds." Antinous is rather pensive. The harsh light accentuates the hollows around his eyes. "He doesn't understand how he came to be surrounded by the ghosts of the future." The workers really do look like ghosts because they all moved a little just when the snapshot was taken. Their outlines are faded as if worn away by time, though most of them are around thirty years old. Maybe the adolescent is anxious as he looks toward the lens because he senses that he already belongs to the past. They all look distinctly older than Antinous, who has the charm of youth and is in perfect focus. It looks as if they are the ones who've just been unearthed. "We're as old as our country," I thought. "We're much older than our ancestors. We ourselves are the ancient Greeks."

Their feet aren't as blurred as their faces. Some are wearing shoes with pompoms. "Antinous is quite fascinated by their shoes." Only one person seems foreign to the photograph's general tone. He's smiling with satisfaction. He has a goatee and from the position of his hands one might think he's rolling a cigarette. He's dressed more elegantly than the others, wearing short trousers like Tintin. He must be a French archeologist. In the lower left you can see a basket thrown on the ground, another one a bit farther over. The mountain of earth behind Antinous is on a low brick wall. His phallus was probably broken off. I think Christians systematically removed the sex organs from statues. What did they do with them? Someday we'll find an enormous pit filled with countless marble phalluses. I gave the magnifying glass back to the librarian.

"Antinous' face will fade gradually," he told me. "As long as they stay underground, statues are beautifully preserved, whether marble or bronze, like the Charioteer. But as soon as they're exposed to the open air, they start to deteriorate. In a way, their discovery means their loss."

We agreed that we'd have lunch together one day. He's Parisian, but he's lived in Athens for years. We usually speak Greek. I spoke to the female student who works next to me too. We were out in the courtyard at the same time. She went down to the garden, straight to the fig tree, and ate a few figs. She brought one for me, already peeled.

"Want it?" she asked me with a pretty smile.

She was wearing a slightly transparent black dress and black sandals. Her legs were a bit thick. I asked her if she had a car, which surprised her.

"We could make a trip to Delphi together," I said to her. "We'll find a good hotel that looks out over the plain. It's covered with olive and cypress trees, it seems. We'll watch the sun rise."

She started laughing.

"But I don't have a car, I told you!"

We spoke in English. She knows German, English, and a few words of Greek. She was born in Switzerland, of a German mother and an Austrian father. Her parents are separated, and she lives with her father in Vienna. Her name is Ilona.

"I don't even know where my mother is at the moment."

"In Italy," I thought. "Her mother is definitely in Italy."

"We'll walk in the sunshine," I continued. "We'll drink from the Castalia fountain when we're thirsty. We'll see Antinous and the Charioteer, of course. I'll point out to you a certain statue my mother liked. It's a little girl smiling. We'll admire the sunset and the red of the rocks around the shrine. We'll walk to the village. It will be nighttime. In the glow of a streetlight, we'll see a snake come shooting down a hill and then speed across the road like an arrow. He'll be chasing a rabbit."

The village of Delphi isn't far from the archeological site. At one time, it was situated on the shrine itself. Travelers who passed through there in the last century didn't see anything very interesting, just a few partial inscriptions on some walls. Flaubert, who visited Delphi in 1850, notes that the men are more beautiful than the women. In his notes on the Athens area, he mentions the name of Stamata. The village had to be moved before the dig could begin.

"We'll eat lamb chops. We'll drink a local wine, which with any luck won't be bad at all."

"Stop it," she said. "I have a boyfriend."

She tried to look serious, but there was still a certain sparkle in her eyes. I saw the blind man. This time I saw only his upper body because he was crossing the garden, downhill from the courtyard. He's a very thin man, his skin tanned by the sun, with sparse gray hair. He was wearing a short-sleeved white shirt and suspenders.

"Who's that?"

"Préaud, the epigraphist," said Ilona.

She anticipated my question: "He reads inscriptions with his fingers. Apparently he manages quite well. They say he corrected a very serious error in the identification of some ruins, but that was before he lost his sight."

The Greek government granted the French the right to dig, but only after ten years of bitter negotiations: they wanted to get a concession from the French to buy more grapes from Corinth. That was the country's main export at the end of the nineteenth century. Greece imported wine, hats, silk, lace, and perfume from France.

"I'm sorry that you have a boyfriend. We could spend the second day looking for someone who can read coffee grounds, a fortuneteller, basically a descendant of the Pythia. We'd certainly find one eventually. She would tell us about fortunate events in our near future. Then we'd make a quick trip to Amphissa, which was once famous for its leather goods and its bells, and which still has a reputation for its oil and its olives. We'd buy a can of oil and another of olives, then we'd head back to Athens, taking our time, along the coastal highway."

"I haven't danced in a long time," I thought as I went down the spiral staircase.

The shrine had been stripped of most of its riches well before the modern era. In classical antiquity, statues of gold, ivory, marble, silver, and especially bronze were so numerous that they couldn't all be seen. They were stacked together like the statuettes on the shelves in tourist shops. I suppose all that wealth, displayed half-way up a bare mountain, must have amazed the visitors, especially when they came upon it suddenly at the bend in the road. For a thousand years, Delphi continually received offerings from Greek cities, but also from foreign kings. After they defeated the Athenians, the Spartans gave the shrine thirty-seven bronze statues.

"A dozen Greek peoples were represented on the amphictyony, the council responsible for Delphi," said the librarian. "That display of cooperation didn't keep them from fighting amongst themselves. The offerings celebrated their victories and they were the trophies of an on-going fratricidal massacre. It's wrong to consider the amphictyony as a forerunner of unity among nations. The Delphic idea is a myth."

Archeologists have unearthed very few statues. We don't know if they were buried by the last pagans, hoping to protect them, or by the first Christians, hoping to make them disappear. A man named Alexandre Condoléon supervised the dig for the Greek Antiquities Service. He held that position for fifty years. The French mention him with veiled exasperation. He was suspicious and a nitpicker. He feared that works of art would be stolen or damaged. I suppose he was reassured by the outbreak of the last war when the Antiquities Service decided to hide all the statues. The Charioteer, wrapped in hay and cotton, found refuge in an ancient tomb. Antinous went back underground. Condoléon played a major part in the operation. He died shortly afterwards, at a time when the Delphi museum was empty.

The star of this spectacular troupe of statues wasn't beautiful, or young, or cultured, or well dressed. She may even have gone barefoot. I imagine that a person unfamiliar with Delphic ritual might have mistaken the Pythia for the temple's cleaning lady. We don't know if she conversed directly with the public, if questions were asked of her directly, or whether they were conveyed to her by the priests. The public was so large that the shrine sometimes employed two Pythias simultaneously. We used to think that the omphalos, the sort of big egg-shaped rock representing the navel of the world, was in the adytum. But that's not certain. We used to think that a laurel, a tree associated with Apollo, was planted there too. But how could it grow with no light? Maybe it was in a pot and taken out to the light from time to time? Examination of the site and the ruins has added to our knowledge, but also to our uncertainties. We had been almost certain, or so I've read, that the Pythia sat on a tripod and that she was enveloped in disturbing vapors from a fissure in the ground. Before the arrival of Apollo, the shrine belonged to Gaea or Ge, the goddess Earth. Perhaps because she received the dead, Gaea was reputed to know all the secrets of life. Plutarch — I did finally read him — seems convinced that there were vapors in the adytum, but apparently that was no longer the case in his time. He simply thinks the spirit of the earth favors the gift of prophecy. It was the Fathers of the Church who wrote most about the telluric vapors, which they describe as "evil." Saint John Chrysostom even claims that the vapors seeped into the prophetess' genitalia and made her delirious. Geological analysis has shown that there weren't ever any emanations, or any fissures, and that no spring waters flowed from the adytum, as some have wrongly thought. Images of the Pythia don't show her with her eyes rolled back in her head or foaming at the mouth. It's not even certain that she sat on a bowl supported by a tripod, which was originally a kitchen implement. Archeologists have discovered a less spectacular Pythia than the one we imagined, a simple and dignified star.

Now and then I think about the children I don't have. How would my life be different if I had children? Does Costas make *youvarlakia* for his daughter? If I had children, I would certainly make *youvarlakia* for them. It's my favorite food and my mother often made it when I came back from Paris. She didn't serve the meatballs in the usual egg and lemon sauce, but in tomato soup with an added lump of butter. I used to watch the butter melt. I'm watching it now and not until it's completely melted do I notice the book on the table, or Ilona's bare arm.

She's writing a study of the death of Alexander the Great to be published in Vienna. An elderly printer, probably the last printer in Vienna who still sets print by hand, will most likely print it on really beautiful paper. He'll have a dog, also very elderly. The print shop will smell of ink and cinnamon. There will be a cinnamon tree in the courtyard in back. When his work is done, the printer, followed by his dog, will go out into the courtyard to water the cinnamon tree. In one of the nearby apartments, someone will be listening to an opera. It will be springtime.

I don't know what Alexander the Great died of. Did someone kill him? Did he drink polluted water? Was he stung by an animal? Did he kill himself? Did he fracture his skull slipping on a rock at the seaside? I know of some rocks that are extremely slippery. Could he have drowned?

The performance started with the sacrifice of a goat, which was roasted and eaten right there. The faithful made an offering of flour paste and honey, which was also burned. The Pythia fumigated by burning laurel and barley flour. And we can assume that they burned grains of incense: the shrine's accounts mention frequent purchases of incense. The atmosphere must not have been very different from an Easter day on the public square of a village, where various odors fill the air, some from the church and some from nearby grills. I notice I often return to images borrowed from Christianity, about which I know very little, to talk about polytheism, about which I know nothing. I'm keeping a record of the dialogue between my ignorances. It's nearly certain that before going down into the adytum, the Pythia drank water from the Castalia and chewed laurel leaves. Perhaps it was a form of communion. She purified her mouth and her mind. Apparently the bowl supported by the tripod held small bones and beans that helped her find the answer when the question was simple. One might reasonably suppose that there were two beans, corresponding to the two possible answers, and that she shook the tripod to make one of the two fall from the bowl. But how could she tell one from the other? I noticed a sack of beans by the door of a grocery store near here. The grocer told me that beans are nearly all white when they're fresh but turn black as they dry out. Let's say that the Pythia used one fresh bean and one dried one.

The questions were generally simple ones: they were from individuals who wanted to know if they should get married, take the boat, leave the country, make a loan, plow the earth. According to Plutarch, the epsilon could stand for the conjunction ei," if," which was the start of every question. When the subjects were weightier matters, the Pythia made a special effort. She answered enigmatically and in verse. When she tells the Athenians to seek protection from the Persians behind a fortress of wood, she is alluding to their fleet. When she tells the Romans that they'll have to fight all peoples at once, she is prophesying the revolt of their slaves, who were in fact of very diverse origins. The Pythia's prophecies were extremely popular in classical antiquity, they were widely commented upon and willingly imitated. Croesus was mocked for not understanding that the empire whose fall the prophetess had foretold was his own. The Pythia answered questions and yet didn't answer them. She offered solutions in the form of problems. The epsilon might have been an oracle, but what question was its enigma intended to answer?

It would be hard to believe that the pronouncements were the work of an uneducated woman — no one has ever believed it, really. Beside her, in the adytum, stood a golden statue of Apollo. The Pythia was the voice of that statue. Her lack of education guaranteed the divine nature of her words, in a way. Apollo's taste for word play and rebus puzzles was so well known that he was called Loxias, the Ambiguous, the Paradoxical. It isn't surprising that his advice might be a bit obscure: he's not only the god of divination, but also the patron of philosophers. That leads Plutarch to suppose that the epsilon could have stood not for the interrogative "if," but for the one so often used by the Dialecticians: "If we accept, my dear Alcibiades . . . ." A third person was present in the adytum, a prophet with no important role to play, in theory. He noted down the oracles, perhaps touched them up a little. We don't know if he did anything else, but nothing prevents us from believing that he was educated and talented enough to improvise a diplomatic response in verse.

While walking home, I felt wings beating beside my neck and just below my right ear. I moved aside, but the bird kept on — I could hear the air vibrate from the fluttering of its wings. I wasn't scared at first. It even seemed like a friendly presence. But I couldn't understand how a bird could be flying that close to me. I stopped, waiting for the wings to stop beating, and it stopped. I didn't see the bird.

I was across from a bus stop where a number of people were waiting. There were a few children among them. "The children must have thrown something at me." But I hadn't been hit any object — the thought of a Frisbee crossed my mind — and the kids seemed well behaved. A few meters later, I heard the same beating of wings, and this time I was scared. My pencils and notebooks fell to the sidewalk. I didn't dare protect my neck with my hand, for fear of irritating the bird. "This fear will come to me more and more often." The attack lasted a few more seconds. I didn't hear the bird fly off. "I'll get used to it," I thought as I picked up my pencils and notebooks. "I'll come to expect an occasional visit from that bird. A person should be able to get used to this sort of situation."

One of my pencils had rolled quite a way down the sloping sidewalk. I found myself across from the bus stop again. People were watching me. I was fiercely irritated and that brought to mind a flood of insults, which I didn't utter, but which made me more and more angry. The bus pulled up between us, and they left. Beside my pencil I found another one that didn't belong to me. It was violet. I took it too. I thought it was a good sign, even though I don't really like violet. I felt like drawing. "It isn't easy to stop doing something you've been doing for so long." I almost became emotional when I thought of all the hours I had dedicated to drawing.

The bird hasn't bothered me since that day. I didn't draw when I returned home. I slept, just like every afternoon. I didn't draw when I woke up around five o'clock either. I don't feel like doing anything at that hour. Even in Paris, where I don't nap, I feel the same weariness. My eyes fix on some object that I don't see while my mind paces off the emptiness in long strides, as if it were measuring it, as if I intended to buy it. The day is far enough along at five o'clock that its meaning is clear. I begin to forget it even before it draws to a close. I've never done anything good after five o'clock.

That same evening I got a call from Véronique Carrier, who asked me for a cover drawing for a new monthly on economics that *Le Miroir de l'Europe* planned to launch soon.

"It won't be for the technocrats," she told me. "They've failed miserably. They haven't even resolved the unemployment problem they claimed they could fix. I think the time has come to review our values. The economic crisis should prompt the Western democracies to reconsider their goals. We have to get back to the individual, understand his basic needs, take his feelings into account. We can't let factions profit from people's distress, can we?"

Well-known intellectuals will contribute to the new magazine, along with philosophers from several European countries. Its title, *The New Humanist*, seemed pretentious to me. She specified that my drawing should target the European Union and that she wanted it to be "caustic."

When I recognized her voice, I thought that she might reproach me for my absence, ask me when I'm returning. She didn't ask any questions, said nothing critical, but instead proved quite understanding.

"It will do you good to spend some time in Greece. It will revive you. Charles is on the Purus River in Peru, with the Kaxinawás .... His best friend's wife died."

Her name was Rava Noora, "She Who Catches Hummingbirds." She always wore the same earrings, wooden ones with hummingbird wings attached to them. Her husband announced her death to the Carriers by sending the earrings in an envelope.

"He had painted the wooden part red, the color of death for them," said Véronique. There was nothing in the envelope except Rava Noora's earrings.

Her call made me feel good. It freed me from any remorse and gave me a flattering reassurance that they still need me at the newspaper. "I don't want people to remember me, and I don't want them to forget me." I'm not sure that Véronique Carrier is the ideal person to head up a humanist publication. But who knows? Her desire to succeed is so strong that she could acquire the humanity she lacks if her career required it.

A little later I got another call, this time from the journalist who was looking for me at Acridakis' bookstore. She works for *Embros Sunday*. I thought of the good-looking writer Caradzoglou had spoken about, but I didn't dare ask her if she had a rosewood bookcase. She had a pleasant voice. She, too, asked me for drawings. She needed ten of them, enough to fill a page, along with a biographical note and a photograph. I told her that I wouldn't give her political caricatures, but humorous cartoons. We decided to meet next Saturday.

I did the ten drawings the same evening. Almost all of them have a cemetery for a background. I wasn't bothered by the smell of India ink. It didn't bring back any bad memories. First I drew a bird (which looks rather like a chicken) sitting on one arm of a cross and leaning over to try and read the name of the deceased, then a marble cross that extends into real roots going deep into the earth. After a dozen unproductive efforts, I had the idea of dropping something on a tomb. So I sketched a cloud from which a few drops of rain, and then a pot of flowers, fall straight down on a cross. I colored the pot red, the flowers yellow, and I drew two violet lines in the sky. The bird trying to read the name of the deceased received multicolored plumage. I drew another bird flying over a grave and a plane dropping a bomb on a cemetery. A tiny man runs toward an abyss with a cross at the bottom. In another drawing, the man is leaning over the abyss and pondering the tomb that awaits him.

Since I didn't have any more ideas, I started drawing crosses. I filled two pages with crosses, until I finally thought of drawing a festive cemetery, with flags and little paper lanterns. I used all of my colored pencils. I have nineteen of them including the violet one I found in the street. The last sketch shows a crocodile weeping in front of a tomb.

At the same time, I thought about the drawing I was supposed to do for Véronique. I wasn't happy about being required, yet again, to represent England as an old woman, the Frenchman with a beret and the Spaniard wearing a matador's *montera*. But I didn't see any other way of identifying them recognizably. I also didn't see how I could wax ironic about the European Union without showing its representatives fighting it out. Every morning, paging through the papers in the newsroom at the *Miroir de l'Europe*, I tried to guess what my fellow cartoonists will draw, to avoid doing the same ones. I don't ever use the first idea that comes to mind for fear that it may already have come to several other cartoonists. Maybe that constant effort, that absurd desire to do better than my colleagues, finally wore me out? Could I be upset about the ephemeral nature of political cartoons? I'm not really interested in politics. That's probably the main cause of my boredom. I forget everything I've read in the press as soon as I've finished my cartoon. The European Union concerns me only to the extent that it makes my travel easier. The only time I was enthusiastic about my work was when I could fight against the junta in Athens. And that, alas, inspired only about thirty cartoons. If I were to publish a collection of cartoons, I would publish only those. It would be a tiny book. Which cartoon would I use on the cover? Probably the one where barbed wire forms the outline of Greece.

I looked over the sketches I'd just finished. I liked the flowerpot best, but since it was perfectly vertical it didn't look like a natural fall. I did the cartoon over again, tilting the pot slightly, and replacing the two violet lines with two tiny blue clouds. While I was making these changes, it occurred to me that Europe had taken the name of a princess who became the mistress of Zeus. I decided to make the European free-for-all look like a scene on an antique vase — I even thought of portraying the brawl on a cracked amphora. I would put a beret on the Frenchman, a Tyrolean hat on the German, but otherwise they'd be completely nude and in affected postures. I imagined a very small Greek wearing an enormous crested helmet. I finally felt like doing that sketch, but it was late and I put it off to the next day. I didn't need to sign all of the cartoons for *Embros Dimanche*, since they would all appear on the same page. Should I sign Pol, as usual? Just when I was about to do so, I changed my mind and I wrote my complete name, Pavlos Nicolaïdis, under the flowerpot cartoon. That was the only one I signed.

When I turned on the television, I recognized Amalia Stathopoulou laughing and looking toward the lights, which made her blond hair shine. The reporter seated across from her said:

"Your interpretation of Electra was a milestone. Aren't you afraid of the judgment of people who were at that historic performance?"

"Do you know how many people write to me every day, even from the provinces, to encourage me? 'You must take the role,' they tell me, 'we're with you.' This morning I even got a telegram from a town on the border."

"A town on the border!" the journalist repeated admiringly.

"I can tell you that I've already discussed the question with the Prime Minister."

"And what did he tell you?" asked the reporter, leaning forward in his chair as if he were about to stand up.

"You must take the role!"

She'll appear at Epidaurus, just like the first time. She will give only one performance and she stressed that all ticket sales would go toward acquiring El Greco's *Saint Peter*, which is to be auctioned in London. I'm sure I read something about the apostle Peter while in the library, but what and where?

She was smoking. I lit my pipe, too. I haven't yet received the tobacco I asked Marie-Christine to send. How long ago did I call her? There are only three packets left. I got the impression that all of Amalia's movements — she crossed her legs from time to time, baring her knees — were carefully planned, studied. She moved languorously. I imagined her rehearsing them in front of a mirror, rejecting some, keeping only the most flattering of them. I thought of Fanny's attractive legs. "I'll ask her to dinner some evening." I wondered if Costas had ever had an affair with her. Every morning I resolve to go out in the evening, but my desire dwindles as the day wears on. I haven't telephoned the friends I used to see, and I haven't called Penelope, Theodoris' student either. Stathopoulou announced the cast of the play. All the actors except Athènodoros Proussalis, who will play Aegisthus, are much younger than her. The actor who will portray Orestes, her brother, could be her grandson — he only recently graduated from the Dramatic Arts Conservatory. The reporter avoided making any comments on the cast. But when she said that the role of Clytemnesta, Electra's mother, would be played by Anna Macraki, who's only about forty, he responded:

"But Macraki ...," he said.

The Minister either didn't understand or pretended not to understand what he meant.

"She's a very good actress, don't you think?"

"Yes, of course. But she's a bit young ...."

"Young?" Stathopoulou repeated, as if she didn't know the word.

She pronounced it tonelessly, in a voice that reminded me of Vasso Manolidou playing Ophelia. I saw her once at the National Theater. She looked at the reporter for a few seconds. Her face had become a mask devoid of expression. The reporter had sunk back into his armchair. He had the same look as my father when he hears the telephone ring. All at once, Amalia threw her head back and laughed. The skin of her neck is perfectly smooth.

"I have to admit that I hadn't thought about it," she said. "She is perhaps a bit young for Clytemnestra, but so what? She's such a good actress."

I got up from my bed and turned off the television. "Maybe she's right," I thought. "Actors are ageless."

It was ten after midnight. I wasn't sleepy. I stood in the middle of the room and made a few quick wrist movements, as if I were holding a ping-pong paddle. I thought about the hands of certain women. One has long fingers, overly long. Another cuts her fingernails so short they look bitten. Another has joints that protrude. I remembered one heavy hand with square fingers and a wide, nearly masculine palm, another small and dimpled, seemingly incapable of the slightest harm.

The desk lamp had stayed on. The bottle of India ink, the green penholder, and the colored pencils were scattered about in its light. They formed a sort of multicolored rain.

I took the sheet of paper with the capital epsilon off the wall and placed it on the table. I sat down and uncorked the India ink. I stared at the epsilon for a long time, trying to discern another form beneath the one it had. I looked at it like you look at those drawings of a landscape where a character is hidden, but I didn't see anything. I drew an E and extended the middle line to the left, which made it look like a trident, the weapon of Poseidon. The God of the Sea also had an altar in the Temple of Apollo. "The upper-case psi (Ψ) looks more like a trident than the epsilon does," I thought. I drew two or three more E's, trying to relate them to something else. I found nothing. "The epsilon doesn't look like anything."

Are all the letters of the Greek alphabet so hard to decipher? I wrote the alphabet in capitals, in two columns. I noticed that it's fairly easy to find an image for the other letters. The alpha (Α) looks like a compass, the beta (Β) like a pregnant woman with a big bust, the gamma (Γ) like a gallows, the delta (Δ) like a pyramid. I left the epsilon aside. The zeta (Ζ), probably because the name of Zeus starts with that letter, made me think of a bolt of lightning. The eta (Η) is a little tiny ladder, and theta (Θ) looks like the head of a screw. I wasn't satisfied with that last image. I reexamined the theta, and finally decided that the line splitting it in half could be the horizon and the circle the rising or setting sun. "Logically, the theta should be at the beginning or at the end of the alphabet." The iota (Ι) reminds me of a lot of things: a candle, a billiard cue. The kappa (Κ) brings to mind a goose-stepping German soldier, the lambda (Λ) a roof, the mu (Μ) a couple holding hands.

I came back to the epsilon. I didn't want to admit that I was incapable of finding a meaning for it. I tipped it forward. It looked like a temple with three columns. Maybe if I tipped it backwards it would look like Apollo's lyre? No, it didn't look like a lyre. In its usual posture, it didn't look like anything. "If there were more horizontal lines, it would look like a comb."

I decided to give up on it for the moment and went back to reading the alphabet. The nu (Ν) is a gate barred with a diagonal board. The xi (Ξ) looks like the moon reflecting on the sea, the omicron (Ο) the moon, or rather the sun — I'd prefer the sun, the star of Apollo. I'm starting to feel rather friendly toward the god who cared about people's problems, who had a taste for paradox, and who loved music. Besides, he was very lenient. The Pythia apparently once answered a young priest who had broken his vow of chastity and came before her to ask how he might expiate his sin, by saying: "All that is done through necessity, the god pardons."

The pi (π) looks like those illegal shacks often built in the woods in a single night, the rho (Ρ) a sturdy tourist loaded down with a bulky backpack, the phi (Φ) like the same tourist seen head on. The sigma (Σ) could be the open mouth of a ravenous fish. The tau (T) is a hammer, the upsilon (Υ) a slingshot, the khi (X) a pair of scissors, the psi (Ψ), as I said, a trident. The omega (Ω) looks like the sun barely above the line of the horizon, just after sunrise or just before sunset. "A half hour is all that separates the omega from the theta (Θ)."

I went back once again to the E. In place of the vertical line, I substituted a man facing to the right, with a trumpet at his mouth and a sword in his hand. But I couldn't manage to replace the last horizontal line. "I can't just give him clown shoes." Despite that setback, I had the feeling that my efforts were leading somewhere. "I'll find it .... I can at least solve this problem." It wasn't long before I came up with something: I drew another man, but this time kneeling, or more precisely sitting on his heels, his legs folded under him and forming another horizontal line. I gave him a long neck, bent sharply forward. He looked like a man praying fervently. That gave me the idea of replacing the middle line with his folded hands. "The epsilon depicts a man praying." I changed my mind immediately and placed a coffee cup in the man's hands: "He's not praying, he's reading coffee grounds." This possibility was much more satisfying to me because it brought me closer to the Pythia.

It was one o'clock in the morning. I was still holding the penholder over the drawing. I started over once again, this time replacing the man with a woman, a woman with long hair — the Pythia had long hair, I thought — and holding not a coffee cup, but a little bowl. "The E is the Pythia," I thought. "She's looking into the bowl to see which one of the beans is still there."

A hundred years after the birth of Christ, at the time when Plutarch was working at Delphi, the amiable Apollo is only a pale shadow of his former self. His lyre no longer charms the multitudes. The Greeks believe less and less in oracles. The Pythia no longer receives visits from foreign kings. More and more, people get by without her opinion. The center of the world has been transferred to another place. Plutarch, who died in 126, never heard of Christ. He knows nothing of the new god rising, but he is obliged to admit that Apollo is on the wane. He's much more worried about this new development than he is about the mystery of the letter E. His text, in the form of a Platonic dialogue, is above all in praise of Apollo. The interpretations of the epsilon that he proposes are all in support of a god who certainly doesn't deserve to disappear. He's writing to save him. He writes about the interrogative "if" in order to exalt Apollo's ability to resolve enigmas, and then about the "if" used in dialectics to remind us that the Lord of

Delphi is the founder of that art. He mentions that among the vowels the E occupies the same place as the sun among the planets (second, after the moon). But the Epsilon could also be the number 5, he says. That hypothesis moves him temporarily away from Apollo—though he's careful to note that there are five rhythms in music. You get the impression that Plutarch lingers over the 5 because he enjoys it: in his youth, he studied Pythagoras at some length. The author remembers.... Most importantly, he remembers that 5 comes from the union of feminine 2 and masculine 3, and so represents the couple, that we have five senses, that the elements which compose all of nature are five (earth, water, fire, air, and light), and so on. He even quotes Plato's astonishing claim that the number of inhabited planets could certainly be no more than five!

The very last explanation he offers allows him to return to his praise of the divinity. The epsilon could be the first letter of the verb "to be," more precisely the second person present tense form, and could signify "you are" (which is still pronounced *ei*). It is not enough to identify the god with the sun, Plutarch writes, although light, the source of life, is one manifestation of celestial goodness. The "you are" formula invites us to ponder the nature of the divine, to understand that Apollo alone truly exists, that he will never age, since he was never young, that he lives in a perpetual present, in short that he is not many. His name — Apollo could be composed from the privative "a" and the word *polys*, numerous — shows precisely that, his unity. As I understand it, to define Apollo apart from his perfection would be the same as denying him. The epsilon could be a theological treatise in a single letter.

Our author turns abruptly toward humans. And what does he see? Their misery, of course. He is surprised that we fear death, when we've already died several times: the baby that we were was killed by the child, the child by the adolescent, the adolescent by the adult. The maxim "Know thyself" is an allusion to the unfortunate human condition, while the E evokes Apollo's immortality. Plutarch simply cannot accept that gods can also grow old, that everything ends, even eternity, and that, at the time when he was writing, the path leading up to the shrine was desperately empty.

Could it be that the religion from Plutarch's time is also going out of fashion? At the funeral, the priest expressed deep worries about its future. He spoke out against young people who don't go to church, but also against those who only go through force of habit and chat during Mass. He deplored our general immorality, randomly stigmatizing drugs, Satanism — the newspapers were talking about a gang of youths, disciples of Satan, who were organizing ceremonies in an abandoned factory — and the exhibitionism present in nightclubs at the seaside, where naked women dance on tables.

He took advantage of our misfortune to tell us about his concerns. He said almost nothing about my mother, who didn't go to church very often. "He's getting even with her," I thought. I didn't like the expression he used to refer to her death one bit: "She has paid the debt we all share," he declared, as if we were there to work out a business deal. When they buried her, he fortunately said nothing. It was my father who spoke. But I'm not ready to describe that scene yet.

I read Plutarch in ancient Greek and in Modern Greek. I understood very little when I read only the original text. Several words on each page are familiar to me, but there aren't many sentences composed entirely of words that I know. I underlined a few, like the one that sums up the author's point of view on fear of death: "We fear only one death, which is ridiculous, since we have already suffered and continue to suffer so many others." I, of course, am not capable of judging the author's style. The translation into Modern Greek is rather boring. Plutarch reminded me of the forgotten voices of my teachers. I remembered the landscape visible out the classroom window: the big packed-dirt playground where we played soccer, the trees behind the wooden fence, and the houses built on a distant hill. I even remembered the sandwiches my mother used to fix for me to take to school. She always gave me two, which she first wrapped in foil and then in white paper on which, in evenly spaced straight letters, she wrote the contents of each one. I didn't have to open them to decide which one I would eat first. She would write, for example, "egg and tomato," "salami and tomato," "feta and butter." They were good, thick sandwiches on sliced bread.

If the epsilon was the first letter of as short a word as *ei*, why didn't they take the trouble to write out the whole word? It really wouldn't have been any harder to write it all out, even if the word were longer. "They probably decided that a mute word was better suited to that place than any word." It may be that the ancient Greeks said nothing about the epsilon not because they knew its meaning, as I once thought, and not because they weren't up to unraveling its meaning, as Caradzoglou claims, but out of respect for its mystery. "To them, interpreting the E seemed like an act of irreverence, of impiety." The effort made by the author of the *Pythic Dialogues* to explain it might mean that the epsilon had already lost its sacred character. "Plutarch has trouble understanding it precisely because he's trying to understand it." I thought, of course, that he wouldn't have understood it any better if he had made no effort. I came to the conclusion that it's just as impossible to interpret the epsilon by looking for its meaning as it is by not looking for its meaning. That reasoning would have discouraged me if it hadn't, like all sophisms, also proved the opposite of what it affirms: it is impossible not to discover what the epsilon means, because, in avoiding trying to explain it, you come closer to its mystery, and if you try to explain it you inevitably come even closer. "Whether or not I try to penetrate the mystery of the epsilon, either I'll succeed or I won't."

Nonetheless, I felt even more demoralized. "All I'm trying to do is keep myself occupied. I'm thinking about the epsilon to stay busy." My ambition is probably limited to getting together forty words to fill up by notebook. Thanks to the ones I borrowed from Plutarch, I have valiantly conquered through page eleven. On page eight, I noted the interrogative "if" and the question *ei apodèmein*, "Should I emigrate?" That question was often asked of the Pythia. I remembered it because it preoccupied me one summer twenty-four years ago. It may torment me again someday. I don't know if I'll go back to France. Maybe my life there is finished, maybe I'm going through one of those transitional periods Plutarch talks about where we outlive ourselves. Though he associates the epsilon with questions asked of the prophetess, he forgets that the word "question," *érotèma*, also begins with E. I wrote that down as well, along with the philosopher's "if," followed by the sentence I improvised above: "If we accept, my dear Alcibiades . . . ." I added *you are* on page eleven.

Plutarch's conjectures didn't really thrill me. The attention he paid to the number 5 seemed especially arbitrary. I didn't write down the 5 in my notebook. The poetry of numbers doesn't move me. There is a 5 in my phone number in France, and another in my birth date. But I don't see any others. I'm forty-six years old. The card the librarian gave me to register the books I've borrowed is number 9618.

I had lunch with the librarian at old Yannis' restaurant in Exarchia. He's the one who chose that tavern. He told me that he loves home cooking and that he avoids restaurants with a cosmopolitan clientele.

"Most of my friends are Greek."

He was carrying a Greek newspaper and an old red leather briefcase. We sat outdoors on the terrace, just outside an open glass door. We would have preferred to sit inside, because it was too hot outside, but there wasn't any room. I noticed the man eating beside us, whose table was framed by the door opening. He was the only customer wearing a suit and tie. We glanced at each other, but I didn't know him.

The librarian is named François. He's about medium height, medium weight, with thinning hair and a gray beard. We probably look something alike.

"Yannis was seriously ill last winter," he told me.

I didn't know that. I don't go to his tavern often. It isn't on my route.

"I'll go see what's good today," he said as he got up. "Shall we drink retsina?"

He obviously enjoyed speaking Greek and he knew it perfectly. He liked using rare words, a bit ostentatiously. He was proud to be among Yannis's close friends. It seems to me that intellectuals often seek the friendship of common people, that they're happy to have among their friends a fisherman, a football player, or a house painter. He entered the tavern through the front door, rather than through the one nearest to us, to avoid bothering our neighbor. A dog was sleeping under the table. I could only see its tail sticking out.

François had left his attaché case and his newspaper on a chair. " A NEW OUTRAGE FROM THE SKOPJE GOVERNMENT," I read. There were two photographs under the headline: one was of a chest found in the tomb of Philip, the father of Alexander the Great, in Greek Macedonia, the other of the red flag of Slavic Macedonia. The sun adorning the cover of Philip's chest, with its alternating shorter and longer rays, also appears on the flag. I turned over the folded paper to see the rest of the front page stories. "LONG-AWAITED VOICE, ARE YOU REALLY HERE?" The question spread across four columns and was followed by a second title in small letters: "THE VOICE OF AMALIA RETURNS TO EPIDAURUS." The performance will take place on August 25, a Saturday. Will I have finished this text by then? But what sort of ending can it have, a text that's nothing more than a private journal? I started writing in the spring, at the time when the shrine at Delphi opened its doors. Perhaps I'll finish it in autumn, the season when the prophetess took her annual vacation. François came back with two glasses and a carafe of retsina.

"I feel right at home in this tavern," he said.

There isn't a single Parisian restaurant where I really feel comfortable. I haven't lived pleasantly in France. The satisfactions Paris gave me were mostly professional. I shared the ill humor and the anxiety of the city's inhabitants. But I don't want to think about the life I led there. I feel like being where I am.

We started using the familiar form of address as soon as the food arrived. We had already drunk two glasses. He had ordered baked meat served with a square pasta called *chylopitès*: he knew the word *chylopitès* too. It was a mistake to write *ainigma* in my notebook. The epsilon at Delphi could not have been mistakenly substituted for the diphthong *ai*, since the ancients pronounced the two letters separately — they said *aï*nigma. Nonetheless, François didn't discount the possibility that the E might have taken the place of another letter.

"The inscriptions at Delphi are full of errors," he said. "The people doing the engraving didn't necessarily understand the texts they were copying. Sometimes they got distracted and repeated the same line twice. It's entirely possible that the epsilon was confused with the eta (η), which became an "i" in Modern Greek, but which originally was a long *ê*, a bit like in the word *bêler*, 'to bleat.' 'Bleat' in ancient Greek was written with the syllable βῆ, pronounced *bê*, but which we read today as *vi*."

I didn't know that the beta was pronounced *b* rather than *v*, or that the eta was pronounced *ê*. My teachers scorned and rejected Erasmus' point of view on ancient Greek pronunciation, which went against their own theory of the language's non-evolution. The onomatopoeic βῆ was missing from the texts we studied because all by itself it would have been enough to show us that we weren't pronouncing the language the same way as Plato. We would have had trouble accepting that sheep had once bleated by going vi, vi ....

"Up until the middle of the fifth century, there's a certain confusion between the epsilon and the eta, each of them often replacing the other. One archeologist even held that the E was nothing more than a simple eta with a smooth breathing mark and a circumflex accent, which means 'he speaks.' Who is it that speaks? Apollo, probably."

I still don't know what verb is hiding behind that ἦ. I need a dictionary of Ancient Greek. "I'll end up getting lost," I thought.

"So do I need to take words starting with eta into account too?" I asked him.

He smiled politely.

"Well, the chances are certainly better that the epsilon is an epsilon, rather than an eta."

We clinked glasses. I was eating artichokes with dill. They were a little tough.

"It's not the season for artichokes," François said to me. "He knows about everything," I thought.

I got up to get more bread. I went in through the glass door. Without intending to, I bumped our neighbor's table, which woke up the dog. He jumped up on me, standing on his hind legs while trying to paw at me with the front ones. I quickly saw that there was no danger: it was Gaour, Vaguelio's dog.

"How's it going, Gaour?"

I held out my hand to pat his head, but just then the man in the suit tugged violently on the leash.

"We know one another!" I said to him, as if to excuse that show of affection.

He wrinkled his nose, glared at Gaour, who hid timidly under the table, and looked toward the street without saying a word. "So he's the one who's with

Vaguelio now." I went on my way. I would have preferred her to be with any other customer in the restaurant than with that man. He looked older than I am, though I could be wrong. The suit and tie no doubt added a few years. I passed by his table again, going back to mine. Gaour was staring at me. "He remembers seeing me crawling on all fours in Vaguelio's apartment." The man didn't look at me again. I think he recognized me as soon as I entered the restaurant, that he'd seen me in a photo he chanced upon at Vaguelio's, in a drawer, hidden under a stack of old telephone bills.

"The epsilon was sometimes pronounced smoothly, sometimes more hoarsely. That second E was preceded by a special sign, which later became a rough breathing mark. The epsilon at Delphi wasn't preceded by that sign, but the sign wasn't always used. For that matter, it's far from certain that they would have appended it to an isolated letter. The word you're looking for could begin with a smooth E, like in the word *éros*, or a rough E, like in *Ellène, ellènikos*."

I'm never sure how to transcribe those words that start with an H in other languages, but actually start with an E in Greek. Should I put the *h* in parentheses, "*(H)ellène*," for example?

I had trouble following him. I kept thinking that Vaguelio was about to appear. Her friend, though, didn't seem to be waiting for anyone. He had nearly finished his meal. I looked down the street. There were very few cars.

The word Hellene revived my attention. "The E was the label of the Hellenes," I thought. "They thought it would be a good idea to hang their trademark over the entrance to the most famous of their religious centers." Even today, the Greek flag often flies over churches.

I was in the midst of telling François how I felt about Plutarch's book when I saw Vaguelio arriving on her motorbike. She stopped just two meters from our table. She hadn't seen me. She looked straight at her friend, as if she knew he was waiting for her here.

"I'm not too late?"

I suddenly realized I'd missed her voice. I remembered the nickname she had given me. She saw me just as she was taking her purse out of the little box on the luggage carrier.

"Well, Pavlos!" she exclaimed. "What are you doing here?"

She was wearing a gray men's jacket with the sleeves rolled up and a wide black skirt with mauve flowers on it. I didn't recognize the clothes. I was about to get up to give her a kiss, but she discouraged me by keeping her distance.

"Are you doing okay?" I said.

"Yes, fine. What are you up to?"

She took a deep breath. Was she feeling emotional? I was.

"He's wondering about the letter E," François explained, "but he hasn't yet told me why."

"I really don't know," I admitted.

I wanted to find out if the letter I'd received in Paris was from her. I asked the question in a low voice. I didn't want to be overheard by her friend.

"Me, write to you?" she said indignantly, almost shouting. "In your dreams, Pavlos! Do you think there's anything left for us to say?"

She was looking at me intensely. "She hates me," I thought.

"Goodbye," she said coldly to François.

I heard Gaour barking gaily behind me. I turned my chair slightly more toward the street. Once again I could feel the tension I felt when I was with her. I heard a vague echo of our quarrels, the endless way we talked things through once the storm had passed, sometimes until three in the morning. She always wanted to make love afterwards, but I really didn't feel like it.

"What were we saying?" I asked François.

"I'm not really taken with Plutarch's suggestions, either, except for one. I'd like to think that the E signifies 'if,' that it's the starting point of an unfinished thought that anyone can complete to suit himself. I don't consider that interpretation more plausible, I just find it more attractive than the others. I would willingly go inside a temple that welcomed me with that word … Am I boring you?"

He asked me that question in French. I answered in Greek: "Not at all."

I didn't want the conversation to go on in French in front of Vaguelio, who couldn't believe that I hadn't taken French citizenship and who accused me of espousing foreign ideas about national problems. She ordered beer and tarama. I heard her laugh. I wouldn't have enjoyed eating with her at all. I preferred hearing François tell me about the epsilon. "No woman has ever intrigued me like this letter." He gestured for the waiter to bring us another half carafe of retsina by placing his hand halfway up the empty carafe. "Someday the epsilon will go back to its usual place among the letters of the alphabet. I'll forget it, like I've forgotten all the rest."

I could hear bits and pieces of what was being said at the next table. They talked about a building lot, then about a store going out of business. They mentioned the names of several islands and they also talked about the guy's sister. He spoke less than Vaguelio and more softly. The building across from us was number 37. The waiter brought us the wine and we clinked glasses again. François told me about one of his colleagues who had become an author of historical novels and who maintained that the E did indeed stand for 5.

"The number, according to him, refers to the four cardinal points, plus the point where the north-south and the east-west lines cross. The 5 gives the coordinates for the center of the world. The problem is that in inscriptions the number 5 is almost never written as the letter E, but rather as five vertical lines, or as the letter pi, the first letter of the word five, *penté*."

"So the epsilon might refer to the number 1, *éna*, since that's the letter it starts with!"

I felt like I'd made an important discovery.

"That's not a bad idea," he agreed. "The 1 was the symbol of Zeus."

Perhaps because 1 is the symbol of Zeus, not Apollo, perhaps for some other reason, he didn't seem to share my enthusiasm.

I wondered if churches have numbers, like houses do. He whispered in my ear, "Your friend is really pretty."

My memory was probably unfair towards Vaguelio, since all it retained were the rough times of our affair. But her presence had been very precious to me during that dark period. I remembered that her smile touched me deeply. She had begun to learn French so that she could chat with my friends when she came to Paris. But the good memories stayed distant. My memory refused to make them accessible. "It's definitely all over."

"Have you heard from Ilona?"

I hadn't seen her at the library for several days. He told me she'd left for the island of Skopélos with her boyfriend. She must have finished her study on the death of Alexander the Great. I remembered Neoptolemus. Why did he hate Apollo so much?

"He considered him responsible for the death of Achilles, his father. The poisoned arrow that wounds him in the foot and brings about his death is guided by Apollo. Achilles had made the mistake of killing Troilus, who was the son of Apollo, and he had shown unbounded arrogance after his victory over Hector, which had also angered the god."

As we were getting up to leave, Vaguelio ordered artichokes with dill.

"Don't order the artichokes," I told her, "they're a little tough."

She gave me a nice smile, which I was pleased to return.

"It isn't the season for artichokes," I added.

5

The ideas about married life I formed from watching my parents aren't good or bad. They're neutral. The two of them certainly had affection for one another, but I'm sure they weren't in love. I rarely saw them kiss. I only rarely heard them argue. I don't think their behavior changed much when they were alone together. They lived together unenthusiastically, through force of habit. I don't think they ever considered separating. Couples didn't separate easily in those days, especially when they had children. What did they share, apart from love for their sons? They both read, but not the same books. My father had a weakness for escape literature, adventure novels and travel stories. My mother's tastes were more classical: she liked Dostoevsky, Pearl Buck, Papadiamantis. She was also interested in studies of Greek history and culture. One of the very rare books they had in common was one whose title I can't remember, about the birth and eruptions of the Santorini volcano.

They had nearly the same attitude about the Church, but for different reasons. Despite her working-class origins, my mother stayed away from politics. But she nonetheless felt that the Orthodox priests were too far to the right. She criticized their lack of culture especially. Their intellectual level appalled her. She found them inadequate. She didn't doubt the existence of God, but she was intrigued by his popularity among the least educated segments of the population. The comments I made about religion in my youth upset her: "But there are some very cultured people who believe in God!" she used to tell me. "Even doctors!"

The alliance of the Greek bishops with the junta pushed her a little farther from the Church. But she never stopped contributing to its charities. She was a good person. People who talked to her always received all the attention she had to give.

As for my father, he doesn't go to church much because churches depress him. The generally elderly clientele gets him down. Maybe he thinks of churches as branch offices of the afterlife. He loves life more than my mother did. I know that he has read the Bible and appreciated it. But he only read it once, like a novel, to see how it turned out. The words he spoke at the burial are the words of a true believer, of course. He was so touching that even one of the two gravediggers, the young one holding the shovel, had tears in his eyes. He stuck the shovel into the earth and rested his chin on the handle. He was about twenty years old. It crossed my mind that he'd been hired that very day and that my mother's burial was his first.

A picture of Jesus hung in our classroom, above the blackboard. Classes began with a group prayer. We stood up. Adoration of God, like that of our ancestors, seemed mandatory. We were taught that there was no break between classical antiquity and the Christian era, that the latter had followed the former peaceably, and was its natural extension. I've already mentioned, I think, that they gave us an idea of classical Greece that conformed to religious precepts. Antigone had the face of a saint, and Aristotle, in his own way, heralded the coming of the Lord. Every day, the schools celebrated the marriage of classical antiquity and Christianity. I wondered why God had taken so long to show himself, to openly declare his existence. What had he been doing in the previous centuries, at the time of the Trojan War or the Peloponnesian War? In the picture above the blackboard, Christ was dressed much like an ancient Greek. He was dressed in a long white chiton and wore a red chlamys over his shoulder — rather elegantly, I must say. His beard was smoother and better combed than Plato's or Socrates'. The relationship between Classical Hellenism and Byzantine Hellenism didn't seem obvious to me. My uncertainty was based on the works of art produced by those two civilizations. I could see nothing in common between the smiling nude Venus, sandal in hand to threaten a harassing satyr, and the Byzantine icons of pallid saints standing motionless in the dark. With their voluminous shining haloes, I imagined them to be the daughters of melancholic goldsmiths. Since I didn't know that the ancient Greeks had the deplorable habit of painting their statues, I associated their art with the light, while Byzantine painting seemed to spring from darkness. God did not have the kind face that my mother attributed to him, but rather the menacing face of a nocturnal creature. As a child, I was convinced that my erroneous ways would cost me dearly. I found no charm whatsoever in churches, not even in the most picturesque of chapels: I viewed them as little courtrooms that sometimes handed down very stiff sentences.

I never stay with one idea for very long. Why did I start talking about my parents' married life? I take long and frequent breaks. I walk around the apartment. I kick the pebbles that work loose from cracks in the floor. When I get back to work, I've generally forgotten what I wanted to say. Did I really intend to say something? My thoughts buzz around like flies. They rarely light on the blank page. Maybe I planned to talk about my relationships with women, explain why I've never thought about getting married. Should I have thought about it? I've probably never felt the need for a permanent presence in my home. My work wouldn't be any better if I were living with a woman. Inevitably, she would move around, make noises that would distract me. She would go into the bathroom from time to time. She would turn on the faucet.

"I especially miss women when I watch television," I said to Theodoris. "I like to comment on the programs. It's just when I watch television that I don't like being alone."

It's true in any case that I've had enough of the solitary life I've led for a month or so — it's the twenty-ninth or thirtieth of June. I go out every night now. I don't often go to the School library anymore. My intellectual curiosity is no longer boundless. I read an essay on the life and work of Anghelos Sikelianos, who tried to bring new life to Delphi. I didn't study it very carefully: I was reading another text between the printed lines, a text that had nothing to do with Delphi or with Sikelianos, a nebulous narrative that groaned faintly. Should I state briefly what I retained from that essay? I'm never sure if I'm explaining things in the right order. I pictured Sikelianos riding a white horse along the beach, wrapped in a white tunic, like a living statue from classical antiquity. Apparently he was very handsome and full of himself. That image saddened me: it reminded me of the sterile narcissism of my education. Sikelianos organized two celebrations at Delphi, in 1927 and in 1930, and tried to bring in an international audience. He was convinced that humanity needed a new start, guided by the peaceful and the elevated thought that, according to him, flourished around the Temple of Apollo. He dreamed of restoring the center of the world to its original location. The events included performances of tragedies. They say that at the première — it was Aeschylus' *Prometheus Bound* — two eagles flew over the theater. The poet thought that the gods were with him. They weren't. The miracle did not take place. The course of time was not reversed. The whole campaign cost his rich American wife a fortune and failed. His poetry pursues the same goal as my childhood education. It tries to unite classicism and Christianity. It's a poetry that mixes ideas, skims over centuries, converses with the invisible. The tone is prophetic and pompous. It's a poetry that doesn't appeal to me.

"Solitude would weigh on me all the time," said Theodoris. "Especially at night, of course. I would hesitate to turn off the lamp, I might sleep with the lights on."

He has never lived alone. He married Niki at age twenty-three. We've been seeing each other very often recently. We've known each other since early childhood. He has a photograph of me at summer camp. I'm half hidden behind an oleander, as if I were intimidated. On the back of the photo, I promise him that as soon as we're back in Athens I'll make him a wooden sword. I don't remember whether I kept my promise and he doesn't remember either. There are subjects I can't broach with anyone but him. He's the only one of my friends who knew my mother well. I'm perfectly aware that time isn't necessarily kind to friendships: it often ends up lifting the veil that hides our weaknesses. We have accepted one another, Theodoris and I, just as we are. We get along very well, even though we're not alike. I wouldn't be able to tolerate Niki for more than a day. Her authoritarianism would drive me away.

"I'm not at peace with myself," he admitted. "I suppose I'm not at peace .... I hide things from myself .... I'm not a creator, silence doesn't inspire me — it means nothing to me. I don't need peace and quiet to write an article or a study. I write about subjects I know by heart, subjects I've lectured on a hundred times .... I don't just want a companion, I want her to be omnipresent, explosive, like Niki."

"Vaguelio liked turbulence too. Orderly ordinary life wasn't interesting for her."

"Niki tried to humiliate me. She treated me like shit. There's no doubt that's what I needed, or I wouldn't have stayed with her for so long."

He was in group therapy a few years ago. Once, I don't have any idea why, he invited my mother to go with him and, strangely enough, she accepted. He was a good friend to her and often visited her in Ano Patissia. Apparently my mother, who must have been seventy at the time, spoke to the group about her sex life with an impressive sincerity. I reminded him of that incident.

"She spoke to us because we asked, because we insisted," he said. "She couldn't refuse us the favor. For her, lying or hiding anything was unthinkable. She understood that we needed to hear the truth and she told us the truth."

One day I asked my mother what she could have said during that public confession.

"This and that," she said, smiling.

"Niki played the father," Theodoris continued. "She was a tyrannical and violent father. Marilena, on the other hand, makes me think of my mother. She opposes things silently, views the course of events sadly."

We were sitting on my bed, in one corner of the room. I'll tell Elias, who knocked down the walls, to fill the holes in the floor with cement and paint the whole apartment. I prefer him to do the work while I'm in Ioannina — I've finally decided to go see my brother Costas. He has problems and he couldn't tell me what was happening, since his wife, Vasso, was at home when I called.

"It's nothing serious," he reassured me. "But it will do me good to see you."

On the way back, I'll stop at Delphi.

Theodoris prefers ping-pong to billiards. He claims that we've played before, when we were kids, at his parents' house. It was a beautiful big house with a yard. They sold it when his father's business went bankrupt. I think that all families have a similar story, made up of difficult times and shining moments. A deaf elderly aunt brings in a tray of silver glasses the size of sewing thimbles. She moves slowly. Everyone is afraid she'll trip on the rug and fall. They recall an uncle who was a doctor, who cured a billionaire for free, and everyone agrees that his kindness bordered on stupidity. His son is already retired. In the photo album, there's a picture of a little girl wearing one sandal. She hasn't had time to put the other one on, and she's carrying it in her hand. The echoes of an altercation about politics that broke out one Sunday can still be heard, along with a few notes of Schubert's *Lindenbaum* played on a violin that was sold during the Occupation. A four-color kite — white, red, yellow, and blue — floats motionless in the sky over a rocky landscape. The elderly aunt finally places the tray on a table. Her hands are trembling, like the liqueur in the glasses.

"I played like a child with Vaguelio," I said. "I've noticed that Marilena acts like a little girl sometimes too."

"A colleague who came by the house saw her drawings and thought we had a child. We're like those tiny troupes of actors where everyone has to take on several roles. Marilena plays the daughter very well, and the nurse too. Niki preferred being sick to taking care of me. I'm sick fairly often, perhaps to justify the presence of a woman beside me. It's a way to avoid asking myself anything more about the nature of my need for her. Basically, I don't think I need a woman because I get sick, I think I get sick because I need a woman!"

He paused for a moment, no doubt to allow me to appreciate his last sentence.

"What will you do if something happens to you?"

I haven't forgotten that the emergency call number is 166. My drawings are a bit clumsy too. I avoid making any show of skill, anything that might allow people to guess that I went to the Beaux Arts School. I rework my cartoons heavily and try to hide that they've been reworked. Humorous cartoons are closer to the doodles that children make in the margins of their notebooks than they are to paintings. They shouldn't be shown in art galleries or published in luxury editions. Newsprint suits them better. They're modest drawings, but with a certain audacity. The first time I visited the Parthenon, I was really impressed by the weeds growing in the cracks on the columns themselves. The temple moved me much less than those insolent weeds.

"I used to speak completely openly with your mother," Theodoris continued. "I could broach any topic. She tried to understand other people. She tried to understand, not to judge."

"Theodoris' mind works *well*," she used to say, stressing that last word.

She liked the way he spoke, admired his command of the language: "His Greek is a pleasure to hear."

For my part, I spoke the Greek of émigrés, with a high percentage of foreign words. My mother seemed not to notice. From time to time, she would remind me of a word. I had forgotten that the word for a pot is *téndzéris*. It's a Turkish word. I've just found it in the Andriotis etymological dictionary. I think that my Greek has improved since I started to write. My pencil now forms certain sentences with relative ease. I continue to consult the dictionary and the encyclopedia, but most of the time I do it out of curiosity rather than need. I write so that I have a reason to open the dictionary. I also look at the words that precede and follow the one I'm looking for. When I'm not looking for anything special, I read the words that start with epsilon. I've been able to write another sentence: *Eptanésios eupatridis éngatestiménos en Ékali énumpheuthi echtès ergatria ekkokkistiriou ekpaglou eumorphias*: A nobleman from Heptanesia living in Ekali yesterday married a cotton carder of spectacular beauty.

I asked Theodoris to give me a word he especially cherished that begins with epsilon. He knows about my interest in the letter. He started thinking.

"I'm not ready to answer that," he finally said. "I'll have to think about it."

I complained that he hadn't yet found the parody of the *Iliad* that he'd promised me. I've noticed that I get serious when anything has to do with my research on the epsilon and the text I'm writing. Most likely I want to persuade myself that I'm doing something meaningful.

I'm looking up old friends, making new contacts. I'm not waiting for others to come to me, I'm going to them. It's something I never did in the past. I didn't take the initiative to cross the threshold of the room where the party was going on. I stayed outside near the door and I smoked. I waited for the hosts to come get me, to ask: "Why are you standing out there? Come on in!"

I needed them to reassure me that I was invited. The living room lights scared me. I probably wasn't sure enough of myself. But I think I also had a fairly high opinion of myself. I both overestimated and underestimated myself. I had all sorts of complexes. One thing that's for sure is that I didn't find myself handsome. I wonder what sort of impression my face would make on me today. I'd have to shave off my beard to find out. I suppose I let my beard grow to hide it and maybe to conform to the style that was de rigueur at the Beaux Arts School.

It isn't hard to meet people in Athens. You can see in peoples' eyes that they expect it. Conversations move along quickly. In an hour, people say things they'd never admit in Paris in ten years, twenty years, a lifetime. It's natural for everyone to know everyone, since it's so easy to form relationships. I've spoken with a lot of people in the past few days. We've exchanged phone numbers. People call me often to invite me for coffee or to ask me if I have plans for the evening. Sometimes they even knock on my door. Rania brought me a pickaxe she'd stolen from a construction site.

"You might need it if you want to plant flowers in your garden!"

She ran off. She had to meet an American musician at the airport. On weekends, she sings in a nightclub on the island of Aegina. I don't know her well. I met her in a bar. We had coffee at my place. Nothing happened between us, and nothing will happen: she has a husband and a lover. At the moment, sleeping alone doesn't bother me.

Athens society is exuberant. It talks incessantly, it expresses its feelings and its point of view, it laughs at nothing, it binges on food, it's always ready to party as if tomorrow weren't a workday, and naturally it needs to see people. It's much more fun than Parisian society, constantly preoccupied with what time it is and unable to forget its obligations. There aren't many clocks in public places in Athens. I think that Parisian society has a certain idea of the future and that it works feverishly in hopes of realizing that vision. Athenians prefer to concern themselves with the present. They apply themselves to shaping it as they please. They live at full tilt, precisely because they don't expect much of the future. The word "progress" gets a lukewarm reception from them, as does the word "tomorrow." In a country so old, one that has seen so many centuries pass, it's tough to still believe in the future. Greek history doesn't encourage anyone to make plans for the future. And so people dream of the present. Theodoris was saying in Stamata that the novel lacks roots in Greece. Here, life itself looks like a novel. Enormous creative energies are expended in cafeterias, bars, and taverns. Perhaps it's a shame. The fact is that people in Athens don't suffer the same boredom that people complain of elsewhere.

One night in the Titanic, a bar in Exarchia, I met Eleni, a blonde with little gray eyes. I was with Theodoris again. He introduced us and then walked away.

"When I was in high school I worked in a bar," she told me. "Everything I know, I've learned in bars. That's where I learned about boss-employee relationships, about fatigue, about politics from customers who became friends. Other customers taught me poetry by reciting verse, at dawn, standing on the bar or on a table. You can't imagine how many people I've met: journalists, doctors, architects. I learned to drink, too, of course."

She stepped closer to me so I could hear her. The music was playing at full blast. She had placed her elbow on my knee. At certain moments I thought her beautiful, others not. There weren't any bars in Athens back in the time of the colonels, when I left the country.

"It isn't true just for me. My entire generation discovered life in bars, finished their studies in bars. They matured at night. The man who was closest to me at the time was Leandros, the bartender at the Bostonians, on Mavili Square. I loved him more than my father. He had had the floor behind the bar raised about thirty centimeters, to look taller. He was very short, the poor guy. He never left his bar except at closing, after the last customer had left."

I thought I heard Theodoris' voice. I turned around, but it wasn't him. I saw him a bit farther away, in a group. He made a few hops, then he laughed. The others laughed too. I remembered seeing him hop the same way on the terrace of the house in Stamata. It seemed to me that the weekend I spent at his place had been decisive for me, but I couldn't justify that impression. What had happened that was so important? Was it the fact that the flat stone near the faucet had reminded me of the epsilon at Delphi?

"Are you listening?" asked Eleni.

She confided that she was in love.

"He's coming back this morning. I'll go wait for him at the bus station. He went up north to Serres, to see his grandmother."

"She's in love with someone who still has his grandmother," I thought. She knew about Serres. She informed me that the region was wealthy, that it produces rice, cotton, clover for animal feed, and a fairly good ouzo called "Magic." I didn't know that ouzo. I don't have it in my collection.

"You don't talk about yourself at all," she remarked.

She hadn't shown any curiosity about me. She smelled my packet of tobacco.

"It doesn't smell good."

"I started to write when I came back from Stamata. Stamata made me want to write. That's the important thing that happened there." She left a bit later, after handing me her phone number, written on the back of a cash register receipt.

I watched her walk away. I liked her square shoulders and her slender arms, and her legs too. She was wearing a gray silk dress. Even her flat-soled shoes looked elegant to me. I liked the way she walked, her confident look. She held herself straight, her chin tilted slightly forward. Her short hair came to a point on the nape of her neck. She looked like she was walking against the wind. I decided to write her name in my notebook. "She'll remind me of the women who beguiled me just as they were leaving." I had the notebook with me, folded in half in the back pocket of my trousers. I think the oracle at Delphi was already active at the time of the beautiful Helen, that Agamemnon went there before he left for Troy. I tried to remember the names of women I'd met whose first names started with E. I didn't know any other Elenis or any Hélènes in France. I remembered Eleonora. We only went out twice. We watched Tati's *Mon Oncle* in an empty cinema. We drank cognac in a café. I was enchanted by her gestures and her eyes. I think I was on the brink of falling in love. A long time after, hearing the music from that film on the radio, I thought of her. The other music that makes me think of her is Verdi's *Il Trovatore*, since the heroine of the story is named Leonora. I've known two Elizabeths, one in Paris and one in Cairo. The second one was Greek. She'd married a businessman. She gave me an apple-green shirt that was a bit tight in the collar. The other was married too. I taught her how to play Greek backgammon. One night, when we were playing at her house, her husband had had enough and went to bed in the bedroom just next to the living room. A few minutes later he was asleep and we lay down on the couch. I didn't think it wise to let the sound of the dice stop suddenly, so I put the box on the floor and kept throwing them with my left hand. The dice rolled less and less frequently.

I thought too of Eva, a twenty-year-old girl I met when I was already forty. We met on the island of Hydra one summer. She was on vacation with her parents. When they found out that we were seeing one another, they forbade her from going out in the evening. I waited for her at the port one night in vain. The sea was calm and perfectly black. There was no light on the quay. The only light was from a clock on the front of a tall building that might have been a church. For a moment, I thought it was the moon — I got a brief impression that the moon had clock hands.

I can't say that the letter E has played much of a role in my love life. The names that have counted the most for me began with other letters: R, M, N, C, another M, another C, D, and V.

The bar was nearly empty now. We could barely hear the music. Grigoris, the bartender, was trying to convince Theodoris to eat a lotus fruit — he pushed a basket full of orange-colored fruit toward him. Was that what Ulysses' companions sampled in the Land of the Lotus Eaters?

"Eat!" he told him. "I brought them back from Mount Athos!"

Theodoris was straightening a frame hanging from a nail.

"That picture is always crooked," said Grigoris.

It was a picture of a blonde with disheveled hair, her large breasts bursting out of a green velour jacket.

"Every picture hung from a single nail hangs crooked, sooner or later," Theodoris declared. "It's impossible to find the exact middle of the cord. Sometimes it's a month later, sometimes six months later, but they're always crooked. The weight of time makes them crooked."

Despite the late hour — it was after three in the morning — there were a lot of cars moving in both directions on Syngrou Avenue. Grigoris dragged us to an open-air cabaret on the beach where two very beautiful and completely naked girls were lying on a glowing runway made of frosted glass. Their bodies were shining. The owner was a friend of Grigoris. He came and sat with us. The dancers had little white towels like the ones they provide in Chinese restaurants, and they were wiping one another gently.

"They're Hungarian," said the owner. "Next week I'll have six Romanians."

He informed us that nightclubs like his get their dancers from Eastern Europe. The tables were arranged in a star pattern around the runway. The tables were long and occupied by groups of relatively young men — their median age couldn't have been over thirty. Years ago, it was nearly impossible to see a naked woman, even in a photograph. Women undressed only in closed rooms with the curtains drawn. I was moved by all those women masked behind their curtains when I was out walking.

One young man seemed fascinated by the dancers. His eyes didn't leave them for a second. He was frowning and he looked worried, as if pondering some difficult problem. He reminded me of the young workman in the Antinous photograph. I remembered attributing his worried expression to some dark premonition, that he was experiencing the vertigo of time. Sitting beside the entranced young customer was a girl slightly older than him who seemed to be having a great time. There were five or six men with them.

The dancers had finished wiping one another and had gotten up. I thought the show was nearly over, but they began to squirt one another with shaving cream. Grigoris was hunched in his seat. He spent most of his time watching his cigarette.

"What were you doing on Mount Athos?" Theodoris asked him.

"I went to see my cousin, a monk. I'm planning to go back. I found the monastery's calm disturbing. I even started to panic. One morning I woke up thinking I was dead. I ran from my cell. I absolutely had to speak to someone to reassure myself that nothing serious had happened to me. But I calmed down quickly. I can never manage to sleep before daybreak, but there I was asleep by ten."

"He brought us here because he's an insomniac," I thought. The music got louder, the spotlights came on, and the dancers climbed up on the tables. One of them chose ours. We had just time enough to grab our glasses so she didn't spill them. I also grabbed the platter of fruit and set it on my lap. I wasn't feeling very comfortable: I had never seen a woman's genitals so close up in public before. My eyes finally fixed on her shoes, the one part of her body that was covered. She was wearing high heels. She knelt down in front of Theodoris, took his head in her hands and rubbed it against her bust, still covered with shaving cream. It got all over Theodoris' face.

"Tatiana, you're wonderful!" said the owner, raising his glass.

This is the sort of show that the Orthodox priest was referring to during my mother's funeral. It's true that there are more and more cabarets. Even the private television channels show strip-tease routines late at night. "Is that an important phenomenon, worth thinking about?" I decided it wasn't worth it. "Nothing ever happens. It's just that we sometimes hear tiny sounds as time shapes the emptiness."

The other girl was dancing on the young man's table. His friend was clapping. She got up, climbed on the table, and began to dance while removing her blouse. She kept her brassiere on. The young man was staring at the table. A few minutes later, he pushed his chair back and left, without ever looking up. I don't know if his friend noticed. In any case, she kept on dancing. Theodoris was wiping off his face with a napkin.

"Let's go," I said to him.

Dawn was breaking when I got home. I hadn't been back since the morning before. On the building security guard's little desk I found the tobacco that Marie-Christine had sent. I thought that Eleni was probably already at the bus station waiting for her friend.

Rania's gift has been useful. I used it to plant a cypress and a mimosa in the garden, just beyond the terrace. The mimosa makes me think of my mother. That's the shrub that keeps her company now. I don't think I chose the cypress because they grow in cemeteries. They grow everywhere, really. The Greek landscape is full of olive trees and cypress trees. Delphi, among others. As a child, I was fascinated by cypress trees because they were the only ones that didn't spread their branches, so I found them impossible to climb. I couldn't explore them. They were withdrawn, mute. The laurel tree that's planted nearby seems especially robust — it's over four meters high — and I hope it doesn't keep the cypress and the mimosa from growing. The earth is absolutely dry. The press is forecasting a heat wave for mid-July, but I don't have much confidence in the papers. They constantly give the impression that extraordinary events are about to happen, disastrous events as a general rule. It's easy enough to see that nothing actually happens and that life doesn't really change. The newspapers displayed around the kiosks are nonetheless frightening. Their headlines are large enough to be seen from the sidewalk across the street. "THE TRAMPING OF BOOTS," "WHERE IS OUR MONEY," "BETRAYED …." People stop to read them, but I've heard they buy them less and less often. Once highly respected daily papers have gotten to the point where they have to offer their readers lotteries for houses or cars. The management team at *Embros Sunday* even thought about proposing a date with a top model as a prize, but in the end they didn't dare do it. One of the paper's editors told me, the one who asked me for the cartoons.

Every evening I pour two pails of water on the cypress and one on the mimosa. I don't want cats drinking the water, so I stay there until all the water has soaked in. During droughts long ago, people threw handfuls of dirt in the face of the Athena statue, to make her understand how dry the earth was and to encourage her to remedy the situation. I'd forgotten that in Greek we don't say "bottle green," but rather "cypress green." Greek wine bottles were colorless for many years. The green ones appeared only recently, after we joined the European Union.

I went into a paint shop near Omonia. They sold cans of house paint, along with Winsor and Newton watercolors. I used to be ecstatic when someone gave me colored pencils. I would take them out of their case and examine them one by one. The red one reminded me of the silhouette of my aunt, walking half-naked through the summerhouse kitchen. The room's floor was red. The blue pencil brought back not only the sea and the summer, but school too. The paper covers for our textbooks and notebooks were blue. The uniform worn by schoolgirls was the same color. The candy-pink pencil seemed so indecent to me that I scarcely dared to look at it. I used to feel like the colors knew my most intimate thoughts.

I spent quite some time in the store, looking at jars, little bottles, tubes, paging through catalogues. I spoke with the employee who sold tempera paints in glass jars. I knew that water colorists really like them, that they dilute them in a mixture of vinegar and egg yolks, but I didn't remember that the dark red was called "Byzantine," or that the bright red, "fire red," is also called "devil red." I asked for a green, without any more specifics. I was curious to see if the clerk would give me a leek green, which would be in line with the etymology of the word *prassino*.

Color perception must be evolving, because he gave me a grass green. I think that a Paris paint store would have thought of the same green. I also asked him for blue. We use the same word in Greek — we say *blè* — but I'm not sure that we're thinking of the same color. The blue he chose for me had the dark color of the sea. In France, they probably would have given me a sky blue. Finally, I asked him to tell me which colors lead to misunderstandings.

"Cherry red," he said. "It's the color of a ripe cherry, but some of our customers think it should have more brown. They're probably thinking of the color of rotten cherries."

I bought the grass green, the ocean blue, and the Byzantine red, and I left. I felt like gray was the dominant color in the street. It occurred to me that, when leaving a paint store, you're bound to find the city a bit dull.

The editor from *Embros Sunday* looked at my cartoons without saying anything, then she reproached me for not giving her a single cartoon based on the news.

"You're known for your caricatures."

"I told you that I wouldn't give you political cartoons."

I was ready to take back my folder, but she guessed my intentions and put her hand on my arm. Her fingers were cold.

"Don't be angry," she said.

We were in the café where I'd met Caradzoglou and his wife. The journalist had a delicate face, but a revolting body. She couldn't be the girl with the rosewood bookcase. She told me that the press and the media are controlled by five industrialists.

"News businesses have become nothing more than common commercial enterprises. Stavrakas, who bought *Embros Sunday*, imports oil from the United States. He comes to work at the newspaper by helicopter and lands on the building's terrace. He's always in a bad mood in the summer, because oil consumption goes down then. We have to wait for winter before asking for a raise!"

She laughed. I wasn't angry with her anymore. It was Stavrakas himself who had the idea of offering his readers a date with a charming companion. He planned to put a limousine and driver at their disposal.

"He'll do it sooner or later," she said. "For the moment, we're using cars as bait to attract readers. They have to have twenty coupons clipped from different issues of the paper to qualify for the drawing. But the impact on our sales is minimal. Everyone has a car."

She didn't know Caradzoglou personally, but she read him regularly.

"His columns give the paper an independent feeling that the readers like."

She couldn't tell me when my sketches would be published. The one I sent to Véronique Carrier, of the Europeans squabbling on an antique vase, will be published in July.

When I was younger, I often drew my face. I was trying to reconcile myself with myself. I gave my face a gravity it probably didn't have. I also drew my hands. I don't draw them anymore. I expect no surprises from them.

We judge artworks by their resemblance to those of the past. Mediocre efforts are judged admirable because they're polite enough not to challenge tradition. There is, in our attitude toward works of past, a certain servility that wrongs them, betrays them. I'm thinking of theater troupes both small and large, who every summer, with the help of the Ministry of Culture, play the same tragedies, often very badly, and also of equally pathetic films based on Sophocles and Euripides. New essays are published incessantly, essays attempting to link the various cultures that have flourished in Greece, attempting to show that the most recent springs from the most ancient. Their authors skim through the centuries in quest of clues tending to prove that we are indeed the descendants of our glorious ancestors. They wonder about the meaning of the word Hellenism. They develop a code of Greek culture, set aside contradictions, forget the influences it has undergone, and reduce it to something very small. They're like those French gardeners who shape nature to whatever look they want. I hope that their research won't result in a definition, which would inevitably deprive Greek culture of its creativity. Definitions are small funeral orations.

I didn't know that Stathopoulou was interested in soccer. About two months ago her Ministry brought out a giant poster to celebrate the national team's qualification for the World Cup. The subject doesn't lend itself to commemorating the past, at first glance. Football belongs to us. Neither the Ancient Greeks nor the Byzantines played it. But it's impossible for us to forget the past, even for an instant. There are still a few of those posters in the street. On it there's a player, and just behind him there's an ancient statue of a hoplite, also playing ball! I suppose that the Ministry, by reminding them of the nobility of their origins, wanted to instill in our soccer players a fervor worthy of the great heroic figures of another time. The message, alas, didn't get through: the national team fell apart in the World Cup, allowed ten goals, and if I remember correctly, didn't score a single one.

The quarrel between Agamemnon and Achilles, the starting point of the *Iliad*, makes me imagine another poster: the two heroes shouting angrily at one another and in the foreground one member of the national assembly punching out another one. I've seen a fight among the members on television and I've seen city dwellers exchanging insults. To me, the Ancient Greeks seem much closer to us when they quarrel than when they philosophize.

Caradzoglou may be right in saying the books of the *Iliad* are each an homage to a letter of the alphabet. The first one does indeed mention a huge number of characters whose names start with A: Achilles, Achaeans, (H)ades, Atreus, Agamemnon, Argos, and Apollo, who also bears the name Argyrotoxos, "with the silver bow." A little later, Athena enters the action. But the characters of the first episode are also present in what follows. And I've noticed that the book that is almost entirely devoted to Diomedes isn't number IV, which would correspond to the letter D, but number V, which relates to the letter E. The words *éris* and *énchos*, the quarrel and the lance, are used frequently. But they give only a very vague idea of the events that take place in V. We witness not only simple quarrels, but scenes of massacre: a severed hand falls to the earth, a lance plants itself in a warrior's cheek and slices off his tongue.

Book II tends to confirm Caradzoglou's theory, since it begins with the convocation of the Achaean Council, the *boulè*, and ends with an analogous meeting among the Trojans. The Greeks are on the point of fleeing, but Agamemnon will manage to dissuade them (along the way, the word *boulè* can be found again — it also means will) and the war will go on. The soldiers are compared to a herd of cattle, a word also beginning with the letter *b* in Greek.

In book III, on the other hand, not a single important word begins with gamma. The word *gyné*, woman, is of course mentioned in reference to Helen, but she makes only a brief appearance. The main subject is the duel between Menelaus and Paris. Maybe Caradzoglou attributes significance to the word "*gynémane*," woman chaser? Among the insults that Hector directs at his brother Paris (yet another quarrel) is the word *gynémane*.

One might allow that book IV, in which the Trojans are tricked by Athena into violating the truce, is based on the word *dolos*, the ruse. The first five episodes of the *Iliad* — the only ones I've read so far — both support Caradzoglou and fail to support him.

I note that the epsilon of Delphi isn't likely to stand for the Hellenes. It was only in the sixth century B.C. that they began to call themselves that. For Homer, Hellade is just a part of Thessaly. He notes that the region is "*calligyne*," rich in beautiful women. He generally calls the Greeks Achaeans or Danaeans. They get along perfectly with the Trojans, which means they most likely speak the same language. Interpreters never enter into it. Negotiations between the Achaeans and the Trojans are in Greek, and it's also in Greek that Helen converses with Paris and with Priam. The poet does mention some of the Trojans' allies communicating in a barbarian language. If the Trojans themselves were "barbarophones," there's no doubt he would tell us.

I admit that I was quite surprised to discover that Hector and his companions spoke Greek. My teachers systematically described the enemies of the Hellenes as cruel and ignorant. Vaguelio wouldn't admit that most of the Slavic Macedonians are Orthodox, that they have at least that much in common with us. I learned in school that nationalism has two faces: one softened by love of country, one hardened by hatred of others. So the Trojans weren't complete foreigners as I'd thought and they enjoyed the support of Apollo. Aphrodite grants her support to the beautiful Helen. As for Zeus, he hesitates, can't choose between Greeks and Trojans, and ends up letting the belligerents sort it out by themselves.

Since I needed to verify Caradzoglou's theory, I had to read the entire original text too. I was pleased to read it, although it's almost completely unintelligible to me. I did find some terms here and there that are still in current usage. I felt a sort of respect for those words, which after having crossed so many centuries are still available and ready to start off on new adventures. Time must have fallen in love with them to have granted them such longevity. Some of them are rather painful, like *dacry*, tear, *penthos*, mourning, *picros*, bitter, *polémos*, war, *thanatos*, death, *nécros*, corpse. Very often they are words which are still used in other languages apart from Greek, like *hégémon*, chief, *laos*, people, *philos*, friend, *géron*, old man, *glossa*, language, *ouranos*, sky, *thalassa*, sea. *Apatè*, swindle, which reappears incessantly on the front pages of newspapers, was already in the *Iliad*.

I would certainly need to study for several years to understand Homeric dialect. The son of an actor friend was telling me that using translations is still forbidden. They require the students to read the classics in the original. The boy admitted to me that he had retained nothing of Plato, Thucydides, and Sophocles, never having read any complete text of theirs. He knew only the few excerpts he had laboriously translated.

"All I've read is the *Iliad*," he told me, "because we read it in translation in the lower grades."

He had never heard of the pornographic version of the poem. Perhaps students who've never had to translate Homer are less prone to laugh at him. Today, like before, schools continue to deny the passage of time, to deny that Ancient Greek has become nearly a foreign language. I don't know how useful teaching the old language is. But it's probable that students won't know Plato as long as they're not permitted to read him in translation. It is strange that the dogma of resemblance between Ancient Greek and Modern Greek is still standard, when in the meantime the State has rejected the old archaistic form, Katharevousa, and has recognized Modern Greek as the official language. I suppose this decision will speed up the evolution of the language and that the students of tomorrow will understand Plato even less than I understood him.

Theodoris finally found me some excerpts from that other Iliad. It's composed in verse, fifteen syllables to the line, which in Greek sounds like Alexandrine verse does in French.

Achaeans and their consorts stand before the mighty gate
And tearfully together they bemoan their awful fate

Ulysses is alone in his tent. He soliloquizes. He calls Menelaus every name there is. Athena appears before him. I will never be fulfilled, she tells him, "as long as I have not tasted your long-desired dick." He permits it. He asks her how the Greeks can enter Troy. "It's written down in Homer," the goddess jokes. Ulysses has the wooden horse built. The Greeks hide in its belly.

In the hollow of its belly the Greeks could clearly see
And through the wooden asshole, they observed the enemy

I'm thinking again of the sandwiches my mother made for me. I see her putting them in my book bag and closing it up. She stands in the open garden gate. We wave to one another just before the building on the corner comes between us. Now it's my father who stands at the garden gate. He asks me the same questions that she used to ask. He has taken over her place in the living room. I wouldn't be surprised if I found him smoking, one day.

I read the words I wrote in my notebook. I stare at them for a long time, spend as much time on each page as if it were entirely filled with writing. *Endélos*, completely, along with the name of Vaguelio, brings back the ghost of a clumsy plumber leaving the field defeated, his head bowed. *Élissomai*, to worm one's way in, reminds me of Acridakis' speech on the dangers threatening our nation, the voice of Amalia Stathopoulou, and the poet in Stamata. His girlfriend, a short dark-haired girl, tells him: "Write something short and pithy! The meal is nearly ready!"

Caradzoglou draws my attention to *éris*, the quarrel, which again reminds me of Vaguelio. My girlfriend's face, purple with rage, makes me think of other faces. Our cries echo endlessly across the city. An enormous demonstration forms, bringing together young people oppressed by their parents as well as illustrious and extremely touchy warriors. I observe the hats upon the surface of this human tide. I can pick out khaki-colored military berets, gray caps, top hats, ecclesiastical hats, fezzes and turbans like the one Macriyannis wore, as well as shining plumed helmets. A blind and very elderly poet, a thin headband holding his hair, is making his laborious way through the crowd. He's wearing a sort of sheet.

"So where are you from?" asks someone who might well be a taxi driver.

The poet gives him a smile in place of an answer.

The verb *eurisko*, to find, written on page four, reminds me of Marika.

"You'll find it," she says.

"Maybe," I thought. I remember the black wings of the cockroach I stepped on and the perfume of the girl who walked by us. François repeats that the diphthong ai was pronounced *aï*, which means I can't stay with the word *ainigma*. I get to *Hermes* and *Hestia* — page six and seven — who take me straight back to the library of the French School of Archeology. They place an impressive stack of books in front of me, bound in burgundy leather, their pages slightly sticky. Do I owe the presence of Ilona beside me to Hermes or to Hestia? To Hermes, probably.

What do gods do once their job is done? Where do they retire to? The all-powerful gods certainly must have a harder time writing off the past than the minor gods do. They must be permanently sullen. Each one has a bench all to himself and speaks to no one. The little gods, I suppose, live a friendlier life. Occasionally they joke, they laugh. In time, perhaps they'll manage to forget they were once gods. The important gods will never forget. The flowering of trees in the spring and the first lightning storms of the autumn will always remind them of their lost power. I imagine them running around pell-mell to get out of the rain. I can see them floundering in the mud. A woman holding an umbrella comes up to Apollo.

"Come," she tells him. "You aren't used to the rain."

She isn't beautiful, or young, or well dressed. Maybe she isn't even wearing any shoes.

Should one leave one's country? That's the question asked on the next page, the one dedicated to the interrogative "if" mentioned by Plutarch. So people were already leaving Greece at the time of the Pythia. My departure for foreign lands was only one more repetition of a very old scene. For centuries now, a woman's hand has been tirelessly waving a white handkerchief. I wonder how the Pythia would answer if I asked her that question today. Page nine contains the word question, *érotèma*. I think she would answer me with some banal proverb like "The pitcher goes to the well so often that it is broken at last" or "You can't make an omelet without breaking a few eggs," which would plunge me into deep reflection.

I understand François' preference for the second *ei*, the beginning of the sentence: "If we accept, my dear Alcibiades . . . ." It has a kindness of words that liberates the mind and encourages it to make use of that liberty. It allows you, for example, to see the third *ei* (which means "you are") not as an homage to divine nature, but as a word of welcome from a god to his visitors. Apollo recognizes them one by one as they enter his temple. He doesn't scorn them: in a few moments, he's going to take a look at their problems. "You are" shows the interest he takes in each one of them. The maxim "Know thyself" doesn't necessarily have the somber meaning that Plutarch gives it. It isn't meant to remind the faithful of their sad destiny, but rather to encourage them to look at themselves with the attention and the kindness that Apollo shows them.

Since the eta was pronounced ê and was sometimes used in place of the epsilon, I thought it might be useful to note down a few words that start with that letter too. First I wrote the eta all by itself (ἥ) as François suggested, which means "he says" (it's a form of the verb *êmi*), and my own contribution, the word *hélios*, the sun. I think the symbol of Apollo deserves a place in my list. "I'll sit on the steps of the temple and I'll wait for the sun to rise. The plain and its olive trees will still be in darkness. A red rag will be nailed to the end of a post lying on the ground."

The Hellenes I talked about earlier make me think of a raucous gathering, of slamming doors. The Delphians, supported by their allies, went to war against their neighbors three times. When they found out that the residents of Amphissa had started to farm the plain sacred to Apollo, they sent Philip of Macedonia to destroy their city. The Greek Church, with its enormous properties, is just as miserly about its lands as the amphictyony of Dephi was. The clergy has always known the value of land. Because they dressed in animal skins, the people of Amphissa were reputed to smell bad, something like the tannery workers in my grandmother's time. I think I read that in Pausanias. "My mother came from a city that the gods probably didn't like." Pausanias describes Greece at the end of the second century A.D. He passed through Delphi a few decades after the death of Plutarch, but he doesn't say a word about the epsilon. Maybe it had already disappeared.

I thought the center of the world couldn't possibly bear the number 5. The number 1, *éna*, is no doubt better suited to it. But I still think that interpretation of the epsilon, the one François wouldn't support, is easily as good as the others I've looked at.

For the moment, the list ends with Eleni, written on page sixteen. I see her moving away from me. I see her shoulders, her short hair. I watch her until she leaves the bar. I kept the cash register receipt with her phone number on it. I don't feel like I'm getting away from my subject when I list words that aren't linked to Delphi. What is my subject anyway? The epsilon, of course, but since I don't know its meaning .... "I'm searching to find out what I'm searching for." I wrote a similar sentence a few pages back. I don't have the energy to go back and find it. I hadn't planned to write so many pages. I'm just chattering, like my father. The epsilon guides me along without ever giving me any direction. It keeps perfectly still, waiting for me to make the first step, as if it were trying to guess my intentions, as if it wanted to understand me. The recommendation to "Know thyself," which some attribute to the Pythia, seems to point to the word *ego*, me.

I write *ego* on page seventeen. While reading the *Iliad*, I paid particular attention to words starting with epsilon. I came across a multitude of *ego*. I was enchanted by the adjective *érateinos*, one of the many words that didn't survive. I don't know how words disappear, whether they just collapse or whether time erases them little by little, whether they die slowly or in an accident. I write down that adjective, which expresses one of Apollo's essential virtues: it means kind.

Just before closing the notebook and changing subjects, I get the idea to give a page to the letter epsilon itself, to acknowledge the strange dialogue I've been having for some time with its silence. "Perhaps it will never tell me anything more than its name." I write *epsilon*, page nineteen.

I also felt like I had to record the word *ethnikismos*, nationalism. The sarcasm of our politicians regarding our neighbors regularly suggests it, as well as our partners in the European Union, the creation of new far-right political parties, television commentaries about foreign workers, and also the systematic praise of Hellenism, especially Byzantine Hellenism. I don't know if the Maastricht agreement is a threat to our national identity. I also don't know what Turkey is cooking up in the Balkans — everyone here is convinced they're cooking something up, as they usually are. But one can't help but notice this explosion of nationalism coinciding with the worsening of the economic situation. The national budget deficit is catastrophic: "WE'RE ON THE BRINK OF BANKRUPTCY," a newspaper announced a few days ago. Apparently that headline, at least, expresses something real.

But in the end it was the speech given by a comedian at the end of an *épithéorissi*, a vaudeville review, that imposed the word "nationalism" on me. It was totally unexpected and didn't relate at all to that sort of show, usually composed of satirical monologues and dance numbers. I was in the wings with an actor friend, Anghelos Yogarakis (the father of the young man who talked to me today about how Ancient Greek is taught). We had left the door of his dressing room open. We could clearly hear the music and what was being said on stage. We could see the chorus girls passing in the hallway. They were running, since they barely had time to change. Their heels made a jaunty noise on the concrete. We were drinking whisky. Anghelos had also changed costumes three or four times. I watched him put on a gigantic pair of false breasts, a woman's black suit, and a brown wig.

"I'm doing a parody of the Prime Minister's mother," he said, looking at himself in the mirror.

He was putting on lipstick. Stuck in the mirror frame were congratulatory telegrams, business cards, and press clippings with his photo, along with a prescription from his doctor advising him to follow a strict diet. I doubt that he wants to lose weight: his obesity is useful on stage. A bit later, when I saw him dress up like a little girl, with a short pink dress, a blond wig with braids, and blue-framed glasses, I thought that his look alone would be enough to make the audience laugh. I wasn't mistaken: his appearance on stage, before he said anything at all, was met with applause. The actor who manages the troupe also uses his physical appearance on stage, the difference being that he is very tall and very skinny.

"I'd like to play Molière or Aristophanes," Anghelos told me as he removed the pink dress. "But it isn't easy to convince the owner of a theater like Dascaleas to offer works from the canon. Subsidized troupes are the only ones who can perform those plays, but to be one of those you have to play the political game."

The chorus girls went by again. They were wearing gold swimsuits with multicolored ribbons in place of skirts. Their legs were bare.

"Are they Hungarian?" I asked Anghelos.

"No, English."

He told me he'd had a fling with one of them, Deborah.

"She wants to stay in Greece. She's from Birmingham. Apparently it's impossible to find work in Birmingham."

While Anghelos was changing, the head of the troupe was playing a policeman listening in on wiretapped phones. He listened in on all the politicians. It made him sick to his stomach to hear them always negotiating a commission, asking for something under the table. He also heard them use blackmail.

"You have to sell out," said Anghelos, "either to a political party or for money. For the moment, I prefer money, I make more."

The policeman on stage holds a press conference to denounce the politicians, but the journalists won't come. He's finally fired by the police. And when he gets home, he notices they've cut off his telephone. The routine was very well received: the applause lasted a long time.

The dancers came by from the other direction, wearing different costumes. Besides the Prime Minister's mother and the little girl, Anghelos played a peasant visiting the capital for the first time and a retiree complaining about the high cost of living. It was essentially a classic *épithéorissi*, like all the others I've seen. The only new elements were the frequent allusions to televisions shows. I think sketches about television personalities were even more numerous than those targeting politicians, as if power were now concentrated in the media. One actress, Stella, came into the dressing room for a moment for a swig of whiskey. She was wearing a blond crew-cut wig. I thought right away of Calogridou. The actress confirmed that she was indeed parodying her.

"She's very well known," she told me. "She gave up her cultural magazine show and now she has a game show with a huge audience."

The show ended as it usually does: the five-piece orchestra playing a lively tune, all the actors and the dancers on stage. I hid behind the curtain and watched the finale. They all bowed and left the stage to warm applause. Only the head of the acting troupe was still on stage. The audience got up.

"Don't leave!" he shouted.

The lights went out.

"Don't leave!" he repeated.

A spotlight came on.

"We had a good time this evening," he said. "It's our job to make you laugh .... We do the same thing as the puppets in shadow plays .... But there are times when the puppets don't feel like laughing .... When puppets cry."

His voice was turning raspy. I noticed he was holding a folded cloth in his hand.

"They cry when foreigners humiliate our country .... When they trample our symbols, steal our history .... When they claim our space, our sea, our islands .... Those European gentlemen don't like the fact that we're Orthodox! Well, tough! The Germans and the French claim that we cost them too much! They forget what they owe to Greece, that they've usurped our culture! Their museums are filled with works they stole from us!"

Anghelos and Stella were standing beside me. She had taken off her wig. Her hair was long and fine.

"Is this the first time he's made this speech?" I asked.

"No, of course not," said Anghelos.

"Those swindlers," the actor continued, "want to lecture us on political economics. Serbian expansionism worries them, but not Turkish expansionism. They don't care about Cyprus, our good friends. Or about the Kurds either."

His voice was getting louder and louder, he was almost shouting. Stella touched my arm with the palm of her hand. I looked at her. I could only see her eyes and her hair shining. I took her hand.

"Greece is alone! Abandoned by all! Our politicians think of nothing but money! We know how they are. We've seen them at work! But the moment is coming when Greece will react! Those gentlemen, Greeks and foreigners alike, don't know what this country is capable of! Long live Greece, my children! Long live our country!"

He unfolded the cloth to wrap it around his body: it was the Greek flag. Then he collapsed, as if he'd been struck down, all the while shouting

"Long live Greece!"

There was applause when he collapsed, but less than for his number about the wiretapped phones. I remembered how tepid the reaction to Acridakis' speech had been. "The audience there was different," I thought.

"Does he really believe what he's saying?" I asked Anghelos.

"Yes .... He believes it, up to a point .... In any case, he believes it during his number!"

The stage lights came back on. The actor got up, still wearing the flag like a tunic, bowed to the audience, then came over to us. He was soaked in sweat, but didn't seem distressed anymore.

"Was I good?" he asked us.

"Very good, as always," Anghelos answered.

He smiled with satisfaction and headed toward the dressing rooms. I was still holding Stella's hand. I drew her to me and kissed her hair. Anghelos left us.

"What are you thinking about?" said Stella.

"I have a notebook," I told her, "where I write down a word from time to time. I think I've just gotten to the middle of the notebook."

6.

Little bats have moved into the rocks of Mount Lycabettus. At night, they visit the neighborhoods around the hill. I've seen them over the streetlights in Kolonaki, Maraslion, and Neapoli. I imagine they're eating the insects attracted by the light. I don't know what they do afterwards. Maybe they go back to their nests, maybe they roost in wide-open windows behind which innocent young women are sleeping. I'm convinced they make the same trip every night, that bats have habits too.

I saw them again when I was on my way to the restaurant with Fanny. They were flying over the lights all along the street.

"What are those birds?" she asked.

I thought about lying to her, but I couldn't think of the name of a bird.

"Bats."

She made a disgusted face. I felt vaguely guilty, like I should have rid my neighborhood of the little beasts before inviting her. We ate near at an Italian restaurant near my apartment. I think the success of Italian restaurants is largely assured by people who can't choose among an ouzo bar, a tavern, a fish restaurant, or a Chinese place. The undecided generally end up with Italian. That's how we ended up on the enclosed patio of the Pizza Maria. Fanny looked up from time to time toward the sky or toward the branches of the tree behind her.

"I didn't know there were bats in Athens."

"Have you noticed that pigeons would rather use their legs than their wings to get around?" I asked to lighten the atmosphere.

It wasn't until she had drunk a little wine that she began to feel better. We ordered an Italian red wine, which was cool and tasted like a Beaujolais. She was wearing black, but she had put on lipstick and eye makeup. I thought she might be happy if I talked about her father, but I knew him so slightly that I didn't know how to start. I don't even know what he did before the accident that left him an invalid.

"I've never been outside of Greece," she said. "I couldn't leave my father alone. I'd like to travel to a foreign country now and I have a friend who wants to go with me. But she wants to go to Europe, she really wants to visit Holland. And I prefer Africa."

We had just about finished the bottle by the time they brought the spaghetti. I ordered another.

"Are we going to drink two bottles?" she asked, wide-eyed.

She wasn't drinking any less than I was, really. I think her glass may well have emptied faster than mine. A pigeon had landed on the empty chair beside Fanny's purse and was watching us. I chased him off by tilting the chair. He moved away toward another table. Fanny looked at the branches again.

"Why Africa?"

"I want to know how people spend their days there. I need to see another way of life. In an album at your father's house I saw that there are superb lakes in Africa. I'd like to be awakened by the sun, along the shore of one of those lakes .... Don't you think tulips are really hideous flowers?"

I hadn't been able to get Costas on the phone to ask if he'd ever made love to her. I didn't know if I really wanted her. The night I'd spent with Stella had done me good. A young olive-skinned man came up to us. He was selling *The Voice of Kurdistan*. I bought a copy. He was carrying the magazines in a woolen bag.

"Do you know who I'd like to visit Africa with? Your father! He'd make the ideal travelling companion. But of course that's not possible."

"Don't you have a boyfriend?"

"Yes, but he's been transferred to Patras .... He's a tax inspector. We still talk on the phone .... He's just a friend — there's nothing bad going on."

The word *bad* took me back to many years ago, when we learned to distinguish the good from the bad. The idea that Fanny had never gotten out of that period overwhelmed me. I brushed against her feet, without meaning to. She didn't move them right away.

"Everything must feel rather cramped here, doesn't it, not as comfortable as Paris?"

"I probably judge people more severely .... I have to look at them as members of my family .... I feel like their actions concern me, their clumsiness bothers me.... The success of the far right in Greece humiliates me, makes me feel guilty, while in France it just scares me. Women who beat their children really disturb me."

"No, mothers don't beat their children anymore. They did in our parents' time. The mother of today doesn't beat her children."

It was clear that she wouldn't tolerate any discussion of the subject. She was eating a cake covered in little waves of whipped cream. A cat had climbed into the tree, its tail was hanging in the air.

"Are you staying in Athens for long?"

Ten- or twelve-year old kids came into the restaurant's patio from time to time, selling flowers. I bought her a gardenia. She unbuttoned the second button of her blouse and slipped the flower into the buttonhole. "We either will or will not make love." We were also accosted by a Serbian who spoke Greek. I took one of his brochures, denouncing the Vatican's plot to infiltrate the Balkans by using Croatian Catholics. He was wearing a long brown jacket with the pockets stuffed full and the collar turned up. He was dressed as if he were hundreds of kilometers farther north.

"So do you have a girlfriend?"

I haven't seen Stella since that night. She didn't give me her phone number. She's living with someone. Through the branches of the tree, I could see the back of an apartment building: all the kitchens with their lights on, the balconies. Now and then a woman in a nightgown or a man in pajamas would come out on a balcony.

"Have you gone to the cemetery yet?" she asked me again.

"No .... I'll go when the time is right."

"I'll go when I get back from Ioannina and Delphi," I thought. Ulysses meets his mother near the Acheron, which separates the land of the living from the territory of the dead. He speaks with her. He wants to kiss her, but he can't: his mother is only a ghost. I'll ask Costas to take me to the Acheron. The river runs fairly close to Ioannina.

Fanny told me that one day she caught my mother studying my cartoons.

"They were cut out of newspapers. She had spread them out on the big bed, close together. There were lots of them: they completely covered the bedspread. She was sitting there on a chair and now and again she would move one of the clippings, after thinking about it for a while. It looked like she was playing solitaire. Sometimes she moved an entire row to leave an open slot in a certain place. She told me she was organizing them by which ones she liked best."

"Do you remember which one she put first?"

She didn't remember. I've already asked my father to find those clippings for me. I suppose they're in an envelope, arranged in the order she put them in. He didn't know that my mother cut out my cartoons or that she saved them.

"I thought she wasn't particularly interested in my work," I said.

"You're wrong."

I imagined my mother sitting on a chair beside the bed. I put out my hand to stroke her back — she was wearing the same beige jacket as in the photograph — but I couldn't touch her. Homer says that Ulysses' mother was "like a dream."

She didn't protest when I ordered more wine, this time a half bottle.

"Would you like more cake?"

"You think I should?"

She didn't have any, though you could see that she would've liked to. The lights in the kitchens were going off one by one. The cat walked all the way to the end of the branch, turned around, then jumped down to the gravel. Fanny started, turned around quickly. The pigeon, too, was frightened and jumped into another chair. A couple with two children were getting ready to leave.

"I'd like to do something useful," she said. "Like take care of handicapped children. There are so many people who need help .... I would gladly move to any distant foreign country, if it gave me the chance to do useful work. I know English quite well and a little Italian. I've had some experience with the sick .... Do you think I could write to the embassies of underdeveloped countries to offer my services?"

She had tears in her eyes. I wiped her cheek with my hand. The family was leaving. To my great surprise, the father, whom I didn't know, bowed to me respectfully. He had mistaken me for someone else, since he said:

"A very good night, Mr. Leonidas!"

Fanny started laughing while the tears were still running down her cheeks. I took her bare arm when we left the restaurant.

"I've had a lot to drink," she said.

I asked her to give me a word that started with epsilon. Without the slightest hesitation, she answered:

"*Elpida*, hope."

A fat woman dressed like a peasant accosted us. She was carrying a basket. She pulled at my shirt.

"Are you crazy or something?" I asked her harshly.

"Don't talk to her like that," Fanny scolded me.

She stopped, pulled the basket away from the woman, and examined its contents. On the edge of the basket were buttons displaying the sun symbol of Philip of Macedonia, the famous sun with alternating short and long rays that now floats on a flag over the new Macedonians. Inside the basket, there were cans of Russian caviar, little triangular banners in the colors of the Greek soccer club of Constantinople, packages of tissues, big boxes of matches, felt markers, marbles in tiny web bags, and aspirin. Fanny took a box of aspirin.

"She's a Greco-Russian," Fanny informed me after the woman walked away.

We continued on our way. I tried to take her arm, but she pulled away.

"Life isn't easy for the immigrants from Albania, Poland, and Russia who've come to us in the past few years. The construction trades take advantage of them, pay them badly or not at all. They have no recourse, since most of them entered Greece illegally."

Apparently there are five hundred thousand of them and they make up five percent of the population.

"I saw refugees on a public square in Thessalonica. I don't think they were illegals. I was with a photographer friend. They refused to let her take their picture. They repudiated their own image."

"It's late," she said.

We were in front of the door to my apartment building.

"Stay."

She looked at me seriously for a moment.

"Okay."

We went to bed.

"You really smoke a lot," she remarked.

She closed her eyes. She hadn't removed anything but her shoes. Both French doors were open. A little breeze came up and I could hear the rustling of the laurel leaves. She opened her eyes and looked toward the garden.

"Don't you want to turn out the light?"

Before I turned off the desk lamp I glanced at the last page of my manuscript: I had started to tell about meeting Eleni at the Titanic.

I took the gardenia from her blouse and put it on the pillow, beside her head. She held her arms straight along her body. She didn't make the slightest movement. All her muscles were tense. I seemed to be caressing a statue. She was breathing heavily.

"What's the matter?"

"I shouldn't have asked her to stay," I thought. All at once, she gripped my wrist.

"Stop."

She sat up on the bed, and put her feet on the floor.

"I'm leaving."

"We could sit on the terrace."

We sat on the terrace. I brought her a glass of water. I hadn't turned any lights on. Her breathing had returned to normal.

"It's never happened."

I said nothing.

"Never," she repeated. "Do you understand?"

She asked for a puff on my pipe. The sky was that same rusty color that the nighttime sky always has over cities.

"I was waiting for the ideal time, the ideal man .... I learned to wait. Little by little, it stopped being a preoccupation .... I thought about it, of course, but as a minor problem. 'I'll take care of it sooner or later,' I said to myself. I always had more important things to do. I'm not unhappy .... Other people think I missed my chance .... I wish I could age faster, so people would stop pitying me, asking me 'So when are you getting married?' I can't stand their sympathy .... I have no regrets about dedicating my life to my father. He couldn't have lived without me .... He was like a child .... You can't abandon a child, can you? I'm not unhappy about not having taken better care of myself, not to have had my own life, not to have anything."

I could clearly see her face. I saw her smile. She sat on my lap, put her head on my shoulder. I rubbed her back. I saw a lot of bats in the sky. "So this is when the bats go home." I thought about the bird that had annoyed me in the street, flying so close to my neck. "He was a messenger .... He was bringing me, far too late, bad news that I already knew."

Pim is pouring water into the radiator of a sky blue Chevrolet. He's working at a filling station just a few kilometers from the railroad that crosses the United States. A huge, hefty, strong guy is watching him. He's wearing a filthy undershirt. His hands are dirty. The barrel of a revolver sticks out of a hole in his pants.

Bill-the-Coward is watching the scene from his office, just behind the gas pumps. He can see that something's coming and he quickly closes the blinds. His wife, a bony Irish woman, is braver than he is. She tries to protect Pim, but the fat man lays her low with a blow to the head with the handle of his revolver. She's out. Pim is forced by the man to go the railroad and there he discovers the fearsome task that awaits him.

That's the beginning of the last episode of the story my father is telling the ladies in his neighborhood every Wednesday afternoon. Fanny was kind enough to repeat it for me. She did it with a humor I didn't know she had. "She's imitating my father," I thought. We stayed on the terrace very late, so late that we were hungry again. We ate yogurt. There was nothing else in my refrigerator.

The fat man is a convict who, in place of serving the rest of his sentence, has agreed to clean half of the trans-continental railroad, from the Atlantic to Santa Fe, with Mirror brand metal polish. The other half, from the Pacific to Santa Fe, is being scrubbed by another convict. There's no doubt in my father's mind that Santa Fe is on the exact middle of the rail line. The contract the two convicts have signed with the authorities also says that the one who gets to that city first, along with his freedom, will also win a ranch outside Salt Lake City, including fifty cows and ten bison.

Pim is doing all the work now, rather than the fat man. They're in the middle of the desert. The heat is unbearable. High in the sky, a buzzard circles ominously. Pim works tirelessly. He spreads the Mirror brand polish with a rag, waits for it to work, and once it's dry — it doesn't take long to dry — he shines the rails with another rag, a woolen one. The polished iron shines like the sun. All this time, the fat man sits on the ground, his back against the barrel of Mirror, and whistles a monotonous tune that he learned in prison. He dreams of the ranch, its fifty cows and ten bison. Far, far away in the mist, he can just make out the houses of Santa Fe.

The whole town is waiting at the railroad station. There are men in sideburns wearing bowler hats, women in long white dresses, and unruly children with freckles. Bill-the-Coward's wife is there too. She's easy to spot because of the enormous bandage held on with adhesive tape. She knows all about Pim's troubles and she keeps murmuring:

"Poor Pim … Poor kid … . "

The crowd first looks left, then right, waiting for the two convicts to arrive. They both appear at the same time, on all fours between the rails, and rubbing like maniacs. The finish line is marked on the rails in red paint.

The fat man took over for Pim just at the edge of town.

"Stay put," he told him.

Pim is certain that if he tries to escape the fat man will kill him sooner or later. He sits on a rock and looks at his bleeding hands. When he looks toward the sky, as if to send out a prayer to the universe, he sees the buzzard circling ever lower.

The two convicts are only a meter away from the finish line. One meter is all that's keeping them from the ranch with its fifty cows and ten bison. They take a deep breath, and then, for the first time, they look at each other. The fat man recognizes the man who betrayed him, his one-time accomplice. He pulls his revolver and fires, as fast as lightning. But the other man fires too, at exactly the same moment. Both men fall dead between the rails.

My father claims that the well-shined transcontinental railroad linking the two oceans across the United States still has one little section, about two meters long, that has never been polished. It's inside the railroad station at Santa Fe.

I was a little jealous of the neighbor ladies when I heard the story.

"I don't understand why he never told us stories when we were children."

"Maybe he thought that you weren't old enough to appreciate them."

I remembered that the hero of Dickens' *Great Expectations* is named Pip. And it seems to me that there are two convicts in the novel who fight ruthlessly. I remembered an old woman, too, dressed in a tattered wedding dress.

"So the episode ends at the railroad station in Santa Fe?"

"No. Pim hears the two shots and guesses that he's free. He doesn't want to go back to the service station and he doesn't want to see anyone. He decides to cross the desert on foot, heads south, where he's heard there's a lake. The buzzard has become his friend. It flies above his head, to shade him. Unfortunately, near the lake, the man with the blue Chevrolet is waiting for him. I have a feeling that this guy is working for Pim's adoptive parents, awful carnival people from New York, but I'm not sure. We're all anxiously awaiting Wednesday to hear what happens next. There isn't a series on television that we like as much as the story of Pim."

I've discovered that my father has a kind of talent. I imagined that he was telling them just any old thing in any old way. I didn't think his stories were so well constructed, with a beginning and an end, so well crafted. "He must work on them all week long," I thought. I underestimated him, like my mother underestimated him. I regretted that she never got the chance to change her mind.

Before I went to sleep, I tried to remember one of my mother's stories. They weren't improvised stories, but stories she'd heard in her childhood. The main character was a girl more often than a boy. I drifted off to sleep.

I slept deeply. I woke up with the gardenia stuck to my cheek. It had already started to dry out.

My father found the cartoons my mother kept in a candy box. I asked him to describe the one on top of the stack.

"They're upstairs," he said.

He put the phone down on the chest. I heard him going up the stairs. He went slowly. Sometimes I think he's gotten older, sometimes he seems younger than I am.

"It's a drawing of a circle and a square," he said.

"Okay, I know which one."

It was one of the very first cartoons I published in Paris.

"The square," my father continued as if he wasn't sure I'd understood, "is telling the circle, 'I don't understand you.'"

He went quiet for a moment, then he added:

"That's funny."

He told me he was going to spend a week in a neighbor's house on the island of Tinos.

"She invited the whole crowd: Anna, Fanny, Mrs. Soussoula .... We'll do nothing but laugh!"

He plans to go to the Church of the Virgin Mary.

"I'll ask them to say masses for mama."

He calls her mama more often that Marika, as if for him she had been primarily the mother of his children. Maybe I should visit the island too, to get a better idea of what Delphi was like. The Pythia was certainly no less popular than the Virgin of Tinos is today. The thousands of pilgrims who assemble every summer probably give some idea of the ambiance around the Delphi shrine at the same season. I know business is good on Tinos, just as it was in Delphi. The ex-voto offerings of today are no doubt more discrete than the ancient offerings, but they too have an incalculable value. Both sanctuaries have a spring with supernatural properties. The Virgin hasn't performed a miracle for several years now, but that doesn't shake the beliefs of the faithful. They pardon her that weakness, the same way that their ancestors excused the Pythia when she was wrong in her assessments, or, worse yet, when she flattered the Persian invaders. Of course, Tinos doesn't allow one to converse with God. The Virgin just listens, if she's listening at all.

"I'll take some sea-water baths," he said. "The doctor has recommended that for my rheumatism."

He finally got his teeth replaced. He doesn't hide them when he speaks anymore. I asked him if he thought he might need the name of an Amazonian Indian for his story."

"Go on," he said.

"Rava Noora, it means 'She-Who-Catches-Hummingbirds.' It's a good name for someone quick and lively. She can be a member of the Kaxinawá tribe, the 'bat-men.' They live on one tributary of the Amazon, in Peru."

"Are they nice?"

"I think so. They don't like red. It's the color of death."

"How do you just happen to know all this?"

I could see the Carriers opening the envelope containing Rava Noora's earrings, painted red. Were they touched? How could they not have been?

I only write in the morning, for two or three hours. I spend the rest of the day walking, chatting, lying in the sun with my eyes closed. It's a pleasure to plunge into an orange sea. Paris seems so far away that I doubt I ever lived there. I have trouble believing the *Miroir de l'Europe* is a real newspaper. When I open the door to my apartment, I no longer feel as if I'm going into a place foreign to me. Evidence of my presence is everywhere. There's also evidence of people who've come to see me. The place has recorded their voices, some of their gestures. When I go out on the terrace, I see Fanny. Stella forgot a bracelet in the bathroom. I finally asked Elias to repaint the apartment, gave him the keys and some money. He'll start after I leave. Today is July 17. I'll leave soon.

Athens has gone back to its true size. I thought about it often, but over the years the picture had blurred. It looked more and more like a cloudy watercolor where the houses are nothing more than an indistinct heap. It was being reduced year by year and its population was shrinking. During my infrequent trips here, I saw only family and a few friends. The city had become the size of a nearly unpopulated village.

I know it a bit better now. I've gotten used to it. I always go to the same café, around noon, and then to the same restaurant. I know the waiters and some of the customers. The vegetable man and the corner grocer have learned my name, though I don't know how. The man who runs the neighborhood newsstand is named Marcos. One Sunday morning, at dawn, when I was returning home, I heard someone singing a sad Epirot song. His voice was so beautiful that I didn't move until the song was finished. I couldn't see where the voice was coming from. Everything was closed and I was alone in the street. Farther on, inside the newsstand, I saw a fairly young man with a thin face and a sparse mustache.

"Was that you singing?"

He said, "Yes," and smiled shyly. We started to talk. It turned out his name is Marcos.

I know where to buy lumber — I bought a board to build a shelf over the refrigerator — retsina in bulk, sheep's milk cheese. I've located the good bookstores, specialty stores for drawing supplies, the stalls with the best kebabs. I've been to about twenty bars — some of them several times. I know that there's a little restaurant in the sailboat harbor in Alimos where the owners and the sailors go. Penelope took me there.

I find my sociability disconcerting. I'm not used to this sort of life. I saw very few people in Paris. What do I expect from other people, exactly? Perhaps that they teach me things, I don't know. I'm more and more enchanted by life in Athens. My new relationships give me a comforting feeling that I'm accepted in Athens society, that I'm not considered an intruder. It's also true that this way of life gets my mind off of things. It allows me to get away from my own thoughts, to leave them unfinished. I sometimes wonder if I listen to other people because I want to learn something, or because I want to forget. My thoughts are always suspended between what I hear and what I don't say.

We took her car to go to Alimos. She drives calmly and fast. I admitted I'd been upset by her remark in Stamata about my pipe ashes. She remembered the incident very well.

"I felt bad about it afterwards," she said. "I talked about it with my spiritual adviser."

I didn't understand that she meant an Orthodox priest. Her hair was tied back in a ribbon. She was wearing little square gold earrings. She talked about the fires that ravage the Greek countryside every summer.

"More often than not they're started by people who own part of the forest. They can't build there as long as the zone is considered forest. They burn thousands of acres just to build a country house, can you imagine?"

For a moment, her voice became just as bitter as it had been back then.

"We're greedy," she continued. "We're pillaging our heritage. We're eating our own flesh."

I remembered that Caradzoglou had also used the word "greedy." "We have the feverish look of gold prospectors," he'd said.

It took us a while to find the restaurant. We walked along the narrow jetties. The masts of the sailboats formed a naked forest around us. There was a full moon. I was rather optimistic about how the evening would go. I was thinking it would have a better outcome than my date with Fanny. The place had soft lights and was decorated with buoys, fishing nets, and little copper anchors. We sat in a corner, by a row of windows through which we could see the owner constantly on the phone behind the counter and at a distance behind him the masts of boats, rocking gently. She asked me to draw her. I told her I'd drawn an imaginary portrait of her in Stamata. I used an advertising notepad that the owner lent me. I colored the cheeks with two drops of wine.

Apparently some art dealers and critics are questioning the authenticity of the El Greco painting of Saint Peter that the Minister of Culture plans to buy.

"It all started with a painter who's plotting to take over Stathopoulou's job. Actually, he's given up on painting. His works don't sell anymore. He has other ambitions."

"What does Theodoris think of the painting?"

"He doesn't have any opinion about its authenticity. He just thinks it isn't very good."

I remembered a book I'd read at the Architecture School that mentioned Saint Peter: it was an essay on Ancient Greek religion and it talked about a temple dedicated to the "unknown god." Saint Peter waxed ironic about that temple: he couldn't understand how any religion might imagine the existence of any gods but its own. The one he himself was teaching didn't encourage speculation.

What will she do, once she's finished the Beaux Arts School? Ceramics, what she's studied most, don't interest her anymore.

"Theodoris argues that an everyday object, however beautiful it may be, can't inspire as much emotion as a work of art. 'I've never had tears in my eyes while looking at a vase, a plate, or a table,' he says. I personally have been moved to tears only once, at the Byzantine museum."

Penelope is twenty-seven. She's not worried about the future. Her father has money. She worked for a few years in the cinema, with director friends.

"I'd like to forget that time," she said. "It did me a lot of harm."

I caressed her breasts.

"Don't be in such a hurry."

I thought of Ilona. "I'll meet her one day in the duty-free shop of the Ottawa airport. We'll have coffee. We'll both be ready to leave, she for Belgium and I for New York. We'll remember the time when we were both studying at the French Archeology School library. I'll confess that I used to look at her breasts. I'll remind her of the peeled fig she once gave me. She'll tell me about the text she was writing at the time. I'll finally learn how Alexander the Great died. Maybe he fell off his horse."

We left the restaurant around midnight. She untied the ribbon from her hair and shook it out. We walked on the jetties. She sat down on a heap of rope. The moon lit up the outline of her hair.

"I want to make love, too, but only when we're married."

"She's joking," I thought. She wasn't joking. She wants to get married and have children. She had a huge number of affairs when she was working in the movies.

"You can't imagine how many guys I slept with. I was disgusted with myself, with men, and with the movies."

That was when she met her spiritual adviser, an elderly Orthodox priest who really understands the young, especially those on the fringes of society, and drug addicts. She spoke with him through an entire night in his parish church.

"He didn't turn on the lights, just lit a few candles. He got up every half hour to replace the burned-out candles."

She told him her whole life, all her affairs. He helped her realize that she was the victim of a materialistic society and an imported culture, one completely incompatible with Greek sensibilities.

We were sitting on a heap of rope. We saw a couple walk by and board a yacht. A few moments later a porthole light came on, adding a second moon to the landscape.

"The icons were watching me, pitying me. I was convinced they'd known me since my childhood. I felt enormous relief that night. I had always believed in God, but that was the first time he'd talked to me. His voice was kind, peaceful, soft. In the early morning, leaving the church, I really thought I'd found myself again."

We talked very little in the car going back to Athens. I've tried to understand why so many people around me, even former communists, are interested in Orthodoxy. Is it because of some need to defend national identity? The rejection of a system, which, as Véronique Carrier would say, doesn't make sufficient allowances for basic human needs? Most of the intellectuals that I meet have gone to Mount Athos two or three times. Are they hoping to find a model for community life? "I'll have to talk to some of them, if the question really interests me."

"Wouldn't you like to go to church with me next Sunday?" she asked.

"I'll no doubt be gone by Sunday."

I thought about noting the word *ecclissia*, church, in my notebook.

"We'll go when you get back. You have to meet my spiritual adviser. He has a vast knowledge and a very open mind."

I sat on the toilet cover, waiting for the tub to fill. I heard the old man coughing. He was coughing constantly, louder and louder, almost as if calling for help. Should I knock on his door, call a doctor, call 166? A moment or two later, a woman's voice said harshly:

"Will you shut up!"

A bit later, the old man quieted down. I got into the bathtub very slowly, the water was boiling hot. It had the same bluish color as window glass when you look at it from a certain angle.

The next day it came to me that I had no reason to stay in Athens any longer. "I've visited enough places. I've looked at enough sidewalks." I went to the Olympic Air office and reserved a ticket for Ioannina, then I went to the French Archeology School. As I was going up Didotos Street, I realized that I had missed the quiet of the library. François wasn't there. He was with a team of archeologists on Delos. I went down to the lower level. No one was sitting in my place. Ilona's chair was empty, too. At random, I took one of the burgundy leather volumes cataloguing discoveries made during the dig at Delphi. It was from 1927. It held an important surprise for me. I knew that neither of the two omphalos found at Delphi was very ancient. The omphalos is that round stone which represents the navel of the world. The ones that have been found are made of gray limestone and of marble and are considered copies. I didn't know that the authentic omphalos had also been discovered, in 1913. It's a Poros stone, crudely shaped into a cone, about thirty centimeters high. That discovery, which created a sensation at the beginning of the century, wouldn't have meant much to me if it weren't for what could be seen carved into the stone near its base, an epsilon facing down. It's a clumsy epsilon, which seemed to me infinitely more beautiful than the one on the Roman coins. I found it much more alive, too, perhaps because the way it's tipped it looks like an animal with three legs. Beside the epsilon are the letters gamma and alpha, which spell the name of the Earth goddess, Ga, the very first mistress of the shrine. Those letters aren't carefully formed, either. The gamma (Γ) is slightly curved and looks something like a lambda (Λ). You get the feeling that the inscription dates back to a time when the letters were still being tried out. I gave the photo and the photographically detailed drawing of the archaic omphalos the same attention I had given to Antinous. I asked for a photocopy of both images. "I'll keep the photocopies with me. I'll look at them from time to time, the way you read a love letter over and over." I didn't feel like reading anything more about Delphi.

It was still early. I visited other departments in the library, examined the spines of the books. When readers borrow a book, they're supposed to leave a little cardboard box with their name on it. I learned that those cardboard boxes marking a book's absence are called "ghosts" in French. There were a lot of ghosts among the books. I opened the *Alexiad* to learn something about the succession struggle between Anna and John, the children of the emperor Alexius I. The author of the preface says that it can be divided into two acts. In the first, Anna tried to assassinate John, with the approval of their mother Irene. In the second, John appeared before the patriarch to announce the death of his father and to be crowned emperor. But Alexius was still alive. Anna and Irene informed him of John's unspeakable conduct, but Alexius did nothing: he had a preference for his son just as his wife did for his daughter. Anna, the author of the *Alexiad*, didn't think much of the language of her era, the vulgar Greek of the twelfth century. She looked on it just as my teachers looked upon Modern Greek, as a second-rate language incapable of expressing elevated thought. When she says she's in love with the language, she means the ancient Attic dialect. It was in that language that she tried to write. Her style is bombastic and apparently she makes lots of mistakes.

I also consulted Henri Estienne's *Treasures of the Greek Language*, re-edited by Firmin Didot — our Didotos — at the beginning of the nineteenth century. I opened it to the letter E. The letter is framed by an engraving of a man about to give up the ghost. He's lying in bed, his head tilted back. A nun is taking care of him, while three men stand by the foot of his bed watching him. Why is the epsilon accompanied by such a sad image? Could it be inspired by the word *étimothanatos*, dying? The man isn't wearing a shirt. His chest is swollen as if he's taking a deep breath. Perhaps his slightly open lips are forming the ancient interjection *é é*, expressing pain or sorrow? In any case, he looks like he's suffering.

I've only seen my mother once in a dream since her death. She was sitting in bed, her back against a mound of pillows. Blood was flowing from her eyes, two big red tears running down her cheeks. It wasn't the color of her tears that upset me, but the fact that she was crying after she died. I knew perfectly well that she was dead. Her face was serene and her eyes were closed. My father was there too, bent over and sitting on a corner of the bed. The room was quite dark. I went closer to my mother to better see her face: she had opened her eyes and she was looking at me too. I immediately thought of the family, of all those people I had informed of her death. Naturally, I had to call them back to tell them that my mother had come back to life. "What if she dies again in the next few minutes?" I thought. "They'll end up not believing me if I keep calling to tell them that she's dead and then that she's alive." I decided to wait a while. Her eyes had stayed open. The half-light made them darker, made them look almost black. I felt like she was making an effort to see me, as if I were some distance away. "My mother's watching me from far away." I didn't wipe away her tears, so as not to worry her. I didn't know if she was aware that she was crying. Anyway, the two red tears had stopped near her mouth. I knelt on the bed, took her under her arms, and drew her toward me. I helped her put her feet on the floor, then stand up. One of my hands was on her arm, the other around her waist. Now I was sure that she was alive. "I'll call the family." My father hadn't moved and said nothing, as if he hadn't noticed any of what was going on around him. I crossed the room with my mother. We stopped in front of the window. The sun was either just setting or had just set. The sky was orange.

"It's beautiful, isn't it?" I said.

She nodded her head in agreement. I tried to remember the date. It was important for me to know what day my mother had come back to life. It seemed to me just as important as the date of her death.

"I think it's the sixth of February," I murmured.

"No, the eighth," she corrected.

Her certainty surprised me. I thought that she was probably right. She looked at the garden in front of the house. The apricot trees didn't have a single leaf on them. The earth was damp and the paving stones of the terrace were glistening as if it had just rained.

"Two little birds," she said.

She pronounced those words with the same satisfaction and with the same difficulty as a child just learning to talk. I saw the two birds sitting on the garden fence. One of them glided to the paving stones. The other followed him a few moments later. My mother looked at them sympathetically. Her face was still very calm.

The next night I went to bed hoping that I would see her again. I woke up at six in the morning without having dreamed at all. I tried to sleep a little more, but I couldn't. I didn't see her again that night, or any other night. I'm afraid that my mother has removed herself permanently from my dreams.

The same color photograph that my father has is hung on the wall of Costas and Vasso's pharmacy in Ioannina. Below it on a shelf is a vase of flowers.

"Costas replaces them every day," says Vasso. "When he's traveling, he calls me every day to be sure that I haven't forgotten to change them."

I look at the cigarette smoke rising along my mother's left arm. I have a photo of her on the bookcase at my place too, a little black and white photo with filigreed edges. She's about thirty years old in the picture and I'm five or six. She's holding me by the hand. We're walking across a square.

Vasso is wearing a white coat. She's standing behind the desk, doesn't have time to sit down, with new customers arriving constantly. It's a wooden desk, painted gray. The top is enclosed on three sides with little columns that form a sort of balcony. The shelves, the cupboards, and the wall separating the counter from the stockroom are also painted gray. Both Vasso and Costas don't think it's worthwhile to update the pharmacy. They've left it just as it was in Vasso's father's time. They've kept a collection of colored glass jars with Latin names on blue labels.

Costas has been at the printer's all morning. He's getting a new issue of his journal ready. In one corner of the pharmacy, just behind the revolving display of baby food, old issues of *Épirotika* are stacked up. The journal is sent out from here and it's here that Costas meets his contributors and various old women who tell him stories of the past. The constant activity doesn't seem to bother Vasso. I have never heard her complain, not even about the financial burden of the journal, which consumes all the profits from the pharmacy. She loves Costas enough to share his passions.

I haven't seen my brother yet. He sent Vasso to the airport to meet me. The fog postponed our landing for quite a while. We circled over the city and the lake without ever seeing either one. Just for an instant I glimpsed the tile roof of an apartment building. In Athens, where it rains less, the apartment buildings end in a roof terrace. It's my third visit to Ioannina, and I'm afraid that once again I won't be able to see the city. It was shrouded in the same fog during my previous visits. Vasso doesn't know if it's because of the lake, the city's altitude, or the mountains that surround it. The highest one is called Mitsikeli. I hope Costas will be able to find the etymology of the name. I've already asked him several times.

We went to their house first, near the lake. I'll sleep on the couch, in Costas' office. Lena, their daughter, wasn't there, but I saw her picture. I barely recognized her with her makeup and short hair.

"She goes out every evening with a group of friends," says Vasso. "Costas doesn't want to upset her. 'Leave her alone,' he says, 'She's on vacation.' But she goes out just as often in the winter. She isn't working. And she's about this close to having to repeat a year in school."

They gave her the names of both of her grandmothers. Maria instead of Marika, and Eleni. But no one calls her Maria-Eleni, the first name has disappeared.

"Is she in a relationship?"

"You mean a really serious relationship?" Vasso said, opening her eyes wide. "Not at that point yet."

She does, however, think that something happened on New Years night. Lena came home at dawn. She was laughing.

"I thought she was drunk, but she hadn't been drinking. She didn't look like she'd been out all night. Her face was radiant! And she was laughing! Everything I said made her laugh! She looked at me and she laughed! She looked at her coffee cup and she laughed! She watched me spreading jam and she laughed! I was exasperated! 'Stop laughing,' I told her! She couldn't!"

The fog is so thick I can't see the street. It plugs up the open windows and doors and some of it even gets into the pharmacy. Customers appear suddenly. I don't see them coming. I only see them when they're already here. They emerge out of the fog the way forgotten profiles sometimes emerge from memory. I have the impression that Vasso's customers belong to a distant past.

It's one o'clock. When is Costas coming home? I want to eat some chickpea soup. To sit down in the back of a tavern and chat with him. Maybe he remembers our mother's stories. He certainly must remember events that we both lived, but that I've forgotten. He has an excellent memory. I hope he can spare me some time. I notice that I rarely call our mother *mana*, a nearly untranslatable word, half way between *mother* and *mama*. The name is too emotional. It reminds me of poetry, songs, and films. *Mitéra*, the mother, creates distance, and lets me talk about her calmly. I'm still looking at her photo. She really admired Vasso.

"She is endlessly kind," she used to say. "And if she weren't, she wouldn't be able to put up with Costas."

When they got married, my mother gave Vasso the only valuable thing she inherited from her mother, a pair of gold earrings.

"How's it going with Costas?"

"He sleeps badly .... He gets up at night .... Maybe he'll tell you what's bothering him."

I ask her for something for my cold. Costas has a perpetual cold too.

"You know that Lena has the same problem?"

She gives me a tiny little bottle of oil extracted from a tree whose name means nothing to me: Niaouli. It has the same smell as camphor.

"You should inhale it every night before going to sleep. You can also put a few drops on your pillow."

Costas is standing in the doorway. He's talking to someone in the street, someone I can't see. I have time to observe my brother. I'd never noticed, in the past, that he looks like our mother. I'd only noticed that he sometimes speaks as carefully as she did. Now I notice that his voice holds an echo of hers. The way he gestures with his right hand and the way he holds his head remind me of her. When he ends his discussion and comes over to me, I have the feeling that I'm hugging her too, at the same time.

"Will you come have lunch with us?" he asks Vasso.

He glances at the letters that have arrived. This is the first time I've seen him since that day. I think about that Wednesday. I know it was a Wednesday, because the stores were closed. I spent a long time looking for an open pharmacy to buy the phials the doctor prescribed. She'd had a bout of fever. Her forehead was burning. I left my father at home with a neighbor, Margarita, and ran off to buy the phials. The doctor didn't seem particularly worried.

"You'll be more comfortable without me," Vasso answers.

"Did anyone call?"

It was twenty minutes to seven in the evening, maybe a quarter to seven, when I left. I wasn't gone more than a half-hour. In the garden, Margarita's husband was pacing.

"You've heard, haven't you?" he said.

"Yes, yes," I answered. "She has a temperature."

He took my arm, squeezed it tightly without saying anything else. As I came into the house, I saw my father coming down the stairs. He was coming down the stairs very carefully, as if he couldn't see them very well. I went to him. His eyes were red and full of tears.

We're walking in the fog.

"Let's go toward the fort," says Costas. "That's where we'll find taverns like the one you're looking for. But you won't be able to eat chickpeas, they don't make soup in the summer."

There's some activity in the streets. Costas stops occasionally to say hello to a friend. I can barely see the cars. They're driving with their lights on. They're not moving much faster than the pedestrians.

"Is something wrong?"

"I'll tell you all about it at the tavern."

Margarita came down the stairs just after my father.

"She went peacefully," she said.

I wanted to know exactly what time it had happened.

"I went upstairs a little before seven. It must've been about five minutes after, no later."

"But I want to know the *exact* time, Margarita!" I exclaimed.

My voice scared her. She didn't understand why I was so insistent.

"It was two minutes, three minutes after seven," she said.

A few days later, I realized I'd reacted like the investigators do in detective novels when they want to know the exact time of the crime.

A bus comes slowly out of the fog. It's going to the university. Behind the windshield, to the left of the driver, there's a sign that says "SCHOOL OF PHILOSOPHY." There are very few passengers on board. Costas tells me that the university operates in the summer as well, that they offer Greek courses for foreigners.

The tavern is just as I'd imagined it: there's a tight wire mesh on the windows, gray-green walls swollen with humidity, a dilapidated mustard-colored floor, an enormous wood-burning stove in the center of the room, a matronly woman standing behind her pots and pans, and an elderly waiter with an absent look. And there's a naïve engraving of the unfortunate lady Phrosyne just when one of Ali Pasha's soldiers is throwing her into the lake at Ioannina. They're in a boat. Phrosyne's feet and hands are tied.

"I met her last year, in the spring," says Costas. "She's an architect. Vasso was in Lefkada. I really wasn't in love with her at first, I just wanted an adventure. I didn't want to make trouble at home. We saw each other at her place two or three times a week."

It crosses my mind that he must've had the affair just after the death of our mother, about when I left Vaguelio. The waiter is incredible: the only dishes he brings us are the ones we didn't order!

"I'm not surprised that I got it wrong," he says. "I can never read my own writing."

He looks at the sheet where he wrote down our order. It's covered with indecipherable scribbling.

"My hands shake.... Tell me what you want again and I'll try to remember."

The matronly woman is looking in our direction.

"It doesn't matter," I say. "We'll eat what you brought us."

"That sort of arrangement seemed to suit her. She never asked for anything more. But two months ago she left for Thessalonica without telling me. She was gone for a month. I didn't hear from her for a month. I've only seen her once since she returned. I haven't been able to get the answers I wanted. She only told me that she wants to feel free, that she's not accustomed to justifying what she does. 'I'm twenty-eight,' she said several times. I finally wrote to her, told her that I couldn't live without her, that I was even ready to leave Vasso."

He hasn't touched any of the food. He's chain smoking.

"The last time we saw each other was at the pharmacy. She came by one day when I was alone. She was badly dressed, wearing no makeup. She was showing herself in a bad light, probably to help me forget her quickly. You know what I felt when I saw her leaving? That all the air in the store was leaving with her."

"We won't talk about our mother." As if he guessed what I was thinking, Costas says: "Maybe I fell in love to get away from the sadness of her death .... Margarita being there did me a lot of good. I was happy when I saw her."

I remind him that the neighbor who closed our mother's eyes is also named Margarita. My remark stuns him.

"Really," he says. "Really."

The soldier who's throwing Phrosyne into the lake has bulging eyes. Her expression is stoic. The scene takes place at night. In the landscape's background you can see the moon. I think Ali Pasha ordered the execution of Phrosyne because she had rejected him. He was crazy about her.

"I feel as if I've been chased away from somewhere beautiful .... From a fabulously wealthy house where an exquisite party is going on ... As if I'd been driven out of paradise! I'm as unhappy as Adam and Eve combined!"

He smiles. His smile rather reminds me of our father. Some of his unusual observations remind me of him too. When he was little, Costas used to say that the trees should keep their leaves in winter to protect us from the rain. But he has no taste for imaginary stories. He's never liked literature. He doesn't know how to lie. He has inherited our mother's seriousness. The stories of elderly ladies of Epirus interest him mostly to the extent that they're part of a very real local culture. He's studying a reality. I wonder if our father reads *Épirotika*. The scientific articles in the journal probably bore him, but maybe he finds things to feed his imagination.

"I can't stop thinking about her. Her absence is my only company, and I don't want to lose that. I talk with her endlessly. She comes to see me in tears, she begs my forgiveness, we fall into each other's arms. The conversations I have with her ghost usually have a happy ending, but not always. Sometimes I get angry, I don't find her explanations good enough, I abuse her, 'Take your things and get out!' I say. I try to convince myself that we separated because that's the way I wanted it."

I'm not used to hearing him confide things so openly. He doesn't confide easily. Some of his secrets he confided only to our mother. I didn't tell him mine, either. His silence left me cold, just as mine perhaps left him cold too. Neither of us has ever tried to break that old silence. "He's talking to me now because our mother isn't here anymore."

"I like the fog. I'm under the constant illusion that Margarita is just a few steps away. I see her all the time. The fog multiplies her presence. I see her silhouette everywhere. I walk for hours hoping I'll come across her eventually."

I don't dare advise him to smoke a bit less. It will just upset him. All he ate was two roasted potatoes. I tell him all about my research on the epsilon.

"Well, that's the first letter of *Éros*!" he remarks. "Do you think that might be what the E at Delphi means?"

"People often asked the Pythia if they should marry."

"I'd like you to write all this down. I sometimes publish articles on subjects outside of Epirus. You should ask the Delphians what they think of the epsilon. All you'd have to do would be to sit in a café and let them talk."

We're walking toward the section of town where the blacksmiths work.

"But we won't be able to see anything!" I tell him.

"It doesn't matter."

We can already hear someone hammering iron. The strokes are slow, calculated, carefully planned. It sounds extremely loud and clear to me, maybe because there's nothing else to notice. We're striding through a place that's been abolished, deprived of images. Other hammer strokes can be heard now. Each blacksmith has his own rhythm. They aren't all working the same metals. More and more varied sounds can be heard. You get the impression they're being led by an orchestra director, since they sometimes all stop at the same moment and then resume their work like a chorus. Their music is sober and grave, but it has a few lighter notes—maybe from a child imitating his father by pounding on a can.

"Do you remember what mama told us about the shepherds of Amphissa? How carefully they selected the little bells for their animals? I always think of her when I come here."

Apparently ironwork is still flourishing in Ioannina. Here, too, they make bells and chimes, but not just that. They produce all sorts of objects made of copper and silver. Costas takes me into a shack that's dark, narrow, and deep. All you can see is the face of the blacksmith, sitting at the far end, leaning over his forge. He pays no attention to us, maybe because he can't interrupt his work. Another man is standing behind him.

"Are you planning to buy something?" I ask Costas.

"I just want to ask him a question."

The second man takes the piece of iron and plunges it into a tub of water. He's wearing a mitten on his right hand.

"I came by a while back with a girl," says Costas. "She ordered a weathervane. Did she come get it?"

"Yes," says the blacksmith. "A few days ago. I'd finished it by Easter."

We hear people running in the street, cries, a howl, whistles.

"Stop them! Stop them!"

The siren of a police car can be heard far away. The blacksmith's assistant throws the iron into the tub, opens the back door, and disappears instantly.

"He's Albanian," the blacksmith laughs. "He doesn't have any papers. He's scared of the cops."

All three of us go out into the alleyway. A neighbor informs us that the people being chased by the police are indeed Albanians.

"As long as there's fog, the police will never catch them. But if the fog lifts . . . ."

We don't hear the running or the shouting anymore. The police siren can still be heard.

"So the girl came by," the blacksmith says again. "I know her slightly. She's an architect, isn't she?"

I look at the postcards in front of a newsstand. Given the weather, it's the only way of visiting the city. I see a mosque and a minaret on a craggy butte protected by the ruins of a fortress. In some pictures, the mosque is reflected in the lake. I see the paving stones of the blacksmiths' district. It may be the alleyway where I was with Costas. There's a little island in the lake. I plan to visit it, but I look at it carefully anyway. I'm sure that I'll find it shrouded in fog. Ali Pasha smoking a chibouk. I know that he suffered from an eye disease and that he wore glasses with blue lenses. Ali Pasha again, in a boat. Ali Pasha and his wife, lady Vassiliki. He married her after doing away with Phrosyne. Vassiliki was also very beautiful. Her hair went all the way to her knees. So the man who left the greatest mark on this city was an Albanian. The tourist brochures that I've read both compliment him and disapprove of him. They remind us that he was deceitful and bloodthirsty, but they also recognize that Epirus became a great power under his rule and that his revolt against the sultans encouraged the Greek insurrection. He's called "the Lion of Epirus." For Greek commentators, one of the best things that Ali Pasha ever did was marry a local woman. Vassiliki became an alcoholic after his death.

The lake waters are calm. The fog just brushes its surface, as if trying to cool off. I can't see more than two meters. From where I'm sitting, in the back of the motorboat, I can barely make out the passengers standing in the front. They make me think of the shades Charon ferries in his boat from one bank of the Acheron to the other. I imagine that the river's waters must be the same gray as the lake and that they must be perpetually shrouded in mist. "There would have to be some sort of screen between the two banks, to keep anyone from seeing what's happening on the other side." Reeds stick up here and there, straight as the lances of an army engulfed by the waters. A wild duck rocks in the little waves from the motorboat. I constantly have the feeling that we're arriving. I think I can make out the outline of the island, but I'm wrong. They say the treasure of Ali Pasha is buried at the bottom of the lake in iron chests. He threw it there to keep it from the sultan's soldiers.

Ali is present on the island too. He took refuge there, on the second floor of a monastery, after he lost the final battle. He was killed by a shot fired from the lower floor: it went through the floor and hit him in the balls. Then they cut off his head and sent it to Istanbul. There are four or five monasteries on the island and I dash through them quickly. The sullen expression of the saints doesn't make me want to converse with them. In any case, it's too late for us to become friends. Reality has been good to me. It has given me everything I need. Inside the church of Saint Nicholas, to the left of the main door, I come across a touchingly naïve mural, an expression of the modern Greek desire to convert classical antiquity to Christianity. In the purest Byzantine style, it portrays Solon, Chilon, Plato, Thucydides, Aristotle, Plutarch, and Apollonius, declaring, "together in a house in Athens, they recognized the divine incarnation and the presence of Christ." Seven centuries, I think, separate Solon from Apollonius. Plutarch is wearing a turban like Macriyannis. The painting dates from 1560.

I didn't expect to find Plutarch here. I sit down in a café and wait for the boat to leave. "I'll have to tell the Pim story to Costas," I think. I imagine my brother in the street, feeling his way through the fog, trying to push it aside so he can see Margarita. The tourists are all sitting outside. I'm the only one inside the café. The television is on. The news anchor is announcing to empty chairs that the government has decided to deport all Albanian illegals. It's supposed to be a response to Tirana for the Albanian Greeks — five of them have been accused of subversive activity and are currently on trial. One Albanian immigrant has climbed up on a utility pole just outside Ioannina, along the highway. You can't see the Albanian very well on the screen. He's hidden by the fog. He's threatening to electrocute himself unless they give him a resident card. There are people around the utility pole. I can even see tourists with backpacks. A few meters away is a squarish building that looks like a stable. It has no windows. I think the Albanian must have been staying there. "Someone must have denounced him to the cops." A police official declares that he has nothing to say.

"We're waiting for the prefect," he says. "You can ask him directly."

The news anchor goes on to another topic. The situation of Albanians in Greece is one that many Greeks have experienced in foreign countries. We should be able to understand the reasons that have made them leave their own countries. All the songs and poems we've written about exile come to my mind. It's one of the dominant themes of our literature. It's a word we've been studying for a very long time. If I remember correctly, Aeschylus' *Suppliants* were women seeking hospitality. Euripides picked up both the title and the theme. Our attitude toward the Albanians would make you think that their pleading look doesn't remind us of anything.

I can't say that I had much difficulty getting a resident card in France. All I had to deal with were the usual vexations. Of course, it wasn't as hard at the time.Tthe far right hadn't collected so many votes, hadn't yet come to power in certain cities, didn't have much influence, wasn't invited to appear on television. I suddenly remember Paris. I remember that the waiters in the cafés wear burgundy colored vests. I remember that the metro is always delayed at Kléber station. While I was watching a delayed broadcast of a tennis match from Roland-Garros, I saw the shadow of a bird flash across the court.

7.

I'm writing in the kitchen. Costas and Vasso are gone. Lena is still sleeping. Yesterday evening we had a visit from Vasso's brother, his wife, and their son, a quiet fourteen-year-old boy. No one was expecting them. They were in a car accident a few kilometers from Ioannina. They were heading toward Igoumenitsa to take the ferry to Corfu, where they were planning to spend their vacation. They drove off the road in the fog and hit a rock. Fortunately, they were only going about thirty kilometers an hour. Vasso put them in the living room. The couple hasn't gotten up yet. I've only seen the young man, who came into the kitchen for a moment. I asked him if he wanted some coffee and he said no. His father is very talkative and knows everything, like a taxi driver. His name is Apostolos, his wife is Anna, and their son is Miltiade. I don't understand why I'm noting down all these details. Maybe I imagine literature as an insatiable ogre who needs to consume a variety of foods, not just substantial dishes, but olives, radishes, and raisins too. From what I can see through the window, the fog is at least as thick as yesterday.

I was awakened by the phone during the night. It was two in the morning. I went out in the hall and saw Costas pick up the receiver, then put it down.

"No one there?"

"No," he said.

"Do you think it was . . . ."

"No, it was some other woman."

Since he wasn't in a hurry to go back to bed, I invited him into the room where I'm staying, into his office. We sat down cross-legged on the couch, covered up our legs with the sheet. "We once sat like this, on a couch, a very long time ago," I thought.

"Darkness is oppressive to me, makes it hard to breathe," he said. "It must be even more awful to break up in November or in December, when the nights are so long .... I try to control my feelings, at times. I listen to songs that remind me of other women I've loved. I felt much better after I wrote to her. I even thought that I was no longer in love. It occurred to me that even the most sincere love letters lie to some extent, since passion diminishes when it is expressed. Love letters are detrimental to feelings."

We talked about the difficulty we used to have in communicating. He attributed it to the friendships that our mother had cultivated with each of us separately.

"The three of us never talked together," he said. "She didn't encourage dialogue between us. She probably thought that we would confide less willingly in her if we spoke more between us. She was our closest friend. I smoked for the first time with her. When you came into the living room I hid my cigarette. I was as embarrassed to smoke in front of you as in front of papa. Our relationship with her was beyond the family framework. It was of a different sort, free."

His theory didn't seem absurd to me, but I still felt incapable of criticizing our mother. I was very surprised at his almost detached way of speaking about her. I supposed he'd often spoken with Vasso about our family relationships, that he had gotten used to analyzing them coldly.

"She was a difficult, solitary woman," he went on. "Even Theodoris' mother, whom she liked very much, she only saw rarely. We're really the only ones she saw .... She must not have spoken much with her parents when she was little .... It seems like she took care of them more than they took care of her. She probably hoped to form bonds with her children different from those she'd had with her parents .... She'd read a great deal about child psychology. She told me one day that she'd started studying the question before we were born. She systematically read every essay that came out, translated from German, from French. I imagine those books must have advised parents to talk to their children, to listen to them .... Strangely enough, she didn't want us to get too attached to her .... She was convinced that children need to become independent quickly .... She had probably picked up that conviction from her readings."

I never saw that sort of book around the house. "She must have thrown them away when we grew up." Our affection for her didn't keep us from leaving home early. It wasn't hard convincing her that I had to leave for Paris. My father, who I rarely spoke to, was more reticent, probably because he didn't know me as well. All at once I saw Costas break down: "You know," he said in a broken voice, "we lost a friend too."

Lena, who went out last evening, suddenly burst into the room. We hadn't heard her open the front door.

"You two aren't sleeping?"

Her good mood immediately changed the atmosphere in the room.

"Am I bothering you?" she asked, half smiling. "Are you talking about girls?"

"Leave us alone," said Costas.

"I was in a new bar, one that just opened, the Pompeii .... You want to go there with me some evening?"

Costas shrugged his shoulders.

"Are you still feeling bad?"

She rubbed his neck.

"You'll get over it, papa."

She told me that she really liked *youvarlakia*, but that she didn't have the chance to eat it very often.

"I'll make you some tomorrow," I said, "using your grandmother's recipe. I'll cook the meatballs in tomato soup."

We were alone again.

"Does Lena know about your affair with Margarita?"

"More or less, yes .... She saw us in the street once .... I try to remember all of Margarita's faults, her imperfections, her quirks, to put together a terrible portrait of her, to convince myself that I'd be better off forgetting her. But that doesn't stop me from thinking about her, even when I'm trying to forget her! I've at least managed to take a disliking to her social and professional circles. She's from an old middle-class family in town. I can't stand the bourgeoisie and I can't stand architects!"

"I live surrounded by ghosts, too .... When I'm eating alone in a restaurant, I hate it when they take away the extra chairs at my table. I'm talking to people who aren't there, I think about conversations I've had or I imagine others I'll have in the future. None of the chairs around me is empty, really."

We chatted until four in the morning. I tried to confide a secret to him, just to show him that it doesn't bother me, but I searched for one in vain. "I must have secrets," I thought, "only I don't know them." I settled for telling him about the women I've met recently in Athens, about Stella, Penelope, Eleni, Ilona. I talked about Fanny, too, but without revealing her secret. I told him about my plans to buy a ping-pong table or a billiard table.

"I dream of a woman who would have Vaguelio's smile, Penelope's hair, Stella's skin, Ilona's breasts, Fanny's legs, Eleni's style, and who knows how to play ping-pong."

Apostolos and Anna have been up for a while. They decided to have their breakfast in the living room so they wouldn't disturb me. Apostolos was getting ready to tell me again about their accident, but his wife stopped him: "We said all that yesterday. Today is another day."

She was wearing a blue nightgown with little red hearts on it. A bit later, Apostolos tried to teach Miltiade how to shave. The lesson took place in the bathroom next to the kitchen. They left the door open. First he showed Miltiade how to spread the shaving cream on his face.

"Spread it with your index finger," he told him. "That works best. Don't use too much foam, or you'll plug your nostrils with it and you won't be able to breathe. I'll show you."

Apostolos put shaving cream on his face, spreading it carefully.

"You see?"

Then he showed his son how to hold the razor.

"You start with the sideburns, then come down slowly. No sudden movements! Slowly, I tell you. You should never get flustered when you're shaving."

He was very worried, as if Miltiade's life was in danger. I made the decision to cut off my own beard, too. I'll go back to the face I had when I left for France, though older, of course.

"The most delicate spots are under your nose and around your mouth," Apostolos continued. "You place the blade vertically, in the middle of your mustache, and you pull it either left or right. But you always start in the middle!"

Since he was already holding a razor, he used it to shave his mustache.

"You see?"

Miltiade, on the other hand, wasn't shaving. He was watching his father in the mirror. I have already seen parents teaching their children things which don't really need any special training, like how to clean your ears, how to tie a package, how to move a table without messing up the floor, how to hammer a nail. Many Greek parents assign great importance to the practical skills they've acquired and want to transmit them in their entirety to the next generation.

"Now shave your chin," said Apostolos. "Do it any way you want. I'd be curious to see."

Miltiade didn't even have time to put the razor to his chin.

"No!" his father cried. "You're going to cut yourself. You have to round out your chin by putting your tongue behind your lower lip, like this!"

Apostolos put his tongue behind his lower lip, which made him look like a monkey. Miltiade didn't laugh: he threw the razor into the sink and quickly walked away across the kitchen. His father, crushed, watched him go, looked at me, then turned toward the mirror and continued shaving.

The woman who cracked my egg in Stamata must have offended me more than I thought, because I haven't forgotten what she did. According to the information that Costas has given me, there's absolutely no reason for my bitterness. Eggs symbolize creation, the renewal of life, they're miniatures of the universe. The Romans ate them during funerals, as did the Byzantines. The custom we're talking about has been around since the thirteenth century. By breaking the shell, we set the forces contained within them free and we evoke Christ's freedom from his tomb. So it's wrong to be happy when the shell stays intact, because only the broken egg can express the mystery of the Resurrection.

The red color is a reminder of the lamb's blood the Hebrews of Egypt smeared on their houses to escape the wrath of the exterminating angel. The cross customarily traced on the lintel of the main door of a house was at one time traced with lamb's blood by the residents of Corfu.

I can't complain, Costas has answered all my questions. The name of Mount Mitsikeli comes from the Slavic word *mečka*, meaning the bear. He even found me one foreign place name that we've changed recently: the village of Kavakia — from Turkish *kavak*, the willow — was rebaptized as Rosebushes. Costas happened to meet one of the residents and asked him if there were really any rosebushes in the village.

"No," he answered, "but we're going to plant some!"

He confirmed that there is no general dictionary of place names, but there are a large number of monographs about the place names of a specific region, for example an island like Mykonos or Ithaca.

"You shouldn't think we're the only ones who change place names when they're foreign," he said. "Our neighbors do too."

I moved to a traditional Epirot-style tourist hotel, built on the fortifications near the mosque that I saw on the postcards. It's one of the highest places in town, with a superb view of the mountains and the lake. I'm sitting facing the window, which is open, but naturally I can't see anything. I will once again leave Ioannina without any image of the city. I'll remember its fog. Ioannina is generous and doesn't overload the visitor with superfluous images, which in any case will fade. It offers a picture of an already-forgotten city. It leaves a little ball of cotton in the visitor's memory.

Costas is coming here to get me at two o'clock. It's easier for him. He has some errands to run downtown. He's going to take me to Amphissa in his car, then turn around right away and get back to Ioannina late. He doesn't want to be gone any longer. We'll make a detour to see the Acheron.

"You'll be disappointed," he warns me. "It's just a stream."

He's much more interested in visiting the Necromanteion, the oracle of death, since he hasn't had a chance to see it yet. It was discovered not long ago, on a hill near the Acheron.

It's Wednesday today. I got to Ioannina the day before yesterday. I planned to stay a while longer, but Costas wants to make the trip today, when the pharmacy is closed. I won't come back to Ioannina. I'll visit Amphissa, then I'll go on to Delphi.

Sometimes I think that if it hadn't happened on a Wednesday, if I hadn't had so much trouble finding a pharmacy open, if I'd run a little faster .... All night long, a neighbor woman I didn't know sat on the second step of the stairway reading psalms. She read by the light of a candle I'd placed on the chest, beside the telephone. There was no other light in the room. I walked by my mother from time to time, but without looking at her. The tranquility from around her touched me gently each time. The air surrounding her was light, as if she were sleeping. Her presence was a great kindness.

The other women were all gathered in the kitchen. They spoke very little. I made coffee and tea for them. When the sun rose, I made breakfast for everyone. I spent the greater part of the night in my parents' bedroom with Vaguelio. We sat on either side of the sewing machine. My father was trying to sleep in the room next door. We were drinking vodka. We hadn't drunk much, maybe a half bottle. I looked at the naked box spring of the bed, the Paris map, and the mark I'd made on the wall, below the map, to show where I live now.

Although I knew a lot of people in Ano Patissia, when I went out the next morning to buy a few things, I met only strangers, mostly young people. Even the grocer was a stranger.

"I'm not new here," he said. "I took over the shop three months ago."

I still had the impression that the neighborhood's population had changed. The woman who read the psalms was certainly among the new arrivals. I had the feeling that several years had passed in a single night.

I rub my cheek, my chin. My head is smaller since I shaved. It's the size of a melon. I touch a face that really isn't familiar to me. I was disappointed in the image that appeared before my eyes after I'd cut my beard. My chin seemed tiny and my lips overly thick. I noticed wrinkles on my neck. Not for a second did I think about the child I once was. I quickly turned my back to the mirror.

Vasso looked at me as if she were seeing a ghost.

"You're unrecognizable!"

But it was Costas who was the most surprised. I was preparing the *youvarlakia* when he came home. I had just put a lump of butter into the soup. I was watching it melt, like I used to. I was rather happy with the results: the smell from the pot was familiar. Costas was speechless when he came into the kitchen. I attributed his reaction to the memories that the smell reawakened in him.

"It's unbelievable how much you look like her!"

"Don't exaggerate," said Vasso. "He certainly does look a bit like your mother . . . ."

I hadn't detected any resemblance to her at all in the mirror.

"For the first few months after my father died," Vasso continued, "I thought that Apostolos looked remarkably like him. But little by little he stopped reminding me of him. Maybe because I was starting to forget him."

"We've reached an age where no one still has both parents," I thought.

"You sometimes use the same words she used," Costas told me.

"Maybe I imitate her without realizing it."

I could see my father sitting in the armchair where she used to sit. "We've divided up her role, just like we divided up her sweaters."

Anna thinks I look better without the beard, that I look younger. I gave her my electric razor as I was leaving, to give to Miltiade.

"Why?" she asked.

"No reason."

I don't plan on staying long in Amphissa. Tomorrow evening I'll be in Delphi. How many days will I spend there? They'll pass quickly and I'll find myself back in Athens without having shed any light on that period, without having made any decisions. How long will I go on pacing in my apartment? Maybe I'm wrong to go to Delphi. The shrine gave me a mystery. Maybe it will take it back once I'm there. "I'm going to Delphi not to find something, but to lose something." That thought relieves me, almost amuses me. I'll see the statue of the smiling little girl that my mother liked and I'll find a moment when the guard isn't looking to touch the archaic omphalos marked with the strange E. I'll notice that time has already marked the face of Antinous. He was unearthed a hundred years ago. Not one of the workers photographed with him would be alive today. Then I'll go to the village café and try to start up a conversation with the Delphians. They, too, will tell me some words whose first letter is E that I'll write down or not write down. The sun will be setting. Through the café's window I'll see the immense cliff that surrounds the shrine and occasionally bombards it with rocks. Its red color, apparently, is due to the iron oxide that it contains. It will be a very bright red at sunset. I'll see the shadow of night climb up it and slowly arrive at the top. Finally there will be just one point of light, looking like it's suspended in the nighttime landscape. I'll wait until it disappears as well. The Delphians — there won't be a single woman among them — will turn their chairs toward the television. They'll watch the news. I didn't find out what became of the Albanian who'd climbed the utility pole. I'll pay the check and I'll leave. I'll take the bus back to Athens. The Delphi chapter will be over. I won't have anything else to write. Maybe I'll read the words in my notebook one last time. The epsilon will be a dead letter.

It's still alive, for the moment. I feel its presence, like Costas sees Margarita's silhouette everywhere. Maybe its silence could be compared to the silence of psychoanalysts, but it's hard for me to say because I've never had any contact with them. Do I still hope to discover something? I wrote down the word *elpida*, hope, that Fanny proposed, as well as *ecclissia*, which I stole from Penelope. Once long ago, the word meant an assembly, large or small, which met regularly. Many texts talk about the *ecclissia* of the members of the amphictyony. What word could I give my father? Costas chose the word *éros*, love, for himself. Could the dying man in the engraving used to illustrate the letter E in the *Treasures of the Greek Language* be their author, Henri Estienne? I wrote down *étimothanatos* and the cry of distress *é é*. The example I chose to accompany the interrogative "if," *ei apodèmein*, is about emigration. I'd nonetheless like to keep one whole page for that word. I've spent most of my life in foreign lands. Most of my friends in Paris are foreigners. I've done several cartoons these last few years on racism. Nowadays, xenophobia is everywhere. You can feel it in legal decisions concerning French citizens of foreign origins, in comments by sports announcers about the French national soccer team, in the look the television anchor gives the Arab Muslim he had to invite because of today's news. He looks upon him with suspicion, tries to flush out the fundamentalist which is bound to be hiding within him, cuts him off when he's speaking. Unfortunately, neither foreigner (*xénos*) nor emigrant (*xénitéménos*) begins with E. It is true that the word "émigré" is also used more and more frequently in Greek (they say *énas émigrès*), but I'm not sure that the language has officially adopted it. So I prefer to write *ekpatrisménos*, expatriate.

While I was shaving, I thought of the word *bamterlélé*. According to Costas, it's a comical deformation of the French expression "*barbe Napoléon III*," "Napoleon III beard." It is indeed exactly that beard that's called a *bamterlélé* in Greek. On the other hand, he couldn't tell me why Stamata is named "Stop:" to whom was the command addressed? And what were they telling him to stop doing? He told me that the name is sometimes given to a girl, in hopes that the mother will have a boy, next time.

The landscape is starting to appear. The fog is lifting. First I see the tops of trees along the lakeshore, then the motor boats tied to the quay. The fog lifts quickly from the whole landscape, unveiling the lake and its shores, the houses built around it, and a small forest. The tableau becomes unbelievably huge, a chain of mountains appears before my eyes, and I see Mitsikeli for the first time. The sun finally appears, giving a metallic gleam to the still waters where then the island miraculously appears. The fog keeps disappearing, fleeing through the mountains that block the horizon. The spectacle would thrill me even more if I didn't know what the sudden disappearance of the fog is likely to mean for certain people.

About twenty kilometers from Ioannina, to the left of the highway, I recognized the stable I'd seen on television. I asked Costas to stop. There was no one around to tell me what had become of the Albanian. At the top of the pole near the power lines, just where two iron bars crossed, a piece of yellow cloth was caught. "His shirt ripped when they were trying to pull him down." Costas stayed in the car, listening to *Il Trovatore*. I rang the doorbell of the only house nearby, but no one answered. The stable door was locked with a nice brass padlock. Before getting back in the car, I cast a last glance at the scrap of cloth floating up there like the flag of misfortune.

"Caterina gave me this opera," said Costas.

I have *Il Trovatore* in Paris, too, but no one gave it to me. I couldn't remember Caterina any more than I could remember that former classmate Fanny told me about.

"Were you in love with Caterina?"

"I think so .... Anyway, I went to a lot of trouble to seduce her .... Do you understand what they're saying there?"

He turned up the music. It was the beginning of the gypsy song.

"They're wondering what makes gypsy life so wonderful and in chorus they all answer 'la zingarella," the gypsy woman."

"I know," I said. "Do you remember the stories she used to tell us?"

He didn't answer. A bit later, he turned down the music. White, hard light was crushing the landscape. I closed my eyes. Now and then I took a puff on my pipe, thinking about nothing.

"I remember a well. A well and three sisters."

"And one of them falls in the well?"

"The most beautiful one, I think .... She wakes up in another world."

"Is it a sinister place?"

"No, not at all. But it's far away. She wants to go home. It's really very far away. I think maybe I'm confusing two stories, because the place is at the top of the world. She can't come down from it without the help of an eagle."

The center of the world was found thanks to two eagles Zeus sent flying from its farthest boundaries. They met at Delphi, just like my father's two convicts meet at the station in Santa Fe. The eagles didn't tear one another apart: they landed quietly on an egg-shaped rock that from then on became the navel of the world.

"Were the sisters princesses?"

"Maybe .... Or maybe they were poor ... Maybe they were poor girls who became princesses."

"I don't remember it at all." Archeologists usually find only the bases of statues. They have cylindrical cavities where the iron that held the statues was fastened. Archeologists linger over those holes, study them, query them about works of art that have disappeared. For me, it's sometimes as difficult to remember the past, as if all that remained were a row of little round black holes. Just at the moment when I was thinking about my poor memory, I remembered that in one of the stories someone was leaving on a long journey.

"Someone had to go somewhere to look for something," I said. "There were pitfalls all along his path."

"Of course! 'Days passed, time passed, and he kept walking,' mama used to say. The journey took months, even years. But he always came back. He came back when no one was expecting him anymore."

"I've waited too long to come back. When you wait too long, it's as if you never came back at all." Manrico, the troubadour, was singing "Addio, Leonora, addio!" I think they throw him in prison, finally.

"You know what else I remember?" he continued. "A big bird that protects a traveler from the sun by flying above his head."

I say that there's a similar scene in the adventure tale that our father is telling the neighbor ladies. I relate the episode I know.

"I don't think he would've borrowed the idea from mama. They didn't tell each other their stories. Mama pretended not to know about papa's taste for telling tales. She was convinced that it could hurt his work at the bank. 'Do you know a lot of tellers who say everything that comes into their heads,' she used to ask him. 'Do you want people to think you're a wise guy?'"

"It was the bird himself who took the initiative to move from one story to the other," I thought. "He went off to the United States to protect Pim after flying over France. It was his shadow that I saw flash across the main court during a match at Roland-Garros. He was heading to the United States to protect Pim." I was suddenly aware of my recent interest in birds. The ancient Greeks perceived signs of the future in their flight. It seemed like the ones I'd thought about related more to the past. I remembered one of the cartoons I'd done for *Embros Sunday* showed a bird flying fast over a grave. "I should have drawn the bird's shadow on the grave." The opera had ended. I went to sleep in spite of myself.

"Here's the Acheron," said Costas.

I looked around me and saw nothing but cultivated fields, reeds, bushes, and, through the car's back window, a hill.

"Get out and you'll see."

I saw it as I opened the car door. It was just below us. We were on a little wooden bridge. I could see the water through the spaces between the planks. Both ends of the bridge were obscured by the weeds and reeds growing along the banks of the stream. It was totally insignificant. It couldn't have been more than three meters wide.

"But why did they need a boat to cross it?"

"I think it's wider elsewhere, when it joins two other streams, the Black and the Mute."

I thought those names were well suited to tributaries of the Acheron—its name means "unsightly." We decided to visit the Necromanteion, which was nearby, before going in search of that confluence. We drove the car to the top of the hill. Hades and Persephone, the rulers of the dead, were lodged in one of the shrine's underground rooms. They had quite a crowd of visitors that afternoon. A bus and several cars were parked in front of the archeological site. A chapel built in the midst of the ruins served as a reminder that monks had taken over the site. What's left of the shrine are walls as much as several meters thick, forming cramped rooms where pilgrims, shut up in total darkness, prepared themselves morally to meet the deceased person of their choice. They were given fresh broad beans to eat that are said to bring about mental confusion. That's the second time I've heard that vegetable associated with an oracle — I remember that the Pythia used beans like dice. There were secret passages inside those Cyclopean walls, making it easier for the priests to set the stage. Archeologists have recovered pieces of machinery that may have allowed the idol representing death to spring up in front of the already-disoriented visitor. That scene must have taken place above the room of Hades and Persephone. We visited it with a Greek couple. We went down a great number of stairs. We came out into a long, vaulted, silent room. Although there was nothing special to see, we stayed there a good while, as if we were hoping that the silence would eventually say something to us. We suddenly heard the very faint ringing of a telephone. The woman took a cell phone from her purse.

"Hello?" she said, in a tiny voice.

She looked really upset. She gave us an apologetic look. The man with her also seemed to deplore the incident.

"I can't talk from here .... I'll call you later .... I'm in a place where you can't talk .... I'll explain later."

She ended the call. In the next few hours, the sentence "I'm in a place where you can't talk" came back to me several times.

It was really difficult to find the confluence of three streams — two, really, since the Black and the Mute join before they meet the Acheron. An endless plain, partly cultivated and partly arid, extends from the hill that shelters the Oracle of the Dead and the sea. The very few roads crossing it are almost impassable for a car and aren't marked at all. But we took a track that seemed to go in the direction of the Acheron. We guessed where the stream was from the vegetation all along its flow. Sometimes we got closer to it, other times farther away. After a few kilometers we were stopped by a hill barring our way. We realized that we'd lost track of the stream. We left the car and continued on foot. We crossed several fields, inspected all the brush and the shrubbery in the area, without finding the Acheron. We looked behind us: we couldn't see the hill anymore, or the car either, for that matter. The colors of the landscape had begun to change. They hadn't gotten darker, but you could already see that they were about to. "We're inside a children's story and we don't know what happens next."

"What should we do?" I asked.

"Shall we turn around?"

The farmer coming toward us put an end to our hesitation. He was quite stout, and walked clumsily.

"What are you doing here?" he asked gruffly.

We were on his land. He told us that the edge of the next field where the Black joined the Acheron was his as well. Did he know that his property was located on the very border of the great beyond? We didn't think it was a good idea to broach the subject. He let us continue on our way and he went on his.

We didn't find the illustrious wood of poplars and willows sacred to Persephone where Ulysses met his mother's shade, according to Homer. The landscape doesn't really look like the one described by the poet. We didn't see the cave that gives access to the kingdom of the dead. We didn't see a single rock.

We did, nonetheless, glimpse a few willows and some clumps of brush at the far end of the second field. The brush became thicker as we went on. We had trouble getting through the last few meters.

The Acheron is dark green, with spots of black under the trees leaning over it. It's a good fifteen meters across at this point. It wasn't covered with mist. We could see the far bank very clearly. I had supposed that its color would be brighter at noon, but I couldn't even imagine it in such light. "The Acheron doesn't take on its true color until the sun sets." Its waters were perfectly calm, even at the spot fifty meters to our right where it joined the Black. The two streams meet quietly, like old friends who don't have much to say to each other.

We smoked. We didn't see anyone on the other side. We didn't see any movement at all. I thought once again of what the woman had said: "I'm in a place where you can't talk." I have never accepted my mother's silence. Sometimes I'm angry with her for not contacting me, as if death weren't enough of an excuse. Her silence doesn't bother me any less when I'm in Paris, because she used to call me often. My reproaches to her are absurd: "Why in the world haven't you called? Did you lose my number? Did you forget?" I imagine the afterlife as a country that is far away, yes, but where you can make a call from time to time. It was fairly easy to accept that I wouldn't see her anymore. I'm resigned to the distance, but not to the silence. Her death reminded me of all the questions I hadn't had time to ask her, all the subjects we hadn't discussed yet. I noticed simultaneously that we couldn't talk anymore and that we had a lot of things to tell one another.

We walked a few steps along the bank. Costas was the first one to see it:

"Look," he said.

Across from us, tied to a tree, was a small, shallow, flat-bottomed boat. It was painted green, which is no doubt why we hadn't see it earlier. It wasn't as bold a green as the stream, but more of an almond green.

We didn't talk much before Amphissa. We stopped only twice, in Agrinio for gas and in Naupactos to eat kebabs. I paged through the most recent issue of *Épirotika*, where there's a large lexicon of the local dialect. The woman who grants her sexual favors readily is called *apalomounida*, "with silky genitals," a very beautiful woman *héliogéni*, "born of the sun." The cemetery is also called *thaphtiko*, "the place where they bury," rather like "burial ground." I liked the word *aka*, which means "no." My mother's father, the one who died on the Albanian front in the last war, came from Zitsa, a village in the Ioannina district. His name was Vryzalas.

I had the idea of making space for colors in my notebook. When drawing, I spend a great deal of time looking at them before choosing one. It seemed to me that there wasn't a color whose name started with an epsilon, but I finally remembered that red is also called *érythro*. I remembered one of the games Vaguelio and I had made up and played.

"Bring me something red," I would say to her.

She would bring me a sock, a bottle of red wine. I remembered the red floor of a kitchen my aunt had crossed bare-breasted — she was wearing a towel around her hips. There was no link whatsoever among the things that came to mind: I thought about the dark red of the eggs at Easter, the funereal red of Rava Noora's earrings, the tears drying on my mother's cheeks as she looked at the two birds on the terrace, the red mark in the center of the railroad in the United States. My thoughts led me to the red of the rocks around Delphi, as if to remind me of the goal of my trip.

But they didn't stop at Delphi. I remembered an enormous moon appearing from behind a cliff in the Peloponnesus. I was traveling with Vaguelio. She was driving. The road ran along the foot of a mountain that rose straight up on our left, hiding half the sky. We hadn't noticed that the moon had risen and we couldn't even suspect that it had, since it was still daylight. On a curve where the road moved a little away from the mountain, we literally saw it leap up in front of us, then at the same lightning speed, hide again behind the rocks. We had the distinct impression that the moon had moved, that it wanted to have a look at the road, as if it'd been expecting us and was beginning to lose patience. Vaguelio braked violently and the motor stalled. We agreed that the threatening apparition boded nothing good. Vaguelio's stepfather was in the hospital then, as was my mother. We wondered which of us the warning was meant for. A few months later, we understood that it was meant for both of us. Every prediction is right, if you just give it time to come true.

Vaguelio was right not to trust me. I thought about Christina. The summer hadn't yet come. It was rather cool outside. Nonetheless she wanted to swim. Her bathing suit had a pattern of fruits in bright colors, including a pineapple on her crotch. I sat on the beach and waited. The day was coming to an end. The shadow of the rocks surrounding the beach was advancing toward us. We made love on the sand. We wanted to finish before the sun disappeared. The shadow came close. We saw it cover our things.

"It won't go any farther," said Christina.

And indeed, it didn't move any more. Christina claimed later that we'd postponed sunset by five minutes.

"Maybe we have problems because we don't know how to keep our hands busy," said Costas. "Unlike feet, eyes, and ears, hands don't have any well-defined role to play. We have to give them a goal, find something for them to do. We learn a trade to keep our hands busy. We learn to drive for the same reason. The pockets of our jackets, worry beads, and cigarettes let us solve the problem temporarily. The ideal pastime is provided by the female body. If we didn't have that problem, we wouldn't fall in love."

He said all that in a cheerful tone, all but the last sentence. He fell silent again. We weren't very far from Amphissa now. Night had fallen. We met a few hares, who looked into the car's headlights for a moment, but who got out of the way in time.

"She went to Thassalonica on my birthday. I'm fifty years old, Pavlos."

He grimaced.

"Fifty," he repeated.

He let the truck pass, the one that had been following us for a while. He had slowed the car down. I was glad, since I didn't want our tête-à-tête to end. I supposed he wasn't in a hurry either.

"I haven't lived much," he said. "I feel that time is charging me far too much for the little I've lived. My age wrongs me. Heraclitus compares time to a child playing dice just for fun. You can't expect fairness from a child, much less from a throw of the dice .... Margarita said that she didn't think our age difference was important .... But she also said a lot of other things that were probably untrue .... I feel like even the memories I have of that affair have been taken from me."

It occurred to me that Heraclitus Street, in Kolonaki, would now always remind me of a child playing dice.

"You'll forget her. You'll forget her phone number. The numbers fade one by one. I think they start fading from the end. In a few months, you'll only remember the first two numbers."

"That's what Lena tells me .... It disturbs me to cause them any pain, to her and to Vasso .... And don't think that Vasso hasn't noticed anything, she knows me .... The princesses in the stories were usually very beautiful .... Maybe I'm nostalgic for the time when my nights were filled with beautiful princesses .... We fall in love with inaccessible, unreal women. I remember a gentle white horse, a long dress embroidered with stars, the mother-of-pearl door of a castle .... We love women who hold the keys to fantastic worlds where the most ordinary sounds are particularly sweet."

We found an old three-story hotel on a square. He asked the woman at the desk to make him some coffee for his Thermos. We sat down in the lobby to wait. We talked a bit about our father, but distractedly — his imminent departure meant that we couldn't concentrate.

The woman soon had his coffee ready. I went to the car with Costas.

"I hope that she calls you," I said.

"And that she tells me she loves me, naturally."

His smile was both ironic and infinitely sad.

"Naturally."

The Museum of Arts and Folk Traditions in Amphissa is located near the cathedral—a commemorative marble plaque says that it was miraculously spared during the bombardments of the last war — on a little street with a butcher shop, the Good Heart café, an agricultural products shop, and the Modelino boutique, which sells wedding dresses and baptismal gifts. It's closed right now, but the owner of my hotel, Mr. Bouras, who's a member of the local folklore study society, will open it for me. The museum has no employees and no revenue. It was created by nostalgic private individuals who are in love with their town. Three orthodox priests get into a car down the street. Finally I see Mr. Bouras with a tall girl following him.

"This is my wife," he tells me. "We were married in September."

He's certainly older than Costas. She lowers her eyes. She's wearing a very elegant dress. A certain disorder reigns in the entrance to the museum, where all sorts of things are piled up: professional tools, kitchen utensils, harnesses, and even an old radio transmitter. In the next rooms, objects are much better organized and are accompanied by explanatory labels. They remind the visitor of craftsmen who have almost completely disappeared, like the tanner and the bell maker, but also the rope maker (I've learned that rope was once among the city's main industries), the farrier, the tinsmith, the barrel maker. I see several rows of bells and chimes arranged by size. I don't feel like an outsider here. We go to the second floor, while the girl stays downstairs in a little office. From the top of the stairs, I look at the bric-a-brac collected at the entrance: my memory must look something like that. I've already told my guide that my grandmother worked in a tannery. I think that's what convinced him to open the museum for me. I would be curious to experience the horrible smell of the mixture they used to soak skins in, but none of the few remaining tanners uses dog turds. So what do the inhabitants of Amphissa do today? They work in technical areas. They work in the Parnassus bauxite quarries. And what inhabitants, for that matter? Most have left.

"We're one of the regions with the lowest population densities in the country, fewer than twenty people per square kilometer. Do you know what that means?"

I look at the old store signs that are leaning against the wall, one against the other. They're made of wood or zinc. I lean them out toward me, resting them against my knee.

"I hope you still produce oil and olives."

"Not so much anymore. Everyone makes the oil he needs. It's not profitable. The majority of people would pull up their olive trees, if the state would allow it. Olive groves are protected, since they're part of the Delphic landscape."

Now I know why my mother sometimes had trouble finding olives from Amphissa.

"They're the charm of our lives, those olive groves. It's only right to protect them. But they're turning purely decorative."

Suddenly, before my eyes is the sign for that bell maker my mother talked about: "Chez Liszt." It's the next to last in the stack, written in yellow script letters on a brown background. From the ground floor we hear the young woman's voice: "I'm going to run a few errands!"

"She's twenty-five," Mr. Bouras tells me confidentially, "I'm fifty-six.... But she's a poet!"

I don't understand what he means: do poets have a different concept of time? Do they enjoy some sort of precocious maturity? It pains me to leave the sign where it is. I would willingly steal it.

He knows that I'm supposed to take the noon bus. He doesn't think much of the Delphians, the only rich inhabitants of the region.

"They're terrible misers, to start with," he tells me.

Like most of the rich, Delphians don't give. They've never given away anything, for that matter. He reminds me that they sent Philip of Macedonia to punish the inhabitants of Amphissa because they'd tried to farm the sacred plain.

"The Delphians' selfishness cost us everything. Philip devastated our city from top to bottom. Our blood was spilled!"

He's as upset as if he himself had witnessed the scene of the disaster. I get the feeling that the blood spilled twenty-three centuries ago still hasn't dried. He does admit, however, that the Delphians never stole or sold antiquities. We go back downstairs into the little office, where he shows me the journal of the folklore study society and some other cultural publications, the *Phocidian Letters* and the *Phocidian Journal*, pamphlets on superstitions, on children's games, on the local figures who played a role in the uprising of 1821. He also has Macriyannis' *Memoirs*. I think once again of my mother, who was proud of the intellectual level of her hometown. Publishing does seem very active for a city of six thousand inhabitants. I buy all the journals I can carry in my hands, along with the general's *Memoirs*, which I hope to finally read. He wants to give me some of the copies, but I prefer to pay for everything. I do allow him to give me a collection of his wife's poems, entitled *Nights*.

"I have to show you one more thing," he tells me.

It's a woolen embroidery hung in the stairwell. The colors are pale. A shepherd and a shepherdess are gazing into one another's eyes. At first glance, it's of no interest.

"Look closely at their eyes," he says. "The woman who created it wanted to make the eyes of the lovers really lifelike, and didn't use wool for them, but her own hair, which was black."

I look more carefully at the image. The eyes of the lovers are shining, as if with tears.

The little plate contains one fried shrimp, a bite of roasted meat, a piece of beef tongue, a piece of sausage, and a roasted potato. I'm drinking ouzo on the terrace of a café on the square. I asked the waiter to bring me a few olives too. I don't want to leave here without tasting the olives of Amphissa.

The publications that I bought at the museum are on the next chair and they make a rather tall stack. The shadow of my glass falls on my manuscript and it's light, transparent, luminous. My text pushes me back imperceptibly, keeps me away, as if it no longer needed my services, as if it could go its own way without me.

I've glanced at the kiosk down the sidewalk a dozen times, but it's only now that I see the *New Humanist* displayed among the foreign magazines. On its cover, I recognize the two-handled amphora I drew. The brick red I had used to outline the Europeans isn't very well reproduced, the color is more of a mustard yellow — I think about Greek mustard, slightly darker than the Dijon kind. The server just brought me the olives. I count five of them, big and shining. In the little bit of oil in the bottom of the plate there's a drop of vinegar.

"I don't want any of your savory olives!" she used to say.

I won't buy olives here, since with a bit of luck I can find the same ones in Athens. I already have too much to carry. But perhaps I'll write the word *élia*, olive tree. I don't see what other word I can borrow from here. I imagine that my mother must have strolled in the olive groves. Time doesn't sound the same everywhere. Here, its passage is marked by the rustling of olive leaves. I try to see the reflection of the square on the olives. I glimpse something, some movement. I look up: a girl is going by on her bicycle.

I walk as far as the kiosk. I can hear the sound of the cockroach I crunched while leaving the café in Kolonaki. How long ago was that? Even though the printer didn't do the red very well, the black of the vase is perfect. The crested helmet I put on the Greek makes him look taller than the other Europeans. Once, I felt immense joy when I saw one of my cartoons published. Time has reduced both the intensity and the duration of that pleasure. I open the magazine as I resume my place at the café table. The pages all look blank in the bright sunlight. I have trouble reading even the headlines. The first article, just after the editor's letter signed by Véronique Carrier, is about a series of economic scandals, misappropriations of funds and influence peddling that compromises some well-known political figures. One minister is already jailed. I imagine the members of the French government dressed like convicts and holding meetings in a prison visiting room. The plate brought with the second ouzo isn't bad either: there are four meatballs, a tomato cut into fourths, and a roasted potato *The New Humanist* slides off and falls on the sidewalk.

"Could you bring me some bread?" I ask the waiter.

The bus terminal is on the other side of the square. "In a few moments, I'll put all my magazines in my bag and cross the square." I see the bus for Delphi. It's still empty.

The funeral took place the next day, a Thursday like today, in the afternoon. At noon I bought all the newspapers where I'd had the obituary printed. The most important news I've ever read in the press was undoubtedly that short text which began with "Our beloved . . . ." I don't really know how things happened after the ceremony in the church. We didn't have to carry the coffin. I saw it sitting on the ground next to the open grave. It was light-colored wood. On the other side of the grave was a mound of earth. The older of the two gravediggers seemed in a hurry. The younger one looked at us with curiosity. We had formed a circle of about fifty people, maybe more. I don't remember the woman who stood in front of me, just her coat, which was blue. Someone had asked that they open the casket, one of my father's sisters I think. I understood that it was customary to open it before placing it in the ground. I moved in front of the woman in the blue coat, but I didn't go much closer. Costas went to kiss her. My father did the same. I stayed a certain distance away. Maybe I wanted to retain the image I had of her. I only saw her face from afar. Other people had approached the casket.

"She's beautiful, isn't she?" Costas said to me.

He wasn't crying. I'd seen him cry a few minutes earlier, while hugging Lena. Vasso was there too, and Fanny, and Theodoris with Marilena, and Yogarakis the actor, and Stelios the photographer, and a few distant relatives I hadn't seen in years. The older gravedigger was just about to close the casket.

"Just a minute," said my father. "I want to say something to her."

Everyone stopped talking. It was then that I realized the concrete building beyond the cemetery wall, partially hidden by cypress trees, was the soccer stadium where I used to go as a child.

"I remember the first time I held your hand. It's been a long time, hasn't it? Over fifty years. Maybe you've forgotten. It was Mardi Gras, and we were in the country, outside of Athens. A man who worked for your father was flying a kite, tied to a stick. He had you hold it, but it slipped out of your hands. I managed to grab it and I started rolling up the string by turning the stick in a circle. 'That's how you roll up the string,' I told you. I must have been trying to look erudite, since you started laughing ... .I dropped the stick too and the kite carried everything off, disappeared into the sky, the employee started yelling, but when he saw that I was holding your hand he stopped talking and left us alone."

His voice was steady. He was standing, nearly straight, beside the casket.

"You chided me sometimes for not showing my feelings. 'But there are things that you can't say,' I told you, 'or at least that I can't say.' You claimed that things that can't be said don't exist .... I wanted to talk to you in the hospital too, but something always kept me from doing it .... I wanted to thank you for keeping me company for so many years, my dear Marika."

He took a few mimosas wrapped in paper from his pocket and placed them between her hands. Then he kissed her hands. I noticed that the young gravedigger was touched. I saw the Orthodox priest, standing behind the family circle, check his watch.

"Don't be sad," he told her. "Everything will be alright. I'll take care of everything. I want you to be at peace. It won't be long before we see one another again. I'll find you. I'll look right, left, and I'll find you eventually, and what happiness that will be, what happiness ...."

His voice was breaking. The gravedigger placed the cover on the casket.

I stand up. I put my things in my bag. I can already see a few passengers on the bus for Delphi.

8.

This place is halfway between the sky and the earth. Its altitude is only five hundred seventy meters, but the slope below the village and the archeological site is so steep that it gives the feeling of being high above the earth. The eye moves down the slope covered with olive trees, pauses at the foot of the mountain opposite with its stream, moves downhill to the right, and ends up on the immense olive tree forest extending all the way to the horizon, where other mountains form lovely curves. The sea is hidden by the mountain opposite it. Only a tiny piece of it can be seen, shimmering at the far edge of the olive trees: framed on all sides by the landscape, it looks like a lake. "This is a place where the sea can and cannot be seen." Cypress trees spring up everywhere among the olives. They're easy to see because they're so dark. It looks like the landscape is punctuated with exclamation points. The sky, unlike the earth, is very near. It seems to rest on the cliffs. They form a kind of amphitheater behind the shrine and are very high. Their color gives the sky a strange intensity. The sky doesn't go unnoticed here. The ceiling of Apollo's temple was blue, red, and gold.

Those rocks have a name. They are called the Phaedriades, the Shining Ones. That's more like their family name. They also have a first name: Phlemboukos, the Flaming, and Rodini, the Red. From the gap between them flow the waters of the Castalian Spring, running down toward the road. I drank a little of that water so celebrated by poets, hoping that it would give me the inspiration indispensable to any talk of Delphi.

The bus left me in the village. I had to check several hotels to find a room. The main street bears the name of Apollo. The hotels, the restaurants, and the tourist shops are named the Pythia, the Dionysus (he filled in for Apollo, who went on vacation in the winter), the Charioteer, the Antinous, the Castalia, the Phaedriades, the Parnassus. Their signs are a good orientation for the visit. I ended up in the Hotel Python, named in memory of the serpent Apollo slew when he settled in Delphi. It isn't certain whether the Pythia's name comes from that snake. Nor is it certain that Delphi is from *delphini*, the dolphin. We can only note that Apollo liked to transform into a dolphin from time to time. They gave me room 8. I would have preferred 5, because of the epsilon, but it wasn't available.

"We have a Danish couple in room 5," said the receptionist.

I didn't do much the first afternoon. I just strolled to the ruins, about two kilometers from the village. I followed the road that cuts the site in two, but not into equal parts, since most of the important ruins are on the higher side. Downhill is the illustrious marble rotunda, but there are also enormous blocks of stone that have fallen from the Phaedriades. I knew that Phlemboukos and Rodini had a taste for destruction, but I didn't know that they used such huge cannonballs. It isn't just natural phenomena that threaten the site: car exhaust and the vibrations from passing vehicles are speeding up its deterioration.

I was completely serene, as if certain that this place would answer all of the questions it had inspired in me. Not far away, I saw the theater and the six columns of the Temple of Apollo. Only one of them has been completely restored and given back its capital. The columns are grouped near the entrance to the temple, where the epsilon was hung. A crowd of tourists covered the Sacred Way and walked nonchalantly along the highway, where dozens of buses were parked. The number of visitors is estimated at one million per year. It occurred to me that Plutarch would have been delighted to see such a crowd. Apparently Apollo has found a new audience. The oracle's popularity could be compared to the first centuries of its existence. I tried to imagine the tourists dressed differently, without cameras. I tried to breathe into them the excitement that ancient pilgrims must have felt. But I couldn't transform them: the constant stream of passing cars didn't make it easy.

Right away I found the café where the locals go. It was the only one on the main street that didn't try to attract tourists. The light was so dim that it looked closed. I sat in the back near a window. I could see the plain and the sea, but not the Phaedriades. The television was on. The only woman in the place was the waitress. I thought about Flaubert, who claimed that Delphian men were better looking than Delphian women. Did he really get the chance to see a lot of Delphian women? The walls, covered in a nondescript wood, were decorated with black and white photos of the Acropolis, of Karamanlis, of Sikelianos, and of an American by the name of Cook, wearing the local costume. I learned that he'd spent the better part of his life here, and that he'd been poisoned. Several Greek flags and an American flag were in a glass on top of the television. The clock on the wall had stopped at a quarter to two. I learned that Sikelianos had had an intense sex life. He often drank a broth made from roosters, reputed to increase ardor. I also learned that Delphians vote mostly for the right. There had been terrible massacres in the region during the civil war. I don't think they'll be forgotten anytime soon. During the Occupation, since radios were confiscated, someone with a megaphone announced the news from atop a mountain.

I started up conversations easily. I talked first with the waitress, who's about seventy. She confirmed that "nearly" all Delphians are rich. Many families have two or three cars. The young aren't very interested in their studies, since their future is guaranteed. Tourism, which began to develop in the 1950s, changed life radically. Livestock farming has been completely abandoned. Couples are separating more and more often. Several villagers have married foreign women who moved here: Americans, English women, New Zealanders. Those mixed couples are among the most stable. The waitress worked on the archeological digs before the last war.

"We all worked on the digs," she said. "The men did the digging, and the women carried away the dirt in baskets. Our workday ended when the shadow reached the top of the Phaedriades."

In the Antinous photograph, two baskets are visible. And yet no women posed with the workers. She knew Alexandre Condoléon, the nit-picking supervisor of the dig.

"'I'm certain that you won't steal anything,' he'd tell us, 'because people don't steal from themselves.' He was particularly fond of the Charioteer. One day he put his own straw hat on the statue and had it photographed. He called the Charioteer 'my boy,' he used to say 'I'm going to see my boy today.'"

Other people joined in the conversation. They assured me that their attachment to antiquities wasn't based solely on the money they bring in. When the Minister of Culture decided to send the Charioteer to the United States, the people rose up, the prefect brought in police from Amphissa and blood was nearly spilled once again. In the end the riot was avoided when the Minister reconsidered his decision. I tell them that I'm writing a study of the Pythia.

"They call us 'the Pythias' in the surrounding villages," said the waitress. "'I'm going to go see the Pythias,' they say. They make fun of us. They insinuate that we never say anything clearly, that we like to complicate things."

I asked them if there was still a fortuneteller or a woman who could read coffee grounds in the village. They were miffed, as if I'd asked them to introduce me to a prostitute. So no, there isn't one. It seemed to me that the waitress wasn't as categorical as the others. "I'll have to ask her again when she's alone." She hesitated, but did tell me that women used to read beans.

"Beans?" I asked, because I wanted to be sure of what she'd said.

"Yes. They spread a handful of beans on the table. They knew every bean exactly: its size, its form, its exterior. They would spend a long time studying how they were arranged on the table. They could tell whether a marriage was going to fall apart, where to find a lost object."

I saw the Pythia in my mind shaking her bowl to see which of the beans fell out. Was it the black bean or the white bean that brought a negative answer? "Probably the black one." The beans made me think of Homeric words that have made it through to us intact. I'm enchanted by words, customs, and myths that survive. They seem to be blessed by eternity, seem to belong to a world of marvels. I always write down analogies between the present and the past. Macriyannis — I read him on the bus — says that when he was publicly humiliated in his youth he went to the chapel of Saint John Prodromos, near Delphi, and asked the saint rather loudly to help him blot out the affront: "I shouted so much that he finally helped me." Macriyannis' shouts reminded me of the ancient Homeric heroes' disputes with the gods. But I don't wish to contribute to cultivating confusion between times, as we do systematically in Greece. I get the feeling that we live in an imaginary place with no perspective, outside of time, where nothing ever starts because nothing ever ends. I didn't feel any bitterness toward the Delphians who had stopped reading beans. "They finally understood that beans have no particular genius, that they're just as dumb as chickpeas."

Night, Hotel Python, room 8. A color photo of the Charioteer hangs above my bed. I asked the receptionist to wake me at seven o'clock, I want to get to the museum before the tourists arrive. I don't think statues like crowds. I think they need a certain privacy to express themselves. I spent the evening at the Castri restaurant — that was the name of the village when it was still on the site of the ruins. It went back to its original name only when it was moved to its current location. It's been called Delphi since it was transplanted and the Castrians have become Delphians. Across from the restaurant, I could see the flashing red lights of the nightclub DELPHI BY NIGHT. A few meters from me, the blind archeologist I'd seen at the French Archeological School was dining. I remembered that his name was Préaud and that he was an epigraphist. "He could no doubt tell me about the epsilon," I thought, but I didn't dare disturb him. He was eating fried eggs. On my way back to the hotel, I noticed that the village has a very large number of jewelry stores. In the window of a souvenir shop, I saw a row of satyrs with outsize erections, standing in front of a row of icons of the Blessed Virgin. Her expression seemed even sadder than usual.

The museum cashier informed me that, in accordance with a decree from Stathopoulou, admission was free for Greeks. I hadn't noticed that we'd visited the Necromanteion for free. I thought that Costas had bought tickets. I got a bit worked up: "I want to pay. I think it's well worth it."

"But I don't have any tickets for Greeks."

A security guard came over to us.

"The Minister hopes to encourage Greeks to take an interest in their heritage," he explained to me quietly. "Mrs. Stathopoulou thinks that we don't love antiquities enough and she's not mistaken about that."

"Doing away with the admission fee isn't going to make us love them more."

The cashier made a face. I thought that she probably shared my opinion. Two Greek couples had come up behind us — the men were wearing Bermuda shorts — along with a skinny little old man wearing a Panama hat. Five or six tourists were waiting in line behind me. They followed the conversation without understanding it.

"We should have to pay more than the tourists, because we're the ones responsible for the deterioration of the monuments," I continued. "I would charge three times the going price for any Athenian who visits the Acropolis!"

I expected some reaction from the Greeks, but they showed none.

"Give me a ticket like the ones you give foreigners."

"It's only natural that we don't have to pay, because these things are part of our heritage," said the little old man.

He looked toward the guard.

"This gentleman has just used the word 'heritage.' People don't pay to see their heritage. The statues are the works of our ancestors, they belong to us!"

His voice had fuzzy inflections. It sounded like it was badly tuned. I looked at him sympathetically, he reminded me vaguely of one of my teachers. "I'm not going to argue with the past."

"I agree that they belong to us, if you mean that we have more responsibilities toward them," I said to him in a friendly tone of voice. "But I refuse to see family portraits in ancient effigies. I don't see myself in them."

"What's going on up there, why aren't we moving?" said a Frenchman.

The line had gotten considerably longer.

"Give him a tourist ticket and let's get on with it," he said to the cashier.

I went toward the first room, accompanied by the little old man. He was pensive. The two couples were just behind us.

"So basically you see the relics of the past as a foreigner would see them?" he asked me in a muted voice.

"Yes .... Like a foreigner who can at least recognize a few words of the inscriptions. And I prefer to see them impartially, not as an heir or an owner would. I claim the right to find them dreadful!"

He removed his Panama hat as he entered the first room, as if he were going into a church. The two couples passed us. I heard one of the women murmur:

"If we all thought like him, we would have given our Macedonia to the Slavs a long time ago!"

The little old man must have heard the remark. As if preoccupied, he immediately asked me: "But if we aren't the descendants of our ancestors, then who are we?"

"I don't know .... I see in myself a certain resemblance to the comic figures of shadow puppet theater ... Like Yannis, the jug merchant who forgets to charge his pretty customers for his wares. Do you remember the couple who starred in the family magazine *Treasure*, tiny Zacharias and his giant wife? Maybe I'm the descendant of Zacharias and the giant woman. Did you read the adventures of Gaour, the Greek Tarzan, that came out in the 1950s? I am the son of Gaour and of Aunt Lena, who hosted the children's shows on the radio! Of the crab in the Tsitsanis song and any of the endless stream of reformed prostitutes in Greek movies!"

He looked at me carefully for a few moments. His eyes were nearly colorless.

"You argue pretty well," he said. "But you do exaggerate a bit."

I asked the security guard where I could find the statue of the smiling little girl and I went straight to it. I can't claim that I looked at it as a foreigner would. It dates from the Hellenistic period and, according to the author of the museum guide, it isn't considered a major work. She has a sweet smile and lovely cheeks that you want to stroke. I felt a certain emotion when I touched them. They were ice cold. I looked around to make sure no one had seen me. At the far end of the room, the old man was standing behind a display case, but I had the impression that it was me he was looking at.

Antinous was rather disappointing. I didn't find him a day older. He looked even younger than in the photo taken before he was cleaned. His body was slightly shiny, as if he'd just come from the bathroom. His beauty is too ostentatious. It's a beauty that shows off, that brags, that's tiresome. His forearms have never been found. It tones down the perfection of the whole statue a little and even gives his face a pained expression. Paradoxically, the missing forearms add something to the statue.

The Charioteer interested me much more. He was driving a quadriga. The horses are gone. Nonetheless, the reins are in his right hand — he has no left hand. He doesn't seem to be making any effort. Only the muscle under his elbow seems a bit strained. The thin cord holding his long tunic goes fairly deeply into the folds of the fabric. Originally he had the golden color of new bronze. His current green patina is the result of time. His eyes are made of a white material, the irises from a brown stone. I sat on the floor and continued to study him. His bare feet are exceptionally fine. What is he looking at? Maybe at the horses who've left. He's looking far away, but not as far as the line of the horizon, to a point just a bit lower. "That's the spot where he finally lost sight of the horses." He doesn't seem surprised or pained, as if he'd known all along that they'd leave. But his look is still melancholy. He's permanently discovering that to foresee an event and to see that it's already taken place are two different things. "He's a spectator resigned to time." I examined the reins. All that's left are little twisted pieces. They make an abstract pattern that looks like what you scribble when trying out a new pen. I stood up and moved a few steps, still looking at them. It looked to me like they formed a capital epsilon, but it was a crude epsilon, barely recognizable. It crossed my mind that the statue's eyes were showing me the distance that separates me from what I'm searching for. "The epsilon stands for the silence around him. It's not the first letter of a word, but of a silence that allows you to hear time passing." As I walked around the statue, I saw the reins take on other shapes. Sometimes they reminded me of a broken theta (Θ), sometimes a stretched-out lambda (Λ), sometimes a lower-case alpha (α). "The epsilon would have meant exactly the same thing had it been an alpha, a lambda, or a theta. The silence would have been the same." It occurred to me that silence sounds louder next to a vowel than it would next to a consonant. The time hadn't yet come to leave the epsilon behind. I still needed it. I wanted to take along a word from my visit to the Charioteer, a word that evokes the passage of time, beginning with an epsilon, or at least with an eta. I felt like the most appropriate one had to be the name of the statue itself, which in Greek is called *Éniochos*, the driver.

I went through the other rooms quickly, looking for the archaic omphalos. All I found was the marble one, from the Roman era. I asked the security guard, who told me that there was another one made of gray limestone on the Sacred Way.

"But that's not the one I mean!"

I showed him the photocopy of the stone inscribed with E and GA.

"We have that omphalos in storage!"

I was shocked.

"Why in storage?"

He didn't know. He told me that access to the storage rooms, located below the museum, was only granted to archeologists.

"You've got to understand that I only came here to see that stone! To read that inscription!"

On the photocopy he still had in his hand, I showed him the epsilon tipped forward.

"That doesn't look like an epsilon," he observed.

There was a break in the stream of visitors just for a moment and I glimpsed the silhouette of Préaud walking by the museum with his white cane. "He's the one who'll let me into the storage rooms." I abandoned the security guard and ran after him.

But I hesitated to speak to him when I caught up with him. He was taller than I am. He was wearing a khaki military-style shirt and stained white trousers, which flapped around his skinny legs. I didn't think he'd noticed that I was there, but he stopped and turned toward me: "Do you want something?" he asked in Greek.

I told him who was I was and what I wanted. I didn't try to hide that the epsilon had attracted my attention purely by chance or that my knowledge of classical antiquity was limited.

"But I've read a few books at the French Archeology School and spoken with François Bouchard, the librarian."

"The history of the archaic omphalos is rather funny," he said.

He walked with the same confidence I'd noticed the first time I saw him through the library windows. He turned on to a little path that led to a grilled gate. The tourists were walking toward the shrine on a different walkway, parallel to ours and lower down. We didn't go as far as the Temple of Apollo. We turned left on a steep path lined with pine trees and started to climb. He was soon out of breath and his face turned red.

"Do you see a cat?"

There was no cat.

"Usually she waits for me here.... It's the School's cat... Her name is Rodini."

We were in front of a modern building, well hidden by trees.

"I'm going to bed soon," he said. "I work nights and sleep during the day. I have the privilege of working at night, in absolute silence."

It came to me that the fried eggs he'd been eating the day before were his breakfast. We went into the house that serves as lodgings for the French archeologists. We sat in a living room with large windows and eclectic furnishings. He told me that he had been interested in the archaic omphalos from the time he arrived at Delphi. He could see perfectly back then. He had first been fascinated by the knife still stuck in a crack running from the top to the bottom of the stone, which his predecessors had not thought it worthwhile to remove. He was also surprised by traces of stucco on the omphalos. So he washed it well, which made the inscription show a little better: he noticed that the long horizontal line supported by three little vertical lines, the tipped-over E, was really two capital pi's (Π) between which an alpha was hidden. He made out the syllable "PAP." He could make out another alpha a little farther to the right. The unbalanced gamma (Γ) was a lambda (Λ) and the alpha of the word ΓΛ, the earth, was really an omicron (O) tied to an upsilon (Y), which made an "OU." What he read, finally, was "PAPALOU." Since there was a family by the name of Papaloukas in Delphi, it wasn't hard to guess that someone in that family had scratched his name into the stone. The knife wasn't very old either: 1860 was the date engraved on its blade. He thought that it had been the top stone of one of those religious shrines dedicated to a saint, like wayside crosses, that spring up along Greek roads and that it had served as the base for an iron cross.

"If you still want to see the 'archaic omphalos,' or rather the Papaloukas stone, I can take you to see it tomorrow."

He was smiling.

"I want to see it."

His story had showed me one aspect of the E that I hadn't thought of, its ironic nature. "The epsilon is making fun of archeologists," I thought. "It's having fun leading the most erudite among them into error." The deceptive E was perhaps a better expression of the Pythia and her god than the mystic letter that Plutarch commented on so seriously. I thought about the ambiguity of oracles. They say that the Pythia advised Nero to fear the seventy-third year — Cavafy mentions the warning in one of his poems. Nero was relieved, since he was still young — but the man who would overthrow him was already seventy-three .... I also thought about Sikelianos, who certainly would have known about this omphalos and who would have thought it was authentic. The metamorphosis of a venerable object into a vulgar neo-Hellenic stone seems to mock not only the romanticism of archeologists, but also the Greek nostalgia for the past. "We'll probably never find the original stone that symbolized the center of the world. We'll have to learn to live without it."

We agreed to meet the next morning at a quarter to seven in front of the museum. I gave him the name of my hotel.

"Sometimes, in winter, the fog packs into the ravines of Mount Parnassus. It looks like a gigantic serpent. I've come to think that's why your ancestors thought a dragon lived here."

I found a path behind the archeologists' house. I followed it away from the ruins. I didn't want to add any other images to what I'd already gathered. My harvest seemed adequate to me. I felt happy, as if I had accomplished a good part of my mission. What mission? I cleared up that question immediately: "It's a mysterious mission, one which I am carrying out satisfactorily." I thought of the little girl's smile, the sad look of the Charioteer, Préaud's mocking expression. It came to me that perhaps the Pythia took this same path when she went home. She lived alone. What did she do when she had her own problems or doubts? Did she ask another oracle? "I really need to find a woman who can read coffee grounds. She's the only one who can explain the meaning of my quest." I was in no hurry. I had the whole day in front of me. It was pleasant walking among the trees. From time to time I kicked a pebble with the inside of my foot, like I used to do as a child. I was up a good deal higher than the museum and the highway and I couldn't hear any cars, apart from the occasional horn. I enjoyed breathing the air, which still had a bit of the morning's coolness. I saw a cat coming toward me, a white cat with red spots. "It's Rodini," I thought. She was running, but not too fast, as if she was only a little late. I walked along the local cemetery. There was a cypress beside each grave. "I'll go see her as soon as I get back . . . . Maybe she's also wondering why she doesn't hear from me." I came to a passable road with a steep incline down toward the village. A beautiful stone house was built on a hill, turned toward the plain and toward the sea. A passerby informed me that it'd been Sikelianos' house and that now it was a museum. I wasn't curious enough to go in.

I called Theodoris from the café and reminded him that he'd promised to get tickets for Epidaurus. I asked him if Marilena would go with us.

"We've broken up," he told me. "One night she started screaming, terrible screams! She woke up the whole building! She's been criticizing me for going out with my students, for giving money to Niki, for letting her use our washing machine for quite some time, but she's always done it quietly. She changed all at once! She threw me out! She reminded me so much of Niki that I almost started crying!"

"Well, you said you needed someone strong near you."

He stopped talking. The waitress was making my coffee on an old spirit stove. At the same time, she was paging through a popular magazine sitting on the table.

"I don't know what I want. I'm completely disconcerted. I told her I thought we should separate. She agrees, on the condition that I leave her the apartment. I'm the one who bought it. I paid every last dime! She wants to drive me out of my own home! She has as much nerve as Niki!"

"Are you going to see Stathopoulou at Epidaurus?" the waitress asked me when I hung up.

She told me that Stathopoulou had gotten married in Delphi, at the village church, thirty years ago. The actress wasn't from the area, she probably chose Delphi for its beauty and to guarantee the favor of all the gods at once. The religious ceremony was followed by a party like nothing anyone had ever seen before. Thousands of people came from all over Greece. Several orchestras played all night long. There were trapeze acts, tightrope walkers, even a lion tamer with two tigers. Stathopoulou gave the beasts an entire lamb.

"We roasted seventy lambs on the square!"

To thank her most distinguished guests, she recited a passage from *Romeo and Juliet* in the ancient theater. The love of her life was an industrialist. They separated six months later.

The waitress showed me the magazine she was reading.

"It's shameful, isn't it?"

A photograph of Stathopoulou in a bikini took up almost all of the right-hand page. It was a recent color photograph. All around Amalia were short descriptions of the plastic surgeries she'd undergone on each part of her body. I handed the magazine back.

"Can you find me a woman who can read coffee grounds?"

She admitted that a former museum maid used to be a practitioner of the art.

"She's still alive," she added, "but she's very ill. I'll ask her daughter if she can see you."

My desire to see that woman was so strong I felt like I could overcome any obstacles. I thought about the humble origins of the Pythia, of her modest clothing.

"What would you ask the Pythia if the shrine were still active?" I asked her.

"About the future of Greece .... We're threatened from all sides .... I heard on television that the government in Skopje plans to claim our Macedonia .... We were once a great country ....Greece once went all the way to the very edge of the world .... Our country is getting smaller and smaller, don't you think?"

At the village library, I found the old handwritten birth records for 1857 to 1930. I noticed that non-Christian first names remained just as popular in Delphi as they are elsewhere, despite the Church's tireless efforts to stamp them out. I found a large number of first names inspired by nature: Rose, Violet, Aurora, Radiant, and others inspired by classical antiquity: Diomedes, Ulysses, Telemachus, Themistocles, Epimanondas, Alcibiades, Aristomenes, Aspasia, Penelope. I even found one Clytemnestra, which surprised me, since the name is understandably not one people like, and I discovered that the names Achilles and Miltiades could be given to women, with the ending changed: Achilloula and Miltiadoula. I noted the birth of one Castalia and of one Olympiad, in 1895, a year before the creation of the modern Olympic games in Athens. But apparently people were better known by their nicknames than by their first names. The librarian gave me a few, which I'll translate as best I can: Sauce, Miser, Existence, Winter, Ailing. I of course thought of Apollo the Paradoxical and of a cynical philosopher known as Planetiades, the Vagabond, quoted by Plutarch.

The library is in one room on the ground floor of the public school. Since they don't have a courtyard, the students play at recess on the square in front of the church, which is just across the street. The village is in danger of asphyxiation: the number of inhabitants, tourists, and cars far outstrips what was planned when it was built. Local authorities who want to extend the city limits are in permanent conflict with the Antiquities Service of the Ministry of Culture, which classes the area as an "absolute protection zone."

I spent my time going from one café to another. Delphi lacks the grace of poor villages. The insolence of money can be seen everywhere. I noticed one little girl with carefully drawn eyebrows. At least ten Delphians talked to me about how the village suffers from lack of space. I learned that apartment prices are just as high as in Athens. The former mayor, who has personally seen blocks of stone fall from Phaedriades and into the valley, told me that when they fell they cut through olive trees "as if they were cucumbers."

"The earth groans terribly when the stones land," he said.

I saw a frog on the paved road. It stopped for some time after each hop, as if worn out by the effort. Nonetheless, it managed to do it again, and so it made progress little by little. "Frogs only move when they have to." I learned that before a fence was built around the archeological site the young people of the village used to go at night to sing in the ancient theater.

I met a poet who assured me that the Pythia retired when she had premonitions of the birth of Christ. There's a poetry contest at Delphi every year in September. I also learned that there are many twins in the area. In the museum are two virtually identical statues of young men. Some say that they are Cleobis and Biton, who were so obliging that they harnessed themselves to a cart to take their mother where she had to go. I thought several times of my father. He should be back soon from Tinos. I could make out the shape of a woman in a mountain. A totally white village was sitting on her belly. Someone told me that you have to go all the way to Lavadia to find women. I learned that there is a snake only twenty centimeters long whose bite means death by sunset.

At the end of the day, I went back to the café where the locals go. The waitress, whose name is Despino, pointed out the restaurant where the former museum maid's daughter works.

"I told her about you .... She'll see what she can do .... Her mother isn't well at all. She's nearly ninety."

She advised me to pay a visit to the daughter the next afternoon. I sat in the same place, near the window. I did a little sketch of the landscape in the margin of my manuscript. The plain was dark. It looked like night was moving up from the far end of the plain. I opened my notebook and reread the last words: *éros*, love, *ekpatrisménos*, the expatriot, *érythro*, red, *élia*, the olive. I added two new words to my collections, *Éniochos*, the Charioteer, and *eironia*, irony. I came to page thirty. The photo of the newly discovered Antinous statue came to my mind. I recalled the worried adolescent who seems to be feeling the vertigo of time. Archeologists usually photograph a worker beside the discovery just to give some idea of its dimensions. I saw a large number of photographs in books at the French Archeology School where the worker, his shirt buttoned all the way to his neck, poses alongside one tambour of a column, a capital, a colossus, an Amazon. It always touched me to see the faces of those workers. I had much more feeling for them than for the colossi or the Amazons. I nearly wrote down *ergatis*, the worker, on page thirty-one, but the presence of the waitress and the memory of my grandmother made me finally choose the feminine form, *ergatria*.

I still hadn't found a suitable word for my father. The bank where he worked is called Emboriki, but he hates that name. I thought about him looking at the phone, terrorized — *éntromos* — but I didn't want to use that word either. "He's a man who's afraid of the phone and who tells stories." I briefly considered *eccentrikos*, eccentric, but thought it too vague. I also considered *épopiia*, the epic: but the adventures of Pim are only the adventures of Pim. The stories told by the Pythia were the work of an inventive mind. And so I came to the word *eufantastos*, which means imaginative, inventive, ingenious. "My father is an ingenious man."

Préaud was waiting for me in front of the museum, as we'd agreed. Rodini was there too.

"Good morning, Mr. Nicolaïdis," he said.

He knows Greek very well, but he's not as accustomed to speaking it as François is. He pronounces each word carefully, as if he were writing a children's story. His speech is monotonous.

We went into the storage rooms. Pieces of statues, reliefs, and vases were stacked up unceremoniously on makeshift shelves, dimly lit by bare bulbs. It felt as if I'd surprised the relics in their private lives. They looked like actors resting in their dressing rooms who forget about their roles for a few minutes. The Papaloukas omphalos was catalogued under the number 17191. The name "PAPA-LOU" was easily readable. Préaud showed me the knife he'd found in the stone. On the blade, just beside the date, was a bird flying off of a branch. The same image was engraved on the other side. I could hear my mother's childlike voice saying:

"Two little birds!"

"Why are you interested in the epsilon?" Préaud asked me as we were leaving the storage rooms.

I could give him no answer but the one I gave to Caradzoglou: "I don't know."

"Heraclites says that the Pythia's prophecies neither hide nor reveal, that they just signify. The epsilon fascinated you. It gave a certain impetus to your thoughts. If I knew its meaning, would you want me to tell you, or not?"

We were following the path that we'd taken the previous evening. Rodini had slipped between the bars of the gate and waited for us to come through. I imagined Préaud on his deathbed, lying in the same posture as the dying man in the letter E engraving in *Treasures of the Greek Language*, murmuring to me a totally incomprehensible word.

"But you don't know, I hope?"

"You can put your mind at rest .... We don't know much, truthfully .... The ruins that we study rarely give away their secrets .... They enlighten us about some points, but they bring up a host of new questions at the same time .... Many mysteries surround us .... The epsilon is only one enigma among many."

His answer flattered me. "I'm a serious student who has managed to earn the confidence of his teacher." He stopped just where the steep path leads up to the archeologists' lodgings.

"I suppose you must be wondering how a blind man reads inscriptions. I'll explain it in a few minutes, if you like. Wait for me in front of the Temple of Apollo."

His last sentence reminded me of films based on classical antiquity, films that I saw as a child. I thought about Kirk Douglas. Préaud started climbing the path. Rodini followed him for a step or two, but she finally went with me. "She's keeping a eye on me." The site was still closed to the public. I went toward the theater, which sits a bit higher than the temple. Rodini walked beside me. "She came with me because my route isn't as tiring." I looked at the theater just for a moment, but soon went down toward the temple. When I got to where the big dark room had been, with its weapons capable of coming down off the walls all by themselves to defend the place, I stopped. Very few things make the eye linger as it looks down toward the plain: the six columns of a temple, the Athenian Treasury — a small marble building, fully reconstructed, even the roof — a few columns here and there. The few stones scattered around this immense space sketch the foundations of a vanished city, make its disappearance visible. Its ghost arises constantly and collapses just as constantly. You don't see the ruins of a city, but a city perpetually falling into ruin. The stones had a soft gray color. They seemed to be still sleeping. The sun, which rises behind the Phaedriades, hadn't appeared yet, but it was already shining on the mountains across the plain. I could hear a bird singing now and again. I remembered that my father had compared the epsilon to the message shipwrecked sailors send out in a bottle. "I'm standing on the bridge of a wrecked ship."

I walked toward the columns. On their shafts, between the drums, I found the same weeds I'd noticed as a child on the Parthenon. I spotted the Altar of Chios in front of the temple. I thought of Neoptolemus and his leap. "I am standing thirteen point five zero meters from the altar." Somewhere, just above where I was standing, the epsilon was hung. I looked up, as if I expected to see it. The sky was very light at that hour of the morning. It had the indefinable color of transparency to it.

I walked through the length of the temple. I walked carefully, trying to make no noise, the way I walked in the French School library. I found the adytum at the far end. It's very shallow, as big as a small room. My readings had prepared me, so I wasn't surprised to see that there were no cracks in the earth. It felt like my thoughts were no longer following me, as if they'd taken leave of Delphi against my will. Rodini, who was at my feet, jumped into the adytum. I was vexed: "Get out of there!" I told her.

She was sitting quietly. She didn't budge. I had to go down into the adytum to get her out. I bent down and looked her straight in the eyes. In a Greek TV comedy I've seen, someone regularly says: "Don't people respect anything anymore?"

"Don't we respect anything anymore, Rodini?"

I caressed her head. I saw Préaud coming toward us, a roll of paper beneath one arm and a pail in the other hand. He looked like a child going off to play. I went to meet him.

"Follow me," he said.

In the pail of water were a sponge and a brush. He started by washing the surface of a big square stone where the inscriptions were barely visible, then on the wet surface he applied the paper, which soaked through immediately. He rubbed it with the brush to make it stick better. He worked out toward the edges all the air bubbles that had formed beneath it.

"Now we have to wait for it to dry. I read inscriptions on the back of the paper, where they show up in relief."

He leaned a hip against the stone and looked around as if he could see.

"I love this hour .... Before I lost my sight, I came here all the time at dawn .... I watched things become gradually sharper, take on color .... In summer, they don't take on their full color until 7:10."

"It's 7:10," I told him.

"Things resurface in the landscape .... They stay damp as long as the sun hasn't noticed them .... They shine a bit .... I suppose they still shine, at this hour."

He took a deep breath, closed his eyes.

"You know," he said, "I really love this spot."

He touched the paper, which was still wet.

"You shouldn't think that I'm the only one who uses this method. It's tough to read inscriptions on site. The sun shines on them at the ideal angle only for five or ten minutes. We know that a certain text is legible at five after eight, another at 8:20, and so on. After that, the letters disappear. Delphi is a thick book — 6,500 inscriptions have been found — but one whose pages are erased before anyone has the time to read them. The epsilon you daydream about sails on an ocean of words that have been erased."

In classical antiquity, the engraved letters were painted black or red. We went for a walk. I was constantly afraid he'd run into a rock, but he knew where every one of them was located. He led me toward the big wall of polygonal stones that supports the terrace of the Temple of Apollo. It was eighty-four meters long and completely covered with tiny letters. I certainly wouldn't have noticed them if he hadn't pointed them out. On that wall, the priests of Apollo had engraved the names of slaves who'd managed to get together enough money to buy their liberty from their owners. The act became official only when the name was recorded on the polygonal wall. Apollo insured the liberty of former slaves.

I asked him to point out a mistake. He showed me the word "archpriest," with one syllable missing. But the engraver had noticed his mistake and added the missing syllable just above the line in tiny letters. Some inscriptions are reminders of quarrels among Greek peoples: the text granting a city the right to priority in consulting the Pythia is crossed out with multiple lines.

He also showed me a marble slab decorated with a relief carving of a double row of perfectly round cylinders. He pointed out that only one carried the mark of the compass used by the sculptor on its top. He must have felt tired just as he was drawing that circle and leaned a bit too heavily on his instrument. I was enchanted by that nearly invisible trace of such ancient fatigue. I thought Préaud had guessed exactly the sort of detail likely to interest me.

We retraced our steps to pick up the paper impression. Only the plain was in shadow now. He carefully detached the paper. I heard the same sound as when I turned the pages of books at the French School. He caressed the back of the sheet with his fingertips. It had turned stiff. The letters were much clearer than on the stone.

"Did you hear the guard's keys clinking?"

I hadn't heard anything and couldn't see the guard.

"You can't see him from here. He goes behind the Athenian Treasury. It won't be long before he opens the gate."

He asked if I'd like to rest for a moment. We both sat on stone, which was still damp in spots. "I may never have the chance to see him again."

"How many words do you want to collect, in total? I imagine you've set a limit."

"Forty .... Does that seem like too few?"

"It's a good number. I think you'd have to find at least forty words if you want to claim to have seriously studied the epsilon. Plutarch only gives six or seven, if memory serves."

I shared my idea that the affirmation "you are" could just as easily be read as a greeting from Apollo to each of his visitors.

"Don't worry about Plutarch. You've found your own way. You should follow it to its end, it will certainly lead you somewhere. I'm only afraid that you'll miss the epsilon once you've put together your forty words .... But perhaps you won't need it anymore. Would you like to tell me which ones you've chosen so far?"

I was scared, as if I were just about to take a difficult exam. I'd never imagined that I would have to read my list aloud just a few steps from where the epsilon once hung. I was intimidated. I had trouble getting the notebook out of my pocket. I read the first words too fast. He interrupted me: "Don't hurry."

I started over, taking my time, delivering each syllable distinctly. I felt like I was reading my intimate diary. The words had faithfully recorded the time that had passed since I arrived in Greece. I saw a procession of people and places. I thought about the days I'd spent reading and writing. When I arrived at the middle of my list, I realized that my presence in Greece had stopped tormenting me and surprising me some time ago, that I was no longer trying to justify it because now it seemed natural. "I'm back," I thought. I read the end of the list joyfully — *irony, female worker, ingenious* — to which I added one word which wasn't yet written down, but which I thought I could finally write: *épistrophi*, the return.

Préaud did not react right away. I didn't even try to guess what he was thinking.

"That's it," he said. "That's it. You have written a text. What you read me is a text."

He gave me a tap on the shoulder.

"I had thought that your investigation was just a way of keeping you busy.... Perhaps you know the advice the Pythia gave to the inhabitants of Delos who had a number of troubles. She told them to double the volume of the altar to Apollo located on their island. Doubling a cube is an extremely difficult problem in geometry. It can't be done by simply multiplying the dimensions by two .... The Pythia furnished the Delians a reason to stop brooding over their problems."

"I've often thought that I was working on the epsilon just to escape. I wrote a few sentences using only words that started with epsilon .... It was a meaningless exercise."

"The words you read to me show that things aren't that simple. I get the feeling that they're a portrait. I don't think it's your portrait, although the word *égo* has a good position, toward the middle of the list."

I saw two tourist buses parking on the highway. I walked Préaud back to his lodgings. He walked more hesitantly than before, using his cane more. He told me that he planned to spend the evening at the Castri tavern with some younger colleagues.

"Come say hello, if you're still around."

Rodini had given us the slip. I shook his hand.

"Do something for me," he said, "since there's still space in your notebook. Write down the word *éos*, the dawn. It's a lovely word."

She lives in the upper part of the village, on Sikelianos Street. We go up endless stairs to get there, her daughter in front and I behind. Now and then she turns around and looks at me out of the corner of her eye. She thinks I'm dawdling. I have a coughing fit. My pipe is in my mouth, but isn't lit.

"Why do you smoke so much?" she asks me.

She cuts through the groups of tourists we meet at every intersection without paying them the slightest attention. She climbs stairs with disconcerting ease. She must be my age.

"Why are you running?" I ask her.

It's an unassuming house with green shutters, the stucco not completely hiding the irregular stones from which it was built. The door alone is relatively new.

"Mama?" she says as she enters.

The air is humid. On the wall I see the Charioteer in embroidery. A certain noise can be heard from the first room on the right, as if someone had moved. The girl goes into that room.

"Mama?" she repeats.

She closes the door behind her. There's glass in the door. A light comes on behind the glass, then goes off. I hear nothing, no conversation at all. I look at the furniture, the knickknacks, the blue raincoat hanging on the stand. "This could be the only poor family in Delphi." The woman who'll read my coffee grounds, if she feels like it and if she's up to it, is named Chryssi. Her daughter comes back into the hallway and seems satisfied.

"She told me to make coffee for you .... Do you take sugar?"

Usually I do take a little, but I tell myself that sugar could distort Chryssi's judgment. I don't want my fortune artificially sweetened.

"No, thank you," I say bravely.

"Don't tell anyone that she agreed to see you, or they'll start coming again. She used to have lots and lots of visits, people from everywhere, from Arachova, from Amphissa, even from Livadia."

I imagine attractive women in tight-fitting red dresses sitting silently in the entryway.

"You swear you won't?" she insists. "She needs to rest."

When was the last time I swore to something? What did I swear to do or not to do? She left the door to the room open.

"Go on in. I'll make coffee."

I stand in the doorway. I hesitate to go any farther. Despite the closed shutters and the drawn drapes, it's quite light in the room. I can clearly see the iron bed in the corner. A burgundy quilt covers Chryssi all the way to her chin: it's exactly the same shade as the book bindings at the French School. "She must be sleeping." I take a few steps. I notice that one of her feet is sticking out from under the quilt. It's bare. I'm bothered by this picture, maybe because I've always imagined the Pythia barefoot.

"Sit down," she says, using the familiar form.

Her voice is harsh and weak. All I see are her eyes, her narrow forehead furrowed with wrinkles, the scarf covering her hair. I sit down on a chair beside the bed.

"I hope I'm not disturbing you."

"I'm very sick. Life has been tough on me. I raised eight children all alone. My man was disabled. I was pregnant twenty-four times .... It was written that only eight children would survive ... .Vassiliki has a twin brother — did she tell you? ... I had twins two other times, but I lost them."

She turns toward me. I look at her feet: both are now sticking out from under the quilt. She worked at the museum for eighteen years. She supplemented her salary with the money she earned as a clairvoyant.

"It was thanks to reading coffee grounds that I was able to feed my family! But that's a secret!"

It occurred to me that she will be the last Delphian to earn a living reading the future. Were there certain statues that she preferred? She mentions the Charioteer and the Naxian Sphinx, a winged woman with a lion's body. Just for an instant I glimpse the electronic sphinx at Omonia Station, the people examining it as they wait for the subway train.

"I dusted the statues with a feather duster, very carefully, as if I were afraid to wake them .... The Charioteer gave me the most trouble, because of the reins he's holding in his hand. They're pieces of twisted iron. Once a feather got stuck there without my noticing and it stayed there all day!"

I imagine an epsilon decorated with a beautiful orange feather. She repeats several times: "Oh, my God ...."

Vassiliki brings the coffee on a tray, places it on the nightstand.

"Aren't you staying?" I ask her.

"No one but you must be here when she speaks to you."

She leaves the room, closing the door behind her. I drink the coffee quickly. It's very bitter. "She won't tell me anything good." I place the cup upside down on the saucer. A little coffee seeps out the sides and forms a dark halo.

"Have you turned the cup over?"

I say "yes" and I wait. Suddenly Chryssi sits up in her bed without pushing herself up from the pillows, her body perfectly straight, and takes the cup from my hands. Her movements are so forceful they scare me. Her scarf slips back and lets her long gray hair flow over her shoulders. Her mouth is small and slightly twisted, shaped like a little wave. "That is not an ordinary mouth." She scrutinizes the bottom of my cup. I'm convinced that the grounds must form a nightmare image.

"You want me to tell you clearly, don't you?"

"Yes," I say, but without much conviction, as if I were expecting to be condemned.

The position she's sitting in reminds me of one of the drawings I did when I was trying to give some meaning to the shape of the epsilon: I drew a woman sitting on her heels, bent over a coffee cup.

"You've had a lot of troubles .... And more are coming .... I see a family scattered and a death. Can you see the death?"

She shows me the cup. I see heavy clouds and spider webs, chains of mountains and dry stream beds, and in the sky black dots like burnt-out stars. I don't see death, but of course I know it's there.

"A person you like has health problems .... and will have to be careful. The woman you're with right now likes you and supports you .... She's well educated."

I am just about to tell her that there isn't any woman, but I hold it in. She reacts as if I had said it, and resumes: "I mean the one who used to be with you, because I see that you've separated. Her name starts with V."

I think of Vaguelio, obviously. It impresses me that she was able to guess her initial. I listen to the rest with much more interest.

"Everything will be better next year. And you'll earn a great deal of money, besides .... You'll meet a woman whose first name starts with an A who'll help you resolve your problems .... A beautiful woman."

"Maybe it's time I started working on another letter of the alphabet," I think.

"A beautiful woman," she says again.

She closes her eyes and lets herself fall back. The cup falls from her hands and rolls on the floor.

"You aren't feeling well?"

"I'm tired," she murmurs.

I arrange the pillows beneath her head as best I can. I slide her hands back under the quilt. "She's cold." Vassiliki comes back into the room.

"Don't worry," she tells me. "Reading coffee grounds always tires her out."

I propose leaving money, but she refuses flatly.

"We don't need it any more .... We have what we need .... And don't say 'thank you' either. If you say 'thank you' none of her predictions will come true."

Before leaving, I pull down the bottom of the quilt to cover up Chryssi's feet.

"So did you ever learn to read coffee grounds?" I ask Vassiliki.

She doesn't answer. She simply smiles. I was probably wrong in thinking that her mother was the last clairvoyant of Delphi.

A French archeologist who's about thirty years old is sitting to my right. She's been in Greece for four years, but she hasn't learned Modern Greek. She's proud of that.

"I don't know a word of it!" she tells me, laughing.

I don't understand what she's proud of. She only sees other French people. I think about François, who systematically avoids them. She asks me this question: "Don't you find that Greeks aren't really all that interesting?"

Does she consider me a Frenchman? She's interested exclusively in ancient Greece. If she compares every Greek she comes across to Plato, she's certainly going to find them mediocre. Préaud, who is sitting to my left, is explaining to her that modern Greece has preserved many of the values of ancient Greece. He confides to us that when he first came to Delphi he spent hours observing farmers in the fields because he thought their movements had an almost classical grace. He tells the young woman that common people have kept a very ancient language alive. He supports his thesis with a series of examples. He's giving her a classroom lecture. She listens to him with a certain incredulity but says nothing. The expression on her face is familiar to me, as are Préaud's arguments. All Hellenists compare today's Greeks to those of the past: some see how similar they are, others how different. I've learned to recognize both, and the ones who see similarities are the only ones who speak Modern Greek.

"What do you think about all that?" Préaud asks me.

"I'd prefer your thesis be supported by you than by my compatriots. I think we're already preoccupied enough with our family tree. Theater productions nowadays give the impression that nothing interesting has been written since Sophocles and Euripides. I remember when the colonels censured a magazine because it had dared to speak of homosexuality among ancient Greeks. Dialogue with our ancestors has never been free and easy."

Préaud seemed to be thinking. He stopped eating.

"I really don't want to convince our friend that I speak the same language as Homer. I admit that I have enormous difficulty reading him in the original. I would simply advise her to see a few plays, listen to some music, read a few modern poets. I have no taste at all for neo-Hellenic compositions. They are what they are, we are what we are."

"So tell me what I should read!" she said eagerly.

Where to start? I mention Cavafy, there are five or six French translations of his poems. From her purse, she takes out a superb pen with a gold nib.

"How do you spell that?"

She doesn't even know Cavafy. She writes the poet's name on a paper napkin that soaks up the ink and shreds. I'm going to start getting angry. Three other people are sitting at our table, but they're engaged in a different conversation.

"Pour me a little retsina," Préaud says to me.

He won't be working this evening. He never works the night of Saturday into Sunday. I would like to ask him about his life, about his disability, but I know I won't have time to do it. I'll leave tomorrow morning on the first bus. As I was leaving Chryssi's, I realized that my trip to Delphi was over. It was only my wish to see Préaud again that kept me from leaving this evening.

"To your health," he says.

He waits for me to clink glasses with him, holding his glass in the air. I learn from the on-going conversation that he's published an article in *Le Monde* where he supports the Greek demand for the return of the Parthenon marbles, now in the British Museum. Apparently his perspective caused a certain amount of agitation even in France, where they're not anxious to open up the question of returning antiquities.

"When I was young," he says, "I often dreamt of finding a beautiful woman's hand on a dig. But I couldn't find the rest of the statue. I learned that she had already been discovered, and that she was scattered over various museums: her head was located in the Vatican, her other hand in Copenhagen, her breasts in the British Museum, her hips in the Louvre, one of her legs in East Berlin and the other in West Berlin. I started on a crusade throughout Europe to try to collect all the pieces and glue them together. I travelled endlessly from one city to another, I begged, but no one wanted to give up what he owned. I was in despair."

I stopped at the café where the locals go to say goodbye to Despino. She was all alone. She was standing by the window, drinking her coffee and looking out at the landscape. The sun was just rising.

I looked at the landscape too as I waited at the bus stop. I was already so accustomed to it that I felt I had known it for years. The bus was nearly empty. It was coming from Amphissa. I sat all the way in the back, on the left side because I would see the Temple of Apollo better from that side.

We went through the village slowly. When we got to the archeological site, my eyes went straight to the columns. I counted them once again, as if to reassure myself that none had been stolen in the night. A man was sitting on the steps of the Temple. I recognized Préaud's khaki shirt. "It's his favorite time," I thought. It looked like he was holding Rodini in his arms.

9.

I'm in Paris with a Greek girl, a student, I think. We're looking for a place to make love, but we can't find one. I don't know her very well. I don't know her name, but she isn't a complete stranger. She's short and slender. I can't really say that I find her that attractive, but we've decided to make love, and I find our difficulties very distressing.

We finally find a place. It's a huge room. It looks like a reception room of an old hotel. Portable screens are scattered here and there, to divide up the space. But we can't really be by ourselves. We lie down on a leather couch. We try to cover ourselves with a sheet that keeps sliding off one side or the other. I think about nailing it to the couch, but it doesn't seem likely that I'll find a hammer and nails there. The leather is smooth. We're on the back of an animal that's trying to buck us off.

We're just starting to make love when five or ten students appear, all friends of the girl, and start packing their suitcases. They're also doing dishes — there's a sink somewhere. They don't pay any attention to us. They pretend not to know that we're there. The girl gets up — she isn't completely naked — and says something to them, then comes back.

"They'll be gone soon," she tells me.

They do actually leave, each with his suitcase in hand. The light isn't nearly as bright as it was. The big doors at the far end of the room open to let in hundreds of people. I notice that we're in the lobby of a movie theater where they've just had the gala showing of a movie by a French director I had lunch with one time. I glimpse him in the crowd. I decide to clear out.

I'm at the airport. I'm running across the runway. They've already moved the steps away from the plane. They tell me that I can only get on the plane by riding on the freight elevator.

"You can't be serious," I say.

But I get onto the freight elevator. It's a bare platform with no rails, lifted mechanically from below. To keep from getting dizzy, I lie down on it and huddle up, make myself as small as possible. Very slowly, creaking slightly, the platform moves upward.

"Was I unhappier than I think I was in Paris? Did I have problems I don't even know about?" I woke up asking myself those questions the morning after my return to Athens. That's the second nightmare I've had about my life in Paris since I've been in Greece. I've already talked about the first one: I'm in a classroom full of immigrants and I'm learning a new language. It's probably a recollection of my first years in France. "The night has its own way of looking at things," I thought. I get the impression that night has a taste for the dramatic.

My first day back in Athens started rather badly and I can't say that it got any better. Just before ten o'clock I got a call from Fanny, who started by telling me that my father's phobias had gotten worse, then launched into me, on the pretext that my French friends, always so fussy about defending human rights, weren't reacting at all to the genocide of the Kurdish people by the Turks.

"They've already killed fifteen thousand Kurds and I assure you that French public opinion doesn't have a single thought about it."

"I know. France has invested heavily in Turkey. I think it may even be the main foreign investor there .... Why are you talking to me about the Kurds?"

"That isn't the question," she said and hung up.

I couldn't ask her about my father's condition. I didn't call him, to avoid making his fears any worse. I took a taxi and went to see him.

He seemed to be in good shape: he was tan from his stay on Tinos, he had put on some weight. But he wouldn't look straight at me. He didn't notice that I'd shaved off my beard. "Maybe I've changed less than Vasso says."

"How did your trip go? How's Costas? Did you solve the epsilon enigma?"

He was questioning me mechanically, as if reciting a lesson. Apparently he wasn't expecting an answer to any of his questions.

"I didn't solve it, but I'm about done with that mystery. A fortuneteller I visited in Delphi pointed me toward the letter A."

"The epsilon is just a letter of the alphabet .... I'm relearning the alphabet. The E is the first letter I studied."

"And how are you doing?" I asked him.

"I was great on Tinos .... I got back last evening .... But during the night I had the feeling that the furniture was moving ... That it was walking around in the dark. I heard noises."

He was looking toward the kitchen. I looked to see what he was staring at and saw that it was the table and chairs where we ate lunch. The legs of the table slope out a bit. It looks like it's ready to run off helter-skelter.

"Don't you get the feeling," he asked in a low voice, "that the table and chairs are holding a council? That they're plotting?"

"Are you serious?"

He sank back in his chair.

"I can tell you that I'm not as scared of the telephone as I was .... Or at least I'm not as afraid of it as I am of the furniture."

He put his hand on the buffet.

"I'm not worried about the buffet .... It can't get to the second floor. It could never get up the stairway. It's too big. I just measured it."

"You were afraid that it would go upstairs on its own?"

"Yes .... I heard creaking on the stairs all night .... They weren't sounds that people make .... They were short, dry, clicking sounds .... It was the furniture going upstairs."

"But why would they go upstairs?"

He looked at me as if he couldn't believe that one of his sons could say something so stupid.

"To crush me, obviously! They want to trample me in my sleep! Don't you see?"

I didn't know what to say. I had to leave the living room for a moment. I went into the kitchen and emptied my pipe into the trash. I forgot my father's problems again. "I'm relearning my mother tongue .... As long as my mother was alive I wasn't afraid of losing contact with the language. I knew that I could get it back anytime .... All I had to do was call her." I went back into the living room. He asked me to close the kitchen door.

"It's the kitchen table that worries you, isn't it?"

"I think it hates me because I use it too often .... Even when I want to saw a piece of wood or paint something .... I've climbed up on it more than once to change a light bulb .... I plan to appease it by giving it gifts .... I already put a nice white ribbon in its drawer. Tomorrow I'll put in an old stamp."

"My father is making offerings of ribbons and stamps to the kitchen table." I told myself that I should visit him more often, that I should spend the night at his place from time to time.

"If you can figure out what causes your fears, you'll be able to overcome them."

"You're probably right," he admitted thoughtfully.

He talked to me about Fanny, who's made friends with a group of Kurds living in Athens, about Pim, who has gotten to the Cape of Good Hope, about the church on Tinos, overrun by immense crowds — but I was only half listening to what he was saying. "The text I've written is just an exercise in my mother tongue .... It's a conversation with the language .... With the language, I'm continuing conversations I had with my mother .... We are children of a language .... I'm looking to claim that identity .... In writing. I'm trying to get words to adopt me.... I'm trying to rediscover the smell of the first books I ever read, The Little Red Hen and The Three Little Pigs."

"The Orthodox priests on Tinos didn't impress me much .... I didn't really like the atmosphere in the church .... I didn't ask them to say a mass. I just lit one of those human-shaped candles they sell there. I didn't do a good job lighting it, it went out right away. I watched the smoke rise .... It drifted up toward the dome, black as the inside of a well .... A priest took care of relighting it for me. I'm sure he collects the candles as soon as the pilgrims turn their backs. Did you know that Soussoula is going to Catholic churches now?"

He half-smiled. I remembered that we'd packed our children's books and our old schoolbooks in a cardboard box.

"She claims that Catholics are better behaved at church, that they talk less than the Orthodox! That they're not as noisy. She finds them more distinguished. She prefers the Catholic Church the way some people prefer American or Greek movies."

"You didn't notice that I look different?"

"Yes I did. You've changed something .... Did you get your hair cut?"

I asked him if he had thrown out our old books.

"No, absolutely not! I've even re-read some of them: *Robinson Crusoe*, *Treasure Island*, *The Count of Monte Cristo* ... But that was a long time ago .... I packed them away in a box, but I don't remember where I put it."

We looked everywhere for it: under beds, in the wardrobe, in the storage closet, in the garden shed. We found it in the wardrobe the second time we looked there, on the top shelf behind a pile of sheets. I didn't find *The Little Red Hen* or *The Three Little Pigs*. But I did locate the illustrated ABC's that my mother used to teach me the alphabet. Each page had one letter on it. I didn't find the alpha on the first page, as I'd expected, but instead, surrounded by an elephant, a church (*ekklasia*), and a pine tree (*élato*) — the capital E.

My cartoons won't be published in *Embros Sunday*. That reporter I met delivered the news. The cartoonists who contribute regularly to the weekly were against publishing them. Do they think I want their job? That didn't really bother me, because in the meantime I've found another paper that wants to publish them. I learned that Caradzoglou resigned from *Embros Sunday* and in an open letter he denounced the "junta of industrialists" who control the press and television. Naturally, the mainstream press and television never mentioned his protest. His letter appeared only in an extreme left-wing bi-monthly. I've thought of calling him several times. I'll do it when I've finished. I wonder how Marika is doing.

"I found something," I'll tell her.

I'll miss the epsilon, of course. I think once again of my first meeting with that letter, in Vaguelio's apartment, and of the plumber who unwittingly led me to read the book on Delphi. The idea that I might never have met the E makes me feel the same retrospective anxiety that lovers feel when they remember the accidental nature of their first meeting. It is very difficult for me to analyze my relationship with the epsilon. One thing that's certain is that without it I would never have left for Delphi. I can see the surprised look on my mother's face: "How can it be that you've never been there?"

I didn't go far, but I still feel worn out. It isn't easy to cross over so many centuries. I'm not overly disappointed at not having deciphered the secret of the ancient letter: its silence has taught me that time brings about permanent divides. The epsilon disguised itself in so many ways that I get the impression I've made the problem even more complicated than it was at the beginning. I console myself by thinking that the goal of writing perhaps isn't to clear up mysteries, but rather to multiply them.

I owe a debt to that letter. It's mostly because of it that I now feel more comfortable in the streets of Kolonaki. I know that Pindar praised the victors of the games at Delphi and that he was given a seat in the Temple of Apollo. Plutarch Street reminds me that we all die several times in our lives and on Heraclitus Street I can almost hear dice being rolled by a child.

There are only two empty pages left in my notebook. I wrote *épistrophi*, the return, on page thirty-three, and *éos*, the dawn, on page thirty-four. Just after that I wanted to note the strange creakings heard in old peoples' houses, and I wrote down the word *éphialtis*. Ephialtes was name of the traitor responsible for the death of Leonidas. In the modern language, the word means nightmare. I dedicated the next page to my mother tongue, *ta ellènika*. It may be that the illustrated ABC book I found at home starts with the letter E because it's the first letter of the language itself. I thought that my mother's death would push me farther away from Greece. On the contrary, it has brought me closer to it. I hope that the country will give me back a little of my mother's presence and that the Greek language will console me for her silence.

Ever since I got back from Delphi, I go to my father's place at noon. We have lunch together, then I leave. He hasn't said another word about his fears. Once when he wasn't looking I opened the drawer of the kitchen table. It's full: I glimpsed a red candle, a bow tie, a hundred-drachma note. I always take a taxi to Ano Patissia. Since the Athens taxi driver has an opinion about everything, I thought I couldn't close my investigation without consulting one, after consulting the Pythia. So I talked to a driver about the epsilon at Delphi.

"I don't know anything about that," he told me.

That may be the first time that I've ever heard a taxi driver admit ignorance.

"But," he added, "if you like, I can give you a word that starts with E and that I really like."

He was weaving in and out, trying to make his way through the backed-up traffic. He passed on the right, crossed over into the oncoming lane, drove on the sidewalk. "He's worming his way in," I thought. When he managed to pass the trolley bus responsible for the backup, he said: "Enthusiasm, my friend! That's what we need, enthusiasm! My customers are sad, teary-eyed, I feel like I'm driving a hearse. My life isn't all that pleasant, either. I have to work twelve hours a day, sometimes fourteen, just to get by. But I don't let it get me down! I don't like misfortune! It's not for me!"

The word delighted me: it reminded me of the Pythia. Originally, to be enthusiastic was to be filled with God. I thought of the prophetess again one day while I was watering the garden. I didn't find either the cypress or the mimosa in very good shape. The laurel, on the other hand, is doing wonderfully well. While I was admiring its beautiful green leaves, I remembered that the Pythia chewed some of them before entering the adytum. I pulled off a few and chewed them. They're very bitter. But I swallowed my saliva before I spit them out. So the Pythia had a rather unpleasant taste in her mouth when she prophesied.

It occurred to me that I could write down a meaningless word in my notebook, to offer my own little enigma to the mysterious E that has been my companion for so long. So I invented the word *ékèlès*. I made sure that it wasn't in any dictionary. It reminds me of the word games that Vaguelio and I used to play when we were first together. I wrote *enthousiasmos*, page thirty-seven, and *ékèlès*, page thirty-eight.

Elias finished all the work I'd asked him to do. The apartment is completely white. Memories of the demolished walls are starting to fade. I'll ask him to paint the floor yellow when I go back to Paris. I'll have to go back, sooner or later. But I don't plan to take up exactly where I left off. I'll propose to Véronique Carrier that my contributions be limited to two or three cartoons a month. I plan to free myself from the obligation of going to the newspaper every day, even of living permanently in Paris. Martha forwarded the letters I'd received. There was nothing interesting, apart from a proposal from an editor who'd like to reprint some of my cartoons to illustrate an account of the Mitterrand presidency. The letter from Greece had been sent by a cousin, the daughter of one of my father's sisters: she needed a medication that isn't sold in Athens.

I finally decided on the ping-pong table. The white walls give the apartment a rather rustic look and the yellow floor will accentuate that. The decor isn't worthy of a billiards table. I don't have the furniture, paintings, or drapes I would need to accommodate one. The ping-pong table will adapt easily to the bare space. I've already visited several sporting goods stores. I've noticed that ping-pong tables have three legs on either side, two at the ends and one in the middle, right below the net. Seen from the side, they look like a tipped-over epsilon, rather like the one that turn-of-the-century archeologists thought they could make out on the Papaloukas stone. I still hope that Chryssi's prediction will come true, that I'll meet an Anna, an Anastassia, or even — why not? — an Antigone. Until then, I'll play ping-pong with Theodoris.

I'll go back to drawing. I want to get back to my pencils, my brushes. I'm beginning to miss colors. The sight of the words I line up endlessly sometimes seem very austere. There's something funereal about that unending parade of Greek letters. Every sentence is a day that begins and ends. Some are fun, but I don't think any are really filled with joy. Funny cartoons suspend time. Flower pots falling from the sky never reach their destinations. Arrows streaking through the air are equally immobile. I'm nostalgic for the gentleness of cartoons. They always put me in a good mood. I always feel relaxed when I sit down at my table to draw. Words make me anxious, as if I had to negotiate the meaning of my life with them.

One night, at midnight exactly, I got a call from Costas.

"Margarita called me," he said. "She begged my forgiveness, she cried. She really never wanted us to be apart .... She explained that she'd gone away to test her feelings for me. Now that she's sure she loves me, she wants us to see each other every day, if possible. We'll see what the future holds .... She told me exactly what I needed to hear. She pronounced those sentences I'd imagined so many times .... Are you busy?"

"No. Wait a minute."

I poured myself a glass of whisky to celebrate. I lit my pipe.

"She called me just before the store closed, like she used to do. I felt enormous relief. 'I'm waiting for you,' she said. The moments after her call were among the happiest of my life."

He really wanted to run straight to her. But he decided to go home first to take a shower and to shave. One doesn't go to such an important rendezvous without some preparation. Unfortunately, the water heater hadn't been lit. He had to wait a half hour before his shower. He used the time to think about the happiness awaiting him. He planned to take Margarita to Florence. The more he thought about it, the more he felt like their relationship was going to flourish. Margarita was no longer a blurry shape lost in the fog, but a woman ready to share her life with him. She would no doubt ask him one day to leave Vasso. He also had time to think about Vasso, Lena, and the pharmacy.

While he was taking his shower he thought about Margarita again. He thought about all her best points, but also about the faults he had so carefully studied when he was trying to forget her. He remembered that she was contemptuous and stingy. He didn't take a taxi to go see her, but decided to walk. He realized that the passion her distance had inspired in him diminished as he approached her house.

"Just as I was about to ring the bell, I understood that I was no longer in love. I stood there in front of her door to think a bit more. I smoked a cigarette, then I left. I'm calling you from the Pompei, Lena's bar. I just had a whisky. And I can tell you that I'm feeling just great."

Two hours before the performance, the Epidaurus Theater was bursting at the seams. I don't know its capacity. There must have been ten thousand people there, maybe even fifteen thousand. We were seated just below the walkway that divides the theater into two sections. A parti-colored crowd filled the upper section. People were dressed more soberly in our section. The celebrities in the first rows were all wearing black. The sky was pink. The day was ending, but it was still very hot: beyond the hubbub of the crowd we could hear the cicadas singing. The set was confined to a massive gray cube placed about ten meters back from the curve of the orchestra pit. It had no openings apart from a small door on the front, framed by two columns with a sign just above it bearing the word *Palace*. Some people found the décor interesting, others didn't. People where chatting, looking at the celebrities. I scrutinized them too, using Theodoris' binoculars. I saw Calogridou in the first row, with Pandelis, Stathopoulou's brother who runs the public television channel, and Acridakis a few rows higher. I felt a sudden and unexpected joy: it was Eleni!

"That's Eleni!" I said the Theodoris. "I'm going to say hello!"

He seemed very surprised that I was in such a hurry. Maybe he'd even forgotten introducing her to me. He made no comment. Just as I was leaving, he said: "Would you get me a beer?"

It took a long time to reach the stairway. When I got there, Eleni had disappeared. I went down the steps to the central circle, followed respectfully around it, and went toward the refreshment stand in the nearby woods. Just by luck, Eleni was there, at the counter. But first I saw Stelios, my father's friend, waiting in line with a young man. Each was loaded down with several cameras. Stelios was wearing a black suit and a bow tie. "He's come to get a photograph with Stathopoulou." He looked very tired to me. He's a little younger than my father, but not much. He confirmed that he had indeed come to pose beside the Minister.

"Stathopoulou is the only Greek public celebrity I'm missing," he said. "I'm thinking of ending my collection with this photo .... How's your father?"

They don't see one another often. Neither of them is very willing to go out. Each reproaches the other for his laziness. My father thinks he's found an explanation for his fears: he claims that he assimilates his environment to his organism, that he projects upon the furniture worries that are really caused by his liver and his heart. The ring of the telephone could be an alarm signal from his body.

"So you can see why I don't want to answer, can't you?" he said. "I don't want to know."

He's perfectly satisfied with his theory, even proud of it, it seemed to me. I don't think I'll every really understand my father. I saw Eleni moving away from the refreshment stand, carrying a can of beer. I ran after her, kissed her on both cheeks. She was taken aback.

"I shaved off my beard!" I told her. "We met at the Titanic. I was with Theodoris."

"Ah ... ," she said, as if she was trying to find me in some obscure corner of her memory.

I imagined her nude in the bluish water of my bathtub. "We'll see each other when her boyfriend is off in Serres .... We'll drink ouzo along the coast, while eating olives from Amphissa." I proposed that we go out some evening.

"When you're alone," I specified.

"But I'm never alone! I live with my boyfriend."

"Doesn't he go to Serres anymore?"

"No," she said. "His grandmother died."

I made my way back to the theater, taking my time. I looked at the people who were coming and going, others running to find a seat, hoping to meet Caradzoglou and Marika, Vaguelio, Stella, Ilona, François, or even Préaud, but I didn't see anyone. Acridakis waved to me. I just waved back. Stathopoulou's brother was holding Calogridou's hand. "They'll be married in Delphi," I thought. "A lion tamer with two old tigers will take part in the festivities."

I'll never understand Theodoris, either. His relationships with women will remain a mystery to me. He separated from Marilena two weeks ago. He left her the apartment, finally. He's not unhappy about the lonely drive to Stamata, where he's living.

"I can finally think freely," he told me. "Niki and Marilena always intervened in my thoughts."

He tolerates being alone better than he thought he would. He's formed new habits. He gets up at six in the morning and works for two hours. He scarcely goes out with his students anymore. When he's bored in the evening he prefers to go have a drink at the village café. The local people claim that Stamata does in fact mean "Stop." Apparently that injunction was shouted by their distant ancestors after the Battle of Marathon to the soldier who was running to Athens to announce the victory over the Persians. He must already have been in a pretty pitiful state by the time he got to where the village now stands.

They turned on the lights for the tiers. The ladies behind us were wondering if the receipts for the performance would reach the estimated price of the El Greco painting. The debate about *Saint Peter's* authenticity was still going on in the press. Both sides exchanged long and venomous letters every day. Theodoris told me about a Poussin painting where Christ is giving a golden key to Saint Peter. Carved into a square column behind them is a capital E.

"It stands for Ecclesia, most likely," he told me. "But I think there's a Poussin specialist who contests that interpretation."

It struck me that the bit part of old keys looks like an epsilon. "I'll end up seeing epsilons everywhere .... The tines of a fork make me think of that letter, and so do the claws of animals, peoples' hands, tree branches, television antennas .... At night the stars form an infinite number of epsilons in the sky."

The Prime Minister arrived five minutes before the performance began. His car, a long black limousine, dropped him just a few meters from the stage. Half of the spectators stood and applauded. A few whistled. He raised a hand to wave to the crowd, then took his seat in the middle of the first row. He was immediately surrounded by two television crews, photographers, and many other people. I watched that little milling crowd through my binoculars. I didn't recognize him right away because his back was turned to me, but I was suspicious because of the little ponytail. It was the poet from Stamata, with a microphone in his hand. I handed the binoculars to Theodoris.

"Looks who's here," I told him.

"I'm not surprised .... He works in radio now. He has a good job .... He's not a bad poet, but his main ambition has always been to get himself a job."

Just as the stage lights were coming on and the tiers going dark, I happened to think of the funny story that Theodoris had told in Stamata and at the Titanic, the one where he hopped in place. I couldn't ask him to tell it to me, because Orestes had already started explaining to an old man how he was going to kill Clytemnestra, his mother, and Aegisthus, her lover. I was fairly familiar with the play: it ends the chain of murders that began with the sacrifice of Iphigenia. As a student, Iphigenia's death had been the only one that troubled me. The death of Agamemnon, who was executed horribly by his wife and Aegisthus, never moved me. It wasn't long before I realized that I wasn't really absorbed by the performance. I was simply curious to hear Stathopoulou tell Orestes, "Long-awaited voice, are you really here?" I think everyone was waiting for that line. The newspapers reminded everyone of it incessantly, recounting Amalia's first triumph in the role of Electra: "She became immortal with a single sentence spoken forty years ago," according to *Éleuthérotypia*. They also published photographs taken during that memorable performance: Stathopoulou wore a fairly short black dress and her hair was pulled back in a bun.

We first heard her voice from inside the palace: "Woe, woe is me!"

The entire theater began to applaud, to cheer her, louder and louder as it became obvious that she would appear soon. As soon as she appeared at the door of the palace, wearing a dress identical to the one she had worn years ago and with her hair in a bun, the entire audience gave her a standing ovation. She looked twenty years old. I had the feeling that she was crossing a line, gaining access to a lighter universe than our own. "We're witnessing a sort of miracle," I thought. She had to bow at least ten times before the applause and the shouts began to fade and the performance could continue.

She recited her rather long text confidently, making liars of those who had spread the rumor that she was no longer capable of learning her lines. For me, it was her youthful, sweet voice that didn't really go well with the fierceness of Electra, who thinks of nothing but avenging Agamemnon. She is impatient for Orestes to arrive, since he alone can punish their mother as she deserves to be punished. She meets him at the beginning of the play, but doesn't recognize him because Orestes was raised far away.

I've always had trouble concentrating. I glanced from time to time at the knees of one of the women behind us. During the dispute between Electra and her sister, who hopes to lead a quiet life, I asked Theodoris to tell me his story.

"A whore offers to give someone a penguin job."

Right then I wanted to laugh.

"She pockets the money, and asks him to drop his pants."

"Shhh!" a lady said.

He had to shut up. We followed the rest of the altercation between the two sisters. I imagined a play made up of the darkest scenes from all the tragedies, where blood would flow like water. A cleaning woman would diligently mop it up. I imagined Chryssi in the role of the cleaning lady. Theodoris used the entry of the chorus to tell me what happens next.

"Just as his pants fall around his ankles, the girl runs off with the money. He tries to catch her, but he can't run, because his pants keep him from moving his legs."

Apparently the chorus wasn't loud enough to cover Theodoris' voice, because the same woman said: "Will you be quiet!"

"All he can do is make little hops, like a penguin."

We were both overcome with one of those irrepressible laughing fits where anything at all can set it off again. The second big fight of the play, between Clytemnestra and Electra, had just begun and it seemed hilarious to us. People around us were exasperated.

"Don't you respect anything?" a man asked.

I remembered Rodini in the adytum and thought of the comedy on television where a character always repeats that same sentence. Complaints just made us laugh harder, as did Electra's growing despair.

"That news is killing me .... Everything has ended for me!"

We didn't manage to settle down until the end of that episode and the beginning of the central scene of the play. Orestes and Electra stand a few meters away from one another. She is convinced that her brother is dead. Orestes lets her cry for a moment. But he ends up revealing the truth to her. She doesn't believe him at first, then finally does believe.

The theater was absolutely quiet at that moment. One would have thought there was no one in the audience.

"Oh happy day!" said Stathopoulou.

She paused for a moment, then added: "Long-awaited voice, are you really here?"

That was the phrase that the audience was waiting for and she was intelligent to enough to say it simply, holding back her surprise and her joy, as if she hadn't spent her entire life looking for her brother's return. I understood why her first portrayal of the role had been talked about so much: it couldn't have been better acted. I wondered if the Modern Greek translator had taken some liberties with Sophocles' text. The audience was silent, as if the actress' voice was still resonating. She took several steps to throw herself into Orestes' arms, then she suddenly lost her balance: she tripped on the bare ground, staggered, put one knee down, made a despairing gesture toward Orestes, then she fell. The audience stood as quickly as she collapsed. She tried to stand up, but even with the help of Orestes, she couldn't. There was blood on her knees, and her hair had come undone. Her brother Pandelis ran to her, closely followed by Calogridou, and several actors came out of the palace to help her. "It was her legs that let her down. She wasn't betrayed by her memory, or by her voice, but she was betrayed by her legs." Pandelis and Orestes managed to stand her up, they took a few steps toward the wings, but the actress resisted, she wanted to bow to her public, so they brought her rather clumsily to the edge of the stage. She looked tiny between the two men. Her hair hid nearly her entire face. She tried to shake loose, to stand just for a moment on her own legs, and she nearly lost her balance. The audience was giving her another ovation, shouting her name. She could bow only by moving her head slightly. "Time has revoked its favor," I thought. Several dozen policemen were trying to protect her from the reporters and photographers who were running in all directions. I didn't see Stelios anywhere. "His collection will remain unfinished." People were applauding wildly. She finally turned her back and walked toward the palace, leaning on the two men.

A number of images came to my mind as I watched her move away — a poet in ancient garb riding a white horse, an ancient Greek playing soccer, a full moon with clock hands, Stelios on the arm of a German champion no one remembers anymore. I thought of the child playing dice, the worried adolescent in the Antinous photo, a word ultimately worn away by time and suspended among six columns, a little boat tied along the bank of a quiet stream. When Stathopoulou disappeared into the palace, I realized that the time had finally come to make the visit I had had postponed for so long.

Theodoris chose the word *éleuthéria*, liberty. He told me when we got back from Epidauraus. It was four in the morning. I wrote it in my notebook right away, page thirty-nine, as if I were afraid of forgetting it. I thought of the freed slaves who put themselves under Apollo's protection and whose names were engraved on the polygonal wall. In May 1969 the workers at the BERLIET plant switched around the letters of their company's name over the entrance gate to the factory to make the word LIBERTE.

I woke up early in the morning. I decided to take the bus. I wasn't in the mood to hear the ramblings of a taxi driver.

The new cemetery was nearly deserted. I found the grave very easily this time. I sat down on the ground. The marble slab is raised toward the back. On top of it is a cross set into a notch in the stone. First I removed the dead leaves from the geraniums planted around the grave, then I sat down. I looked at the mimosa. It's bigger than mine, but it still looks fragile. Its stem is still very slender. It's tied to an olive-green plastic stake. Will it ever become a tree? Its leaves are nothing more than a multitude of little lines on either side of the branch. They are leaves that make no shade. They rustle constantly, even when the air is calm.

The slab was slightly dusty. There was a little more dust inside the engraved letters of her name. I bent down and blew the dust away. I thought again of the epsilon. The name of my mother, Marika Nicolaïdis, doesn't contain that letter. Mine doesn't either, for that matter. But I was still certain that the word I needed to complete my notebook was there somewhere. I looked at the thin gravel border around the geraniums. Two birds were foraging not far away. I suddenly thought of the word *ellipsi*, to miss.

"We've missed you, Marika," I thought.

I'm not sure that I didn't say those words aloud. The emotion that I managed to control on the day of her death and on the day of her burial, which I had never stopped controlling since then, finally escaped. At one point I heard steps coming closer and then moving away. I could hear the chirping of the birds. I rested my head on my knees. I remembered the cheering of the soccer fans that had erupted during my last visit. They would certainly have helped me recover, if I'd heard them again. But the soccer stadium was silent and that was better. I was in no hurry to recover.

I got up after a long moment. The two birds were still there. They looked like the ones I'd seen with my mother in one of my dreams. Before I left, I asked them to land on her grave from time to time, to sweep away the dust with their wings.

Afterword: Vassilis Alexakis and *Mother Tongue*
By Marianne Bessy

Vassilis Alexakis is the rare bilingual writer who not only writes and publishes in two languages, but — like Samuel Beckett and Vladimir Nabokov before him — also self translates his work. Since 1974, he has published fourteen novels—some written first in French and others in Greek, depending on the chosen location for the text, but all of them later translated into the other language by the author. His dual cultural belonging has become a trademark of Alexakis's novels, which — like *Mother Tongue* — address questions of identity, language, and loss.

Such books are an important contribution to contemporary writings in French and Greek but it is his unique artistic engagement with his two writing languages as well as his creative range — along with writing prose he has also worked as a cartoonist, children's book author, and film director — that set him apart from other French and Greek authors. Alexakis's texts are routinely shortlisted for major literary awards. He received the Prix Médicis in 1995 for *Mother Tongue* and the Grand prix du roman de l'Académie française in 2007 for A.D. In 2012, Alexakis was awarded the Prix de la langue française in recognition of the scope of his literary work to date. *Mother Tongue*, only his second book to be published in English, is among his most important texts in part because it confirms self-translation as Alexakis's preferred creative writing practice.

Born in 1943 in Athens, Alexakis left Greece for France to study journalism in Lille in 1961. In 1964, he returned to Greece to complete his military service but the military coup pushed him to leave his country once again in 1967. He then settled in Paris where he worked for French newspapers *La Croix* and *Le Monde* and participated in radio shows at France-Culture before turning his attention to literature. His first novel, *The Sandwich*, was published in Paris in 1974. In the years that followed, Alexakis continued to distance himself artistically from

Greece and the Greek language, pushed in part by the intellectually paralyzing dictatorship back home as well as by the exhilarating freedom of his busy Parisian life.

In the early 1980s, hoping to bridge this gap, the author embarked on a new creative adventure: he painstakingly relearned his atrophied mother tongue and produced the book *Talgo* which was published in Greek in 1980 before being self-translated into French. With *Talgo*, Alexakis opened the door to an exploration of his cultural in-betweenness in his fictional work, which has allowed him to reconnect with his Greek self not only on a creative but also on a personal level. This relearning of Greece and things Greek was confirmed and explored further fifteen years later in *Mother Tongue*.

Like most of Alexakis's fictional works, *Mother Tongue* includes autobiographical elements. As he once told me, "In *Mother Tongue*, I deal with the death of my mother. I wanted to talk about it without talking about it. And I relied on something I found fascinating: the mystery of the Delphic Epsilon. The novel is an investigation on a letter that has disappeared, a letter that stands for the mother tongue, the tongue of the mother."

In the novel, the protagonist Pavlos returns to Greece from Paris where he has worked as a newspaper cartoonist for the past twenty years. He does not explain why he came back or for how long he intends to stay. At first he feels like an outsider who has lost touch with Greek traditions and culture, but he eventually finds himself reconnecting with his friends, his country, as well as its language, and its history. Pavlos becomes obsessed with an ancient mystery: he wants to know why the letter "E" used to hang at the entrance of Apollo's temple in Delphi.

His investigation into ancient Greece sends him on trips to a variety of Greek locales (Delphi, Ioannina, etc.) where he interviews many fellow countrymen and collects words that start with the letter Epsilon. Thanks to this seemingly random list of words, and thanks to his Delphic musing, Pavlos eventually embraces his mother tongue (*ellènika*), comes to terms with his status as an expatriate (*ekpatrisménos*) and opens up to the loss of his mother (*ellipsi*), whose death — the reader learns — was what had brought him home in the first place.

The themes Alexakis tackles in this novel — memory, loss, language, identity, belonging, history — are serious ones and yet, his voice remains light, intimate, even funny at times. The author's talent lies in his ability to paint human emotions all readers can relate to, even if the trajectory of his main character — caught in his Greek-French identity dilemma — seems, at first glance, unique. The attempt to reconcile broken selves, the past and the present (collective and personal), or the living and the dead, is what *Mother Tongue* sets out to explore, and it does so in a way that resonates with readers. Much as Pavlos longed to rediscover his Greek identity, many of us wish for a more cohesive self.

Mother Tongue stands right in the middle of a career that now spans more than four decades. Alexakis is a literary veteran. His work draws attention to the growing contingent of non-French authors who, by making the French language their own, are resisting the prevailing Franco-centrism of the Parisian literary scene. Since *Talgo*, Alexakis's systematic use of two writing languages has not only allowed him to negotiate his own in-betweenness, it has also helped showcase the complexities of contemporary European identities in the face of heightened nationalistic discourses.

Today Alexakis lives in Paris, Athens, and the island of Tinos. He is a busy author who — when not writing, translating, researching the topic of his next novel, or participating in speaking engagements about his books or the Greek economic crisis — volunteers with refugees and homeless compatriots in Athens.